# AFTER THE SPY SEDUCES

## ANNA HARRINGTON

# COPYRIGHT

NYLA Publishing
121 W 27th St., Suite 1201, New York, NY 10001
http://www.nyliterary.com

## A NOTE BEFORE YOU BEGIN READING...

This novel contains references to the War Office, the War Department, the Home Office, and the Foreign Office. It can be quite confusing trying to keep all of them straight and to remember which office is responsible for what jurisdictions. To brush up on your knowledge about which is which, please see the Historical Note at the end of the novel.

*Happy reading!*

# CHAPTER 1

May 1824
Surrey, England

"Come here, m' lovely!" Christopher Carlisle grabbed the barmaid around the waist as she sashayed past and yanked her down onto his lap. He whispered a dirty joke into her ear about drivers and the length of their whips that made her laugh loudly enough to attract the attention of the men sitting around him in the crowded tavern.

She smiled and looped her arm around his neck, pressing her bosom into his chest. Not that he minded. She was lively and pretty, and clearly hoping to snag him for an evening's pleasure in one of the rooms upstairs. "Ye tell that story as if ye have firsthand experience, sir."

"I do." He took the opportunity to glance around the tavern's taproom at all the people who had crowded inside in the past two hours since he'd been sitting here. "I'm a fierce driver myself."

She laughed at his bawdy entendre, just as he'd hoped, and he rewarded her with a bounce on his knee. Tonight, he wanted the kind of attention her loud laughter would bring.

With a satisfied smile, he raised the tankard to his lips and took another look around the barroom. His focus never strayed far from the door.

The tavern was filled with people seeking shelter from the foggy and damp weather, which promised to unleash even more rain by dawn. Mostly local men crowded into the room, gathered for a few hours of drink, cards, and escape from their wives. A handful of lightskirts looking to make rent and a few travelers who had no place else to spend the night in this part of Surrey mixed into the lot of them.

Always, Kit kept his attention on the men. He could dismiss the women, likewise the local villagers and the handful of hostlers who'd come inside after tending to the last of the coaches for the night. Those two groups of men were easy to spot by the familiar way they strode through the door without hesitation and warmly greeted the barkeeper, by how they ordered their food and drink with a wave and a wink to the serving wenches.

No, the men he watched for tonight would be outsiders. Their unfamiliarity with the place would require a hesitation at the door that would mark them as strangers. So would the length of time it would take for the barmaids to serve them, because the women's attentions would be on those men who returned night after night, who'd paid in the past to tup them and would most likely do so again. They wouldn't waste much effort on men who weren't important to their continuing ability to buy bread and pay rent.

His own bar wench, whom he'd spent the past hour slipping coins to and flirting with so he could disguise himself as a local, teased at his waistcoat buttons. "Yer not from 'round here."

"No, indeed." He grimaced into his ale. Good to know that a

decade of training as a Home Office agent had brought his skills on par with a barmaid's.

Ten years. *Good God.*

How could he have known when the Home Office came looking for new agents among the army's ranks that he'd still be working for them a decade later? But then, he'd been damned surprised that they'd wanted him in the first place. After all, he was the worst possible sort to be an officer in His Majesty's army. A man who chafed at regulations and who'd repeatedly escaped punishment by the skin of his teeth. The same man whom the generals recommended to the Home Office most likely just to be rid of him.

But to everyone's surprise—and his most of all—he'd thrived as an operative, all the while keeping his work secret. To the rest of the world he was simply a shiftless younger son, wasting his allowance on cards, drink, and women, without ambition or prospects. Only his brother, Ross, and new sister-in-law, the Home Secretary himself, and the undersecretary who directly gave him his orders knew that beneath his scapegrace exterior he was completely dedicated to England.

He claimed to all who'd listen that he was waiting for a living in the Church to open so he could make his future there. But the truth was that his life had to be lived in suspension—no wife, no family, no commitments of any kind. No future path. Couldn't have those, not when he had to be free to be sent on a mission at a moment's notice. Not when he didn't know whom to trust, and since Peterloo, that included the Crown and its administrators. Hell, he couldn't even follow the lead of other gentlemen and take a mistress because he couldn't risk her learning the truth about him. Too high a chance to be blackmailed or simply handed over to his enemies. God knew he'd certainly made enough of them on both sides of the Channel.

All of that meant he had to lead a life that others mistook for rakish impropriety and laziness, because limited relationships and broken commitments were all that he could offer as long as the Home Office owned his loyalty.

Or was it his soul they possessed?

After ten years, all the suspicions, false identities, secrets, and lies had festered into a churning blackness inside him that made it nearly impossible to trust anyone, save for his brother. Not the people he interacted with at society events and clubs. Not the women he bedded. Certainly not the other men at the Home Office. He couldn't even trust his cousins on the Trent side of the family with the true work he'd been doing for fear that they might accidentally divulge how he'd been spending his time. After all, he'd already learned the hard way that real lives hung in the balance behind all the lies.

His existence had become nothing but doubt and mistrust, detachment and dispassion. But since that night six months ago, the relentless hell of it had become intolerable. His singular focus was now set on revenge.

But if he wasn't careful, if he couldn't extricate himself from the web ensnaring him, the dark place would completely claim his soul.

"What's yer name?" the barmaid asked with a friendly smile as she tangled her fingers in his jacket lapels.

"Christopher." He gave her a grin. "But my friends all call me Kit."

"Why're ye here tonight?"

He took a long look around the tavern, coolly assessing the crowd. "I'm here to meet someone."

"*Found* someone already, looks like." She artfully wiggled her bottom against his lap with such enthusiasm that he couldn't stifle a genuine laugh of amusement.

Had this been any other night, he might very well have taken her up on her offer to provide sexual pleasure. She was vivacious and spirited. Full of life. Exactly the kind of woman he could easily lose himself in for a few hours of precious distraction.

But not tonight. "I'm waiting for a man."

"A friend?"

*The enemy.*

Garrett Morgan. A less likely man to be meeting with French agents Kit couldn't imagine. For all that he'd personally seen of the man, Morgan had always struck Kit as...well, *annoying*. Eager to blame his failings on others. Never happy with his situation and always complaining that life had given him a raw deal. Mostly, he blamed his father, whining to his chums at the gambling hells that General Thaddeus Morgan possessed unrealistic expectations for him, ones he could never live up to.

While there might have been some truth in that last—after all, Kit had served under the general and knew how demanding he could be—Garrett Morgan's failures were largely his own. He'd fallen short first in the army where he didn't have the discipline to thrive, then later at university where he lacked the intellect necessary to distinguish himself. Now, at an age when he should have already been established in some sort of career and a household of his own, he still resided with his father and two sisters, living off the graces of his family and shirking all sense of responsibility.

Kit grimaced inwardly. The exact same could be said of him.

The difference, however, was that Kit was a decorated agent of the Crown who had to keep his work with the Home Office secret, while Garrett Morgan had murdered James Fitch-Batten in cold blood.

Fitch...His chest tightened with the sickening pang of guilt that he'd come to expect but would never grow used to. Because his long-time partner and best friend had been beaten nearly beyond recognition one night six months ago, then had his throat slit from ear to ear. Because it was Kit's fault.

Because it should have been him instead.

But tonight he would finally catch the man responsible. And make the bastard pay.

The tavern door opened. A man paused in the doorway, his large frame silhouetted by the lamp hanging from the doorpost outside.

Awareness spooled down Kit's spine. One of the Frenchmen arriving for tonight's meeting, he was certain. And early, just as expected. Just as Kit would have done himself if he'd been meeting with a new contact. Most likely, somewhere in the tavern crowd around him, sat more Frenchmen, waiting and watching. All of them, just like Kit, pretending to be nothing more than another man out for an evening's entertainment.

As his gaze followed the man across the tavern to an empty table in the corner, that old, familiar sensation sparked inside him that nothing was as it seemed. Instantly, he grew suspicious of every man in the room, especially the ones who seemed to belong there. Like him.

But tonight, there was no reprieve from suspicion and distrust. After six months of pursuit, the endgame was finally in motion, and his heart pounded brutally at knowing that justice would be granted. If everything went according to plan, Kit would have not only the man who'd murdered his partner but also the evidence necessary to make him swing.

Now he simply had to wait for Morgan to arrive.

The barmaid fluttered her hand temptingly over his shoulder. "Perhaps when yer through talkin' with your friend," she suggested, "ye'd like to go upstairs an' relax." Her fingers kneaded into his hard muscle. "I'm good at makin' gentlemen relaxed, and yer in sore need of some attention."

His lips twisted at the irony. She had no idea how much he needed exactly that. Every muscle in his body was so tight that he was nothing but a ball of knots, every inch of him tensed and ready to spring at a moment's notice. Yet tonight he didn't have the luxury of losing himself in comforting arms, if only for a few hours before the harsh light of day arrived and reminded him of exactly who he was.

"That sounds enticing," he answered instead. "But what about my horse?"

She blinked, bewildered. "Your...horse?"

"Surely you're curious to see it." He trailed a fingertip across the top swells of her breasts, her bodice so low that she was nearly spilling out of it. "After all, you know what they say about the size of a man's horse."

"No." She toyed with his dark blond hair where it curled against his jacket collar and in her curiosity was unable to resist asking, "What do they say?"

He brought his mouth to her ear and drawled such a lewd description of horses and naked women that the barmaid shifted back on his knee to stare at him, her eyes wide with shock.

Feigning innocence, he asked, "Does this mean you won't wear spurs?"

She slapped him. Hard.

A thunder of laughter erupted from the men around him who had witnessed the skirmish, and she scrambled off his lap with whatever last bit of dignity she could summon. For a moment, he thought she might slap him again, just for good measure. But with a loud *humph!* she jabbed her nose into the air and stomped away.

Kit happily watched her go. He wouldn't receive another offer by her or any of the other barmaids tonight.

*Good.* The last thing he needed now was distraction.

The door opened again a few minutes later, right as the long case clock in the common room struck the hour. Kit casually took a sip of ale and watched another man pause in the doorway. Another stranger who raised the hairs on his nape, then set them into full-out tingling when the young man looked slowly around the room, searching the crowd...and found the Frenchman in the corner.

Short and slight of build, with slender shoulders and narrow hips beneath a brown jacket and breeches that were both too big for him, the young man reached between his legs to adjust himself before sauntering toward the Frenchman. His collar was turned up against the rain outside, an old tricorne pulled down low over his ears. Just enough of his face remained visible to reveal a thin moustache.

*Not* Garrett Morgan.

Could his contacts have been wrong, and Morgan wasn't meeting with French operatives tonight in the tavern? No. Kit had never been misled by the men who'd pointed him here.

Something else was going on, something that put him on alert as he watched the young man enter the barroom. Not more than fifteen or sixteen based on the size of him and the smoothness of his cheeks, the lad sat across the small table from the Frenchman. He hunched down, drawing up his shoulders, then wiped his nose on his sleeve.

Kit's eyes narrowed. Who *was* he? And where the hell was Morgan?

The French agent and the lad exchanged a few words. Then the young man glanced around the tavern, skimming his gaze over the room, once more searching...But based upon the frustrated tightening of his lips, he didn't find who he was looking for.

The boy turned back to the Frenchman and leaned further across the table toward him, tapping his finger on the tabletop in a way that reminded Kit of an irritated governess.

The Frenchman answered curtly with a visible snarl.

Apparently, whatever the Frenchman said wasn't at all what the young man wanted to hear. Shaking his head, he reached into his inside breast pocket and removed a handful of pages, neatly folded and tied together with string.

Kit sat up straight, his eyes glued to the papers.

Perhaps his contacts weren't wrong after all. Perhaps this young man had been sent to negotiate in Morgan's place, or had somehow gotten the papers from Morgan and took it upon himself to make the exchange. Whatever the reason, that boy was here because of Garrett Morgan and would be able to connect those pages back to him under interrogation. Or torture. Kit didn't particularly care which as long as he gained the information necessary to arrest Morgan. His heart skipped at the thought, not with vindication but absolution.

At the table, the discussion grew heated, with tapping fingers turning into pounding fists from both sides. Suddenly, the lad jumped to his feet so quickly that he knocked over his chair. He snatched up the bundle of papers and shoved them at the Frenchman, demanding the man take them, then gestured almost pleadingly at the crowded tavern around them.

The Frenchman threw the papers back with a curse and brought himself to his feet.

Which brought Kit immediately to his.

Whatever was about to happen wouldn't be good. He didn't give a damn if Morgan's proxy got the pulping of his young life, but Kit needed the lad alive to swear out a statement. And he needed those papers to force the boy into doing it.

He started forward slowly as their voices rose, then broke into a run when the Frenchman lunged, grabbing the boy by his throat and tossing him backwards halfway across the room. The lad stumbled and fell onto a nearby table, knocking it over and spilling drinks, cards, and coins onto the floor.

A melee erupted as the roomful of drunken men and desperate lightskirts scrambled after the money. Fists flew and loud curses went up, accompanied by fierce shoving and kicking, and followed by thrown tankards and plates, smashed glass and chairs, the flash of knives—

The Frenchman raced out of the tavern into the night.

The boy charged after him.

With a curse, Kit chased after the boy. *Christ.* He was getting too old for this!

He rushed out the door and into the inn yard only a few strides behind the much slower lad who ran with his arms swinging at his sides. With each pounding length, he gained ground quickly on the boy, until he was almost close enough to reach for him.

But the boy kept running, foolishly chasing after the Frenchman who was several yards ahead and increasing the distance as he raced toward one of the horses standing at the hitching posts at the edge of the yard. He untied the horse and leapt up onto the animal's back. Grabbing the reins in one hand, he spun the horse toward the road. His hand dove beneath his coat, and metal flashed in the dim lamplight.

"Get down!" Kit yelled at the boy and lunged.

He tackled the lad to the ground as the sound of gunfire shattered the night, followed instantly by the ball striking the cobblestones just inches from his head.

The Frenchman dug in his heels and charged the horse straight at them.

Kit grabbed the boy as he lay winded from the force of the tackle and rolled him over across the muddy ground. Pounding hooves flew past, barely missing them, and thudded onward to disappear into the night.

"Damn fool!" With a growl, Kit grabbed the lad by his lapels and threw him onto his back with no more effort than tossing a sack of potatoes. The boy was even younger and slighter than he'd thought. That coward Morgan had sent a mere child in his place. "Are you trying to get yourself killed?"

But the boy lay motionless on the ground.

Fear plunged through him. Had the boy had been injured—or worse? Straddling him to keep him pinned to the ground in case he caught back his breath and came up swinging, Kit ran his hands over the lad's head to check for wounds, then carefully down his neck. Nothing. He swept his hands over the boy's slender shoulders, then along his arms, feeling for broken bones.

Worried that he might have crushed the lad's ribs when he rolled him across the cobblestones, he slipped his hands beneath the jacket to feel for the ribcage, tracing his fingers upward along each rib, moving systematically higher.

He froze. His hand cupped around a soft fullness for one baffling moment when his confused brain couldn't comprehend what he was feeling—

A breast.

He yanked his hand away. *What the hell?*

He grabbed for the boy's hat to snatch it off and accidentally released a curtain of golden tresses. With a curse, he reached for the fake moustache which now drooped low over the woman's ripe lips, ripped it away, and revealed the face beneath. The very beautiful face. One he recognized even in the darkness.

"Diana Morgan," he murmured in disbelief.

Her blue eyes flew open, blazing as she stared up at him.

Of all the women— *Good God.* "What the hell are you—"

Her small fist plowed into his chin.

# CHAPTER 2

"Get your hands off me!" Diana bit out as she drew back her fist to punch him a second time.

But he grabbed her wrist before her knuckles made contact. "Then stop trying to hit me!"

She drew her other hand into a fist and swung, but the devil dodged the blow with all the skill of a natural-born athlete.

When her elbow landed a hard blow to his stomach, he winced and let out a growl of aggravation. He pinned both of her arms to the ground beside her head, holding her immobile beneath his heavy body.

"You cad!" She knew him, this man who'd tackled her to the ground and had his hands in places they had no business being. Oh, that made all of this so much worse! "You—you *Carlisle!*"

That last was accompanied by such venom that his head snapped back in surprise. "Hey now," he chastised. "No reason to bring my ancestry into this."

"Every reason," she ground out through clenched teeth. Despite the sharp pain in her side where she'd hit the ground so hard that the air had been knocked from her lungs, she struggled fiercely against him, only to barely move at all. "Let go of me!"

"The hell I will," he snarled, placing his long leg over both of hers as she kicked at him to free herself. "Not until you stop fighting me."

She twisted futilely with a cry of rising panic. "He's getting away!"

"He's *gotten* away." He glared down at her with a harsh grimace, not at all happy with her.

And she certainly wasn't pleased with him! "I have to ride after him. I have to give him those papers, make him—"

"He doesn't want them."

"He does." He *had* to! That man was the only link to her brother, the only way to free him from the men who had kidnapped him. Hot tears of frustration stung at her eyes, knowing that with every second she delayed her brother's life was put in increasing danger. "Let me up!"

"So you can go riding after him and get yourself killed? How do I explain that to the general?"

"So you can keep me here, lying on top of me?" She somehow managed to jab up her chin defiantly despite being on her back on the ground. "How do you explain *that*?"

"I was checking for wounds on the *boy* I saved from being killed." His eyes narrowed as he lowered his head, bringing his face so close to hers that she could feel the heat of his lips shadowing hers and the anger pulsating from him. "And you were meeting with unauthorized foreign agents on English soil to give them military documents." When her lips parted, stunned into silence, he pressed in a low yet carefully controlled voice, "How do *you* explain that?"

Her heart plummeted to her knees with a dizzying jolt. Sweet mercy, she was going to be sick!

She asked hoarsely, her voice lost beneath her shock, "How do you know about that?"

"I'm looking for your brother and heard that he'd be here tonight. Imagine my surprise to find you instead." He raked his gaze over her with a look that made her skin sizzle. "Dressed like this."

"I certainly couldn't have come here as myself." So she'd donned some of Garrett's old clothes from his Eton days, and with the help of a fake moustache adhered to her lip, she'd called on every detail she could remember from her bother's boyhood about how he'd swaggered and behaved and gestured. It had worked, too, so well that even Christopher Carlisle had no idea that she wasn't a man. Until he'd accidentally touched her breast.

Her face heated from humiliation, and from something else just as hot. Something she had no business feeling for this man in particular and on this night of all nights, when her focus should have been on her brother.

"Let me go," she pleaded. "I can still catch up with him and—"

"He's gone. The exchange failed." The finality in his voice sliced through her like a knife. "All you'll do if you try to go after him is get yourself hurt."

*Or worse.* The words hung between them as clearly as if he'd uttered them.

She didn't care about herself. But her brother— Dear God, Garrett was gone. What might have been her only chance to save him had vanished into the night along with the Frenchman, and the enormous guilt that swept over her left her trembling with helplessness. His life had rested in her hands, and she'd failed him.

She turned her face away before Carlisle could see the tears swelling in her eyes, before one slipped free in self-recrimination and grief. To break down in front of him, a Carlisle no less— She couldn't have borne it.

"Miss Morgan."

The formality of that struck her as absurd, given the way he lay on top of her, his body pressed along the length of hers.

But an anger simmered inside him as well, and not just because she'd accidentally started a fight from which he'd felt compelled to save her. It went much deeper than that. An anger she knew involved Garrett.

"Where are the papers now?"

"Didn't you feel them when you were running your hands over me?" she asked caustically, letting her own anger push away her mounting worry.

In reply, he took her chin and turned her head back until she had no choice but to look at him. He shot her a warning glare so stern that she knew not to try his patience further.

"In my left jacket pocket," she snapped out.

Not trusting her even then, he took both of her wrists into one large hand and delved into her pocket with the other. He pulled the papers free, then slipped them inside his own jacket.

"What are you doing?" she demanded. She needed those pages to free Garrett.

"Taking these." He muttered, "After all, you might decide to give them to the Americans next."

She glowered at him, her hands drawing once more into fists. "I am *not*—"

"Where is your brother?"

The unintended irony of his question pierced her like a blade of ice. "I wish I knew."

His eyes flashed. That wasn't at all what he'd wanted to hear, apparently.

"I was told that Morgan was meeting with that Frenchman here tonight." From the tone of his voice, he was furious to find her in her brother's place.

"A Morgan did meet with him," she confirmed. "Me. But *not* for the reason you think."

"Tell me," he ordered, easing his hold on her wrists but not enough to let her go.

She bit her lip. How much could she trust a Carlisle? And this Carlisle, in particular? "I received a message a few days ago."

"From the man you met with tonight?"

She nodded warily. "A ransom note, telling me that Garrett had been kidnapped." She sucked in a deep breath to gather herself. "The man said he had Garret and would let him go in exchange for those pages, pages he wanted me to deliver tonight. Alone. If I told anyone, he—" She choked, then found the strength to force out in a whisper, "He threatened to kill Garret."

"That's why you're here?" He spoke slowly, as if hoping she would contradict him. "Because you believe your brother was kidnapped for these pages?"

"I know so."

"And that was all you received—just the note?"

She blinked. "Isn't that enough?"

"No. Ransom notes usually come with proof that the victim has been taken—a scrap of handwriting, a lock of hair, an ear or finger."

The blood drained from her face. Dear God, she was going to be sick!

"No." She swallowed to keep down her accounts. Hard. "Nothing like that."

"But you acted upon it."

"Yes. I brought the papers, just as I was told to do. But the man didn't want them."

"So I saw. Why not?"

"I don't know." Grief clawed at her belly. "He looked at them and said they weren't the right ones."

He frowned. "What did he mean by that?"

"I don't know. But those are the pages asked for in the note. I'm certain of it."

"Pages from what?"

"*Not* military documents." She didn't like his earlier accusation that she was giving away secrets. Her father had been a distinguished general in His Majesty's army, for God's sake! She would *never* do anything that would even remotely aid the French. So he might as well just forget any chance at gaining a reward from turning her in for it. "They're from the general's memoirs. Just scribblings that he's been trying to put together into a book."

Disbelief darkened his face. "Why would the French want those?"

"I don't know. And I don't care." Her eyes burned with self-recrimination at how she'd failed to exchange the papers. "All that matters is saving Garrett's life."

No sympathy showed in Carlisle at that. If anything, his jaw clenched even tighter at the mention of the danger her brother was in. "You think that the Frenchman who sent that note and met with you tonight is going to kill your brother because he didn't take those pages?"

"Yes." The word emerged as a desolate rasp, and a single tear slipped free.

"Then you can stop the tears." With a fleeting expression of sympathy, he brushed it away with the pad of his thumb. "Because most likely your brother hasn't even been kidnapped."

Not kidnapped? She searched his face, desperate for answers. Clearly, he believed that, but his words brought no spark of hope. "They have him, I know it."

"Because you received a note?"

"Because he's *missing*. He left two weeks ago to visit friends in the North, but when I received the note, I didn't know what to believe, if it were true or simply some childish joke that his chums were playing on us. So I hired a messenger and attempted to reach him. But his friends replied that Garrett wasn't with them, that he had never arrived." She gave voice to her deepest fears. "I think he was captured just after he left home."

He paused for a moment, chewing that over. Then he mumbled, half to himself, "Why don't I trust you?"

"Why would I lie?" she shot back.

"Because people are seldom as they appear and rarely tell the truth." To make his point, he replaced the fake moustache on her upper lip and tapped it into place with his fingertip. But there was nothing at all teasing about the black expression on his face. "Even beautiful ladies."

Her belly fluttered at what was little more than an empty compliment, and one given in chastisement at that. What a goose she was! *This* was why she avoided men like Christopher Carlisle. Far too easy to be caught up in their web of charms, even when lying on her bruised bottom in an inn yard in what she hoped was nothing more than mud.

A loud shattering came from the tavern. He glanced across the yard toward the fight. His face hardened, and he let out a soft curse.

"What is it?" She twisted around to follow his gaze, just in time to see two very large men stumble outside. They paused to search the night, as if looking for someone to blame for the fight.

"We have to get out of here. *Now.*" He dropped his gaze back to her face—no, to her mouth—and she could have sworn regret flitted across his features at being interrupted.

But before she could be certain, he released her wrists and rolled away. He took her arm and pulled her to her feet, then quickly led her across the yard toward the horses. She struggled to keep up with his long strides. Worse—she winced at the sharp aches that portended nasty bruises in all kinds of unmentionable places from the way he'd tackled her to the ground.

When they reached a large gray gelding who stood calmly amid the commotion, he released her arm to untie it and swung up onto its back. The horse instantly came alert, his eyes clear and bright, his nostrils flaring.

He leaned down in the saddle and held out his hand to her.

She hesitated.

Of all the men to come rushing to her defense tonight, like a parody of a well-intentioned knight in shining armor—of course, it had to be *him*. Christopher Carlisle. One of the men formerly under her father's command, who now belonged to the same clubs and attended the same sporting events as her brother. A noted rake and scoundrel who seemed determined to bed every woman in society, just for the sport of it.

And now the only ally she had.

Surely, fate was laughing at her.

"There!" An excited shout went up from the two men. "That's them!"

With a curse, Carlisle grabbed her arm and swung her onto the horse behind him.

"Hang on," he ordered as the gelding danced beneath them. "We're in for a wild ride."

She wrapped her arms around his waist as he kicked his heels into the horse's sides and sent it racing into the night.

# CHAPTER 3

By the time Kit reined his horse to a stop in the fog-drenched shadows behind the old stone stables, the anger that had pulsed inside him at the tavern had dulled into simmering resentment. At Morgan for not being there as expected. At Diana for coming in his place. And especially at himself, for letting his hopes rise that he'd finally find justice for Fitch tonight.

Nothing. Months of investigating and desperately tracking down leads, of risking his career...and *nothing* to show for it. None of the pieces of information he'd learned tonight fit together. Especially not Diana's piece of the puzzle. Morgan had been kidnapped and was being held ransom for a few memoir pages? He couldn't believe that story.

Nor did he want to believe that his only lead was a society miss who had nearly gotten herself killed.

*Damnation.* He was just as far from finding answers now as he'd been six months ago.

Pushing down his irritation, he scoured his gaze across her father's small manor house. Idlewild was shuttered against the darkness, except for the first floor, where the glow of lamplight shined through one of the windows.

"All locked up for the night," he muttered. Any chance he might have had of searching her father's house for answers disappeared like the shadows as the moon slid out from behind the thickening clouds.

She loosened her hold around his waist and shook her head, misunderstanding. "I can slip inside without anyone seeing."

Of course she could. She'd set out to commit espionage, after all. And a woman who had enough cunning to not only dress like a man but also study a man's movements and gestures to fool everyone in the tavern—including him—would have had the forethought to leave one of the doors or windows unlocked.

He glanced over his shoulder at her. Garrett Morgan was a traitor and murderer. But where did his sister fit into all this?

He saw the pain and distress on her face when he'd questioned her at the tavern. She wasn't good enough of an actress to fake that. But her belief that her brother had truly been kidnapped kicked up even more questions inside his head. Because whatever Diana's role in all of this, Morgan hadn't been taken. Kit knew that the way old sailors sensed oncoming storms. In his bones.

So where in the hell *was* he?

Forcing back his frustration, Kit dropped to the ground, then reached up to clasp her around the waist to help her down. He bit back a curse. Everything about this personal mission had just grown ten times more complicated.

Diana lost her balance and fell forward as she slipped down into his arms. His hands tightened on her hips, but not in time to stop the press of her body against his as she stumbled into him, or the flattening of her breasts against his chest as she threw her arms around his neck to catch herself.

Kit sucked in a mouthful of air at the contact, all of him stiff-ening as a jolt of pleasure-pain sped through him.

"Apologies," she murmured.

"None necessary." But his gut twisted when he looked down at her as she regained her balance.

Her blonde hair lay around her shoulders like a silver curtain in the moonlight, and her full lips were parted temptingly in a look of befuddled surprise to find herself once more in his arms. Soft and warm against him, with a faint scent of lavender surrounding her... What would she do if he dared to kiss her?

He bit back a groan and set her away from him. *Ten times?* He nearly laughed. His mission had just gotten a helluva lot more complicated than that.

Mumbling her goodbyes, she began to slip past him for the house.

"Not so fast." He grabbed her arm and stopped her.

She wasn't leaving until he had answers, or at least until he knew in what direction to head next. Simply tracking down Morgan wasn't enough. Kit also had to find irrefutable proof that he'd committed crimes against England and murdered Fitch. That's what tonight should have been—Morgan caught with the papers in his hand, and the door of the trap finally swinging closed.

Instead, Kit found himself in the thick of a new mess, with Diana as the only path out.

"When was the last time you saw your brother?" he demanded.

"A fortnight ago."

"Here?"

"Yes." Her eyes dulled as the moon slid behind a thick cloud. "When he'd told me goodbye."

"And everyone in the household knew that he'd planned to visit friends?"

"Yes." Her mouth turned down grimly. She was sharp enough to realize the suspicion lingering behind his question. "You think that one of the servants was involved?"

"Very likely."

She slid an icy glance down to his hand on her arm. "Our staff has worked for us for years. Many of them served with my father in the army. They're loyal and would never do as you're implying."

In his experience, people did all kinds of unlikely things, especially when desperate. Whether the servants had anything to do with Morgan's disappearance, he had no idea. But someone inside the house had contacted the French, of that he was certain. "Those pages they asked for—they're from your father's memoirs?"

Her brows drew together, wary of where he was leading her. "Yes."

"How many pages has the general completed so far, do you estimate?"

Confusion visibly stiffened her limbs. "A few hundred. But I don't see—"

"Tell me this then." He leaned toward her, bringing his face level with hers. "How did the kidnappers know which pages to ask for out of all those hundreds if no one inside your household told them?"

If her face wasn't awash in shadows, he was certain he would have seen her pale. "You think—" The words choked off. She cleared her throat and tried again. "You think someone inside our house kidnapped my brother?"

He thought it might be much worse than that. If he had to place odds in the book at White's, he'd venture that Garrett Morgan might already be dead. That was why the French had to coerce Diana into handing over the pages rather than receiving them from Morgan himself, whom Kit's contacts had assured him was already working with the French. And that was most likely why Morgan wasn't in the tavern for the trade, waiting to be freed.

But upsetting her by telling her that would do no good. So he asked instead, "What does the general know about tonight?"

"Nothing. It was all my own doing."

*That* he easily believed. "Good," he bit out, releasing her arm. Then warned, "Keep it that way. Tell no one about your missing brother or what you did tonight. You can't trust anyone."

"Not even you?"

His mouth twisted as he leaned in to murmur, *"Especially not me."*

A threat lingered behind his words, one he didn't bother attempting to hide.

But instead of keeping her distance, the frustrating woman stepped closer. Every inch of him tingled with an awareness of her that crackled on the rain-scented air around them.

She studied him in the shadows. "Why are you looking for Garrett?"

"I can't tell you."

"Because you don't trust me?"

"I don't trust anyone." More truth existed behind that quiet comment than he wanted to admit.

"Not even me?"

Responding to her challenge, he raked a slow, languid look over her, letting his gaze linger on all those tell-tale places that marked her for a woman beneath boy's clothing. Good Lord, how could he have ever confused her for a lad? Long legs accentuated by breeches that rounded into full hips and a narrow waist. Full, ripe lips that were now pressed into an irritated line, which he was certain she'd meant as a chastisement but which only had him wanting to kiss them until they softened beneath his.

"Especially not a beautiful woman," he murmured. The night was full of confessions, apparently.

Despite the darkness, he saw her cheeks flush. Damnation if that didn't make him want to kiss her even more.

He'd known Diana for years—from a distance. As two people living on the fringes of society, they'd attended several of the same events since the general and his family had returned from India three years ago. Kit's cousin Robert had courted Diana, before they'd mutually broken off. Kit himself had once served under her father's command during the last skirmish with the Americans, in the early days of his commission.

And always, Kit had avoided Diana. Like the plague.

Oh, she was beautiful, certainly, possessing soft and ethereal qualities that reminded him of an angel, right down to that golden hair and those deep blue eyes that could beckon a man to his ruin if he wasn't careful. Intelligent and accomplished, and in far more areas than that drivel of music lessons, watercolors, and drawing room French that society misses believed constituted an education. She was a general's daughter, after all, disciplined and composed, and she'd already traveled to more places around the world in her father's wake than most women ever traveled in their entire lives.

But no good could have come from Kit pursuing her, so he'd never tried. He didn't seduce unmarried innocents, and anything more serious was simply impossible. Hell, he couldn't even ask her for a waltz or turn about the garden because he couldn't risk her seeing right through his façade if he let her get too close. Ironic, given that getting close to Diana Morgan was the goal of half the unmarried gentlemen in England.

Tonight proved that he'd been right to stay away. Was she playing a role in her brother's treason? Or was she simply a pawn for the French?

And why, for God's sake, did he ache to kiss her? Her. The *worst* woman in the world to long to taste.

Like a siren sensing the effect she had on him, she shifted closer, and near enough that her lavender scent wafted over him like a cloud. She placed her palm on his chest. Right over his startled heart.

"Do you have any idea at all where my brother is?" Her whispered entreaty twined uncomfortably around his spine, because the only answers he could give would wound her. "If he's safe and unhurt?"

"No."

As if recognizing that for the lie it was, she searched his face, but she wouldn't find any answers there. He was too good to let his secrets escape so easily. Not even to a beautiful angel wrapped in the moonlit fog. "Would you tell me if you did?"

"No." *That* was the brutal truth.

Her frustration flared for one unguarded moment. "But you *have* to tell me." Her fingers clutched pleadingly at his waistcoat. "Don't you see? I'm the only one who can help him."

He tightened his jaw. Her pleas of mercy for her brother grated. So did the realization that she was only touching him because of that murderous bastard. "Maybe he doesn't deserve to be helped."

She stiffened. "My brother is an innocent victim."

"Your brother is anything but innocent."

Her hand dropped away, and the loss of her touch chilled him. "So you think I'm lying?"

He folded his arms across his chest, to keep from grabbing her and shaking sense into her. Or kissing her. At that moment, given the anger and yearning warring inside him, the result would be a toss-up. "I think you're in over your head."

Her eyes iced over. "Actually, Mr. Carlisle, I don't really care what you think of me."

"You should." He was deadly serious. Did she really have no idea how much danger she'd put herself into tonight? To sneak off in disguise without telling anyone, to meet foreign operatives and exchange documents— She was damned lucky that he'd been there to save her. "Right now I'm the only thing standing between you and the gallows for treason."

Her face turned ghostly white in the shadows. *Good.*

Calling what she'd done treason was a grand exaggeration. But if it took that threat to convince her to keep herself from danger, then so be it. God only knew what might happen if she tried to rescue Morgan again. He couldn't bear to have another death bloodying his hands.

"I am not a traitor. I would never..." Her voice faded away as softly as the mists lingering around them and ended in a hard swallow. She whispered so breathlessly that he had to lean in to hear, "But I did, didn't I?" Her hand went to her chest, as if needing a physical reminder to keep breathing. "Dear God..."

"So what I *think*, Miss Morgan," he said, lowering his head until their eyes were even, his mouth so close to hers that he could feel the warmth of her nervous breath skittering across his lips, "is that you love your brother and would go to any lengths to ensure his safety. You even put yourself into danger tonight to save him." Removing his right glove and letting it drop to the ground, he murmured, "Very brave of you."

Also damnably foolish. But he knew better than to utter that thought aloud. After all, if he was going to be slapped, he might as well make it worthwhile. So he audaciously brushed his bare knuckles across her smooth cheek to soothe her fears.

In truth, though, he simply couldn't resist touching her.

"But I wasn't successful." She trembled as he dared to stroke his thumb over her bottom lip, yet she didn't push his hand away. A low thrill of triumph warmed through him when she faintly turned her face to nuzzle his palm. "They still have Garrett."

If he had any sense in him, he'd simply walk away right now and return to his work with the Home Office, work he'd been seriously neglecting of late. He'd let her brother's role in all this play out and let her discover on her own what her brother had really been doing. His head knew it. The instinct in his gut was certain of it.

Instead, against all reason, he heard himself proposing the exact thing he shouldn't—"I can help you find out what happened to him."

The same expression of stunned disbelief gripped her beautiful face that he was certain was also flitting across his at his momentary lapse of sanity. The lapse that put ten years of secrecy in jeopardy because he'd just offered to let her get close to him. *Very* close.

"You said it was dangerous." She pulled in a ragged breath when he gently angled her face up toward his, anticipating the kiss he so very much wanted to give her. "Why would you help me?"

His mouth hovered only a hairsbreadth from hers. "Because I think you're in danger." The harsh truth followed. "And I couldn't bear to see you get hurt."

He lowered his lips to hers—

"And *I* think you're not at all what you seem."

His head jerked back. He stared down at her, stunned.

*Impossible.* She didn't know that he worked for the Home Office. Couldn't possibly have known. Yet surprise electrified him.

Leaning his forearm against the barn wall beside her, he shifted rakishly closer and forced a grin, to once again slip behind the safety of false facades. "I'm just a man who wants to become a vicar."

She lifted a brow, seeing right though him. "You are a liar."

"Vicar, liar..." He clucked his tongue and fussed with the man's neckcloth at her delicate throat, as if contemplating stripping it off her...and what a damnable shame that he couldn't. "Such insults, Miss Morgan! And to the man who saved your life."

"To the man who had his hands where they shouldn't have been," she muttered.

Her scolding comment only earned her a mischievous smile. "To the man who will help you find your brother, if you're honest with me." *Or what's left of him.*

He straightened and took a step back from her to demonstrate his sincerity.

"Yet you still think him a traitor," she said softly.

*No. A murderer.* His eyes fixed on hers. "I think his disappearance might not have had anything to do with the Frenchman you met with tonight."

A glimmer of hope flashed in her eyes, chased immediately by a pang of guilt in his chest. He was misleading her, purposefully so, in order to keep her out of harm.

But if Morgan were still alive, then Diana was the only path to the man. And if Morgan were dead, then Kit damned well wanted proof.

"We won't know anything for certain until we find your brother. And the only way to do that is to work together."

She bit her bottom lip at the temptation of his proposition and looked warily at him as if he were the devil himself, come to bargain away her soul.

Perhaps he was. But he would never be able to absolve himself of Fitch's murder without her help. In that, she might truly be an angel leading him to his salvation, after all.

"If I agree to help you, you'll tell me if you discover anything about where he might be?" she asked.

Not a question, he understood. Terms of negotiation.

But in the end, any negotiation always included terms of surrender for at least one side, and his heart skipped that she'd so easily relented. "Immediately."

The tension eased from her shoulders. "All right. Then we're in this together."

"Together," he repeated, far more huskily than he'd intended, and stepped forward once more to close the space between them, to once more cup her face and tilt her mouth toward his.

She arched a brow at his obvious intention. "Sealing our agreement with a kiss, are we?"

"My favorite way."

"The gentlemen at White's must find that fascinating."

He paused for a beat, his mouth so close to hers that the heat of her lips teased at his. Then he grinned at her audacity. "You'd be surprised."

Her gaze lowered longingly to his mouth. "Actually, I've heard—"

He brought his mouth over hers, capturing her lips beneath his and finally taking the kiss that he'd ached to claim since he'd discovered her at the tavern.

*Sweet Jesus.* He nearly groaned. She tasted of vanilla and cherries, of warm summer afternoons and rose gardens, and of something spicier beneath that he couldn't quite place but found himself craving. Shoving his fingers into the silky waves of her hair, he traced the tip of his tongue across the seam of her lips, coaxing her to grant him an even deeper taste.

She hesitated for one heart-stuttering moment when he thought she might stop him, only to relax with a sigh and open her mouth to his. Her arm drifted up to encircle his neck and pull herself closer in silent permission.

He eagerly accepted and slipped his tongue between her lips in a silken glide, to drink in the sweetness hidden inside. Dear Lord, how delicious she tasted! And how hungry he was as he kissed her, open-mouth and feverish… Starving, in fact. Enough to devour her if she'd let him.

"Who's there?" A shout broke through the foggy silence surrounding them. "Show yourself! And be warned—I've got a gun."

# CHAPTER 4

S tartled, Diana opened her eyes just in time to see an annoyed grimace twist Carlisle's lips as they lingered above hers, their kiss interrupted. Full, sensuous lips...close enough for their warmth to heat hers, their deliciously masculine taste still lingering on her tongue.

A lightning bolt of realization slammed through her. Christopher Carlisle had been kissing her. Worse, she'd wanted him to do exactly that.

*Good Lord.* She'd gone mad!

She shoved at his shoulder to push him away, horrified at herself. "What are you doing?"

Not letting her out of his arms, he glanced toward the house as a second warning shout went up. "Apparently, waiting to be shot."

"It's Higgins, our steward." She dug her fingers into his shoulder and caught her breath at the way the hard muscle flexed invitingly beneath her fingertips. Heavens, but she couldn't stop herself from squeezing his shoulder again. "He couldn't hit the side of a barn."

"Convenient," he muttered, "because he doesn't have to if I'm standing in front of it."

When he tried to pull her back into the shadows with him, safely out of Higgins's sight, panic spilled through her. To be alone with him in the darkness, to risk that he'd kiss her again, that she'd crave another embrace after that, the way she'd so shamelessly craved this first one—

*Lord help her!* "You have to go." Hiding her ruefulness at being so weak as to kiss him, she grabbed his shoulders and turned him toward his horse. "*Now.*"

Higgins called out again, this time much closer.

She shoved him as hard as she could, but the man was a mountain of solid muscle and barely moved an inch. Oh, the frustrating devil!

He grinned lazily at her over his shoulder. "Worried about me, are you, angel?"

She scowled, more so because her belly fluttered at the flirtatious endearment than at his audacity. Then she shoved him again with all her strength, forcing him to take a step forward. "Will you go already?"

His grin faded. "All right." He turned to face her and walked backwards into the shadows, his eyes never leaving hers. "But we're not finished with this."

Oh yes. They *very* much were.

In one fluid movement, he mounted his horse and pulled the large gelding in a tight circle as he found his seat in the saddle. He leaned forward, and the gray horse leapt to canter off, disappearing into the fog like a ghost.

Diana held her breath and listened as the hoof beats faded into the night and silence descended.

Then she let out a long, trembling sigh. Had tonight really happened? The tavern, the Frenchman, Christopher Carlisle...

kisses. Her head swam with it all, in a foggy confusion as dream-like as the white-shrouded night around her.

Higgins's approaching footsteps crunched loudly behind her on the gravel.

There would be time later to sort through it all. Now, she had to deal with more immediate matters.

Squaring her shoulders, she turned and plastered a bright smile on her face. "Mr. Higgins!"

"Lassie?" Surprise filled the older man's voice, and he rested his hunting gun across the crook of his arm. "I thought I heard horses. What on earth are you doing out here at this hour?"

*Kissing London's biggest scapegrace.* "I came out to check on the new foal." *Because he'd saved me, apparently after I attempted to commit treason.* "I wanted to make certain that she was nursing properly." *Because my brother has been kidnapped, and I'm the only one who can free him.* "And that the stall had enough straw to keep her warm." *Because Carlisle is right, that I am so very much in over my head that I don't even know how to begin to swim back to shore...*

"Is everythin' all right?"

She nodded with resolve. "It will be."

"You an' those horses," the older man chuckled as he came forward. "Still fascinated with 'em, even after all these years."

"I suppose I am." A twinge of guilt at lying to her closest confidante among the staff pricked at the backs of her knees. But what was this one little lie compared to the grand ones she was keeping? "You know how much I love to ride."

"Aye." His eyes sparkled even in the darkness. "Your thinkin' of trainin' the yearling colt yourself, aren't you?"

"We'll win the Derby at Epsom." She winked. "Just wait and see."

He laughed and reached out to chuck her affectionately on the chin.

AFTER THE SPY SEDUCES 35

He'd done that since the first day they met, when she'd been only eight and the general and Mama had just purchased Idlewild. They'd hired Angus Higgins to run the little estate for them, and a better steward couldn't have been found. Higgins had understood how difficult it was to be a soldier's child and a general's most of all, so he did everything he could to make the farm a happy home for both her and Garret whenever they visited.

Unfortunately, with wars on the continent and troubles in the far-flung corners of the empire, visits to Idlewild were few and far between until they returned for good three years ago. When they came back to the farm, Higgins was there to welcome them home —including baby Meredith, who had been born en route from India and shown to all their friends and servants by Mama with beaming pride.

Higgins had been especially kind to Garrett these past few years, as if he realized the weight her brother carried on his shoulders as General Thaddeus "Never Surrender" Morgan's only son.

Oh, how she wished she could confide in Higgins about Garret! But she couldn't. Especially now that Carlisle had set doubts swirling inside her about her brother's disappearance and suspicions about who might have given information to the French. Of course it wasn't Higgins. She knew that in her heart. But Higgins talked to the other servants and staff, and she simply couldn't risk putting Garrett's life in further danger, certainly not after how badly tonight's exchange had gone. And not if Carlisle's intuition was correct, that Garrett's disappearance had nothing to do with the French. If so, then her brother might very well still be alive and waiting to be rescued.

"You need to be careful, lassie," he warned. "Never know who you might run into out here in the darkness an' fog."

She sighed. Wasn't that the truth? "I'm heading inside right now."

"Need me to escort you to the door?"

Her chest warmed at his thoughtfulness. "I'll be fine."

"Sleep tight, then."

"Thank you, Higgins." Impulsively, she hugged the old steward. "For everything."

Then she was gone, hurrying away through the fog and darkness toward the house. By the time she'd reached the unlocked kitchen door, so much roiling guilt and fear and worry tangled in a lump in the pit of her stomach that she feared she might cast up her accounts right there, all over the stone floor.

She squeezed her eyes shut and leaned against the wall to take several deep, slow breaths to calm herself, but she knew that the only way to make herself truly feel better was to tell the general about Garrett and her failed attempt to rescue him. The exact thing Carlisle had warned her not to do.

But what did Christopher Carlisle know about her family, for heaven's sake? Or how much she owed her brother for all he'd done for her since they left India? Did Carlisle care about anyone or anything except himself? He was nothing more than a scoundrel, content to shiftlessly waste away his allowance on cards, women, and drink, while seeking no sort of gainful living. Even his concern over her brother was only so he could be paid whatever gambling debts Garrett owed him. *Had* to be. Lately, since Mama died, Garrett had become little more than a scapegrace himself, spending far too many nights in gambling hells and seedy locales of all kinds.

That would all change, though, as soon as Garrett took the position at the Inns of Court that he'd been waiting for. It broke the general's heart to know that his son hadn't been able to thrive in the army, that he'd not been able to capitalize on any of the other opportunities that had been available to him. But Garrett liked the law, argued well, and would do a grand job of it in London, she knew. Perhaps someday he might even take the silks and become a King's Counsel. Then, the general would have to admit that he was proud of Garrett. He would *have* to.

But none of that would come to pass if he didn't return safely.

With a burst of steely resolve, she shoved herself away from the wall and slipped quickly through the dark house. She hurried up the stairs toward the first floor study where her father liked to spend his evenings, surrounded by his papers and books, warmed as much by a glass of fine cognac as by the fire.

And that was where she found him, slumped down in his favorite leather chair, a book lying open across his lap, and his chin resting on his chest.

She paused in the doorway. Even in his sleep, the general possessed the dignity and stateliness of a man of his rank and grand accomplishments. A soldier who had dedicated his life to the army, he'd been thwarted from being named field marshal only because his family wasn't connected to the aristocracy, and by the time Prinny had handed out the rank to several worthless royals and aristocrats, there had been none left for the true heroes like her father. A true hero he was, too, saving countless men's lives at Toulouse and Vittoria and playing a pivotal role in the Waterloo campaign. When the wars with Boney and America were finally over, he'd gone on to save lives in India.

"They don't make men like you anymore, do they, general?" she whispered. Men so dedicated to Crown and country that they were willing to sacrifice everything for a greater cause and for no gain of their own. Men who were willing to be sent wherever His Majesty needed them. Men who knew that war was never glorious, and that gallantry in the midst of battle was a damn lie.

Her throat tightened with emotion. A man willing to protect his family at all costs, even at the price of his own career.

That was why she loved him, and why it tore at her heart to know that he and Garrett were always at odds.

Dread pierced her, so hard that she winced. How could she tell him that his only son was in danger and that she'd failed to bring him home? That she'd unwittingly attempted to commit treason tonight herself in a futile attempt to save him?

Papa had sacrificed so much for her. How would he ever be able to forgive her for that?

The general stirred in his sleep, waking himself with a loud snore. He glanced around, as if sensing that he wasn't alone. He saw her lingering in the doorway, blinked hard for a moment to clear the fog of sleep, and smiled.

"Diana." His expression faded into confusion. "Why are you dressed like that?" He squinted at the mantel clock. "At this hour?"

"I was checking on the new foal in the stables." The same lie she'd given Higgins, followed by the same pang of guilt. "I didn't want to dirty my dress, so I put on Garrett's old clothes."

"Just like you to fuss over those horses." He closed the book and set it onto the round side table at his elbow. "I wish I could convince you to be as interested in soirees and outings."

With a wry smile, she approached him. "Ah, but horses are so much better at intelligent conversation than all those society dandies, far better at dancing, and never spill punch on my dress."

He grimaced. "They never ask to court you, you mean."

"That, too. Find me a husband whom I can put out to pasture when I'm tired of him, and then I might consider it." At her father's exaggerated look of exasperation, she squatted down beside the chair and rocked back onto the heels of her boots, more than happy to change the direction of this conversation. "Why are you still up? You should have gone to bed hours ago."

"I spent the evening going over the last of the preparations for the party next week." He gestured an irritated hand at a stack of papers on his desk and exhaled a long sigh. "Your mother always did the planning for these things. All I had to do was stand at the front door and greet the guests."

"Before slinking off to join the men for port and cigars for the rest of the night," she reminded with a chastising purse of her lips.

"Exactly."

"Well, if this party is too much of a strain for you, we can always cancel it." How much she wished he would do just that!

"We're on the offensive, sergeant." He emphasized his old nickname for her with a wag of his finger. "It's the perfect opportunity to remind everyone that you're still a highly eligible young lady." His lifted a bushy brow. "And that you're receptive to being courted again."

She bit back a long-suffering sigh. Since Mama died, the general's primary mission had become steering her successfully into matrimony. Diana knew it was because he worried about her and wanted her to find someone who would take care of her. Yet it grated.

"But if I find a husband, then who will be here to take care of you?" She softened her teasing with a pat to his arm. "It would only be you and Major Paxton, pouring over your memoir pages and locking yourselves away from society."

"Not if you marry the major."

*Oh no.* Diana fought to keep from rolling her eyes. Not this again.

Major Reginald Paxton had served as her father's aide-de-camp since the end of the wars with Boney, and since the general's retirement, the man had been spending hours helping with the general's memoirs. More often than not, though, she'd caught the two men wasting time sharing stories over glasses of cognac and cigars rather than organizing her father's writing.

Despite the major's attentions, she wasn't at all interested in letting him court her and turned him down gently at every opportunity. Of which there had been many. The man was quite candid about his interest in her. Lately, that interest had become downright stubborn, accepting neither subtle hints nor outright rebukes, and she'd become incredibly uncomfortable around him. Thankfully, Garrett had cut off the man's entreaties at every chance, saving her from having to be bluntly rude to the major and upsetting Papa.

Oh, the major seemed like a good man, devoted to her father and to England, with a lauded army career and a no-nonsense bearing that did his uniform proud. But Diana had no intention of marrying him.

"I am not interested in Major Paxton," she countered firmly. "Nor anyone else in uniform."

Her father bristled. "What's wrong with a man in uniform?"

For her, what was right? A man in His Majesty's service had little say over his life or where he would be posted, especially an ambitious officer with promise. She couldn't bear the thought of being sent to the other side of the empire, where she might be away from her family for years, unable to help Garrett find his way, watch Meri grow up, or help the general as he aged. Or worse, if her soldier husband was killed...

She pulled in a deep breath, knowing first-hand how terrible a life connected to the military could be. But those trials they'd endured in India seemed to have happened so long ago now, were never spoken of once they were back in England— She couldn't blame her father for forgetting, even if her own heart still bled.

Not wanting to wound him with an answer, she placed a kiss to his forehead. "Leave all the party plans to me." She hid her purposeful dodge of his question with a long-suffering sigh at the frustrating truth that army officers made for poor party planners. "I'll take care of everything."

"You always do."

That innocent comment cut her. Because she hadn't, not tonight. She hadn't been able to rescue Garrett from his kidnappers. *If* he'd been kidnapped at all. The more she thought about what Carlisle had told her, the more doubts began to plague her.

"Robert Carlisle and his wife will most likely be in attendance at the party," Papa said quietly.

"I know."

Given the Duke of Trent's influence on the War Department and King's Cabinet, of course invitations had been extended to the entire Carlisle family, including his brother Robert and Robert's new wife. But the general needn't have worried about any lingering awkwardness between the two of them. They'd made the right decision in mutually breaking off their courtship.

Besides, Robert wasn't the Carlisle who bothered her now.

She asked as casually as possible, "His cousin Christopher... What do you think of him?"

He frowned, puzzled. "But you know him."

"Only in passing." Only enough to avoid him. Until tonight, when she'd lost her mind and fallen for the charms and good looks that he relied upon to make his way through the world. "What do *you* think of him? He is a Carlisle, after all."

The general's brow softened with a low chuckle. "That he's most likely the best of the lot of them."

She blinked. "*Christopher* Carlisle?"

His eyes shined as he shook his head. "The most unlikely officer ever commissioned into the British army, I'll grant you. Always did as ordered in the end, but in the most unconventional ways imaginable. If he'd stayed in uniform, he would have been destined for generalship."

Her chest sank. This wasn't at all what she wanted to hear. She'd wanted to know without doubt that he truly was the idle scoundrel that gossip made him out to be, so she'd have good reason to never be tempted to kiss him again.

"Or handed over to the enemy by his own soldiers," the general continued. "When he served under me, it was still a toss-up."

She twisted her mouth in silent chastisement. The general was bamming her. But her initial suspicions of Carlisle as nothing more than a scapegrace simply *had* to be correct, no matter what glimpse of goodness she'd seen in him tonight that made her lose her mind. "Why did he leave the army? Surely a second son would have thrived there, unless..." Unless he'd done something absolutely disgraceful. Oh, she prayed that he had!

The general paused, as if contemplating what to tell her. But then he simply shrugged. "The wars were ending, his father had fallen ill, his brother took a diplomatic position... Lots of reasons. But it was a good decision in the end." He grinned with ironic amusement. "England's all the better for it."

He expected her to smile at his enigmatic quip, so she did. But inside, her stomach twisted so tightly with disappointment that she sucked in a mouthful of air to tamp it down before it overwhelmed her.

"Nothing passed by him unnoticed, no opportunity he didn't exploit."

*That* she believed. She leaned forward, clinging by her fingertips to a last scrap of hope. "So he's just as bad as everyone claims, then?" Seducer of widows and wives, relentless cardsharp and gambler, lazy and unambitious...

"Not at all."

*Drat it.*

"He's better than most second sons, I'd wager. But don't believe the stories about him wanting to become a vicar."

No. She had firsthand knowledge of that. A man of the cloth? Ha! For heaven's sake, he'd made her toes curl with one kiss. God only knew what he could have done to her if Higgins hadn't interrupted them. And it wouldn't have been leading her in Bible study.

"Keen as a knife, that one," the general muttered with a private chuckle, half to himself. "Even in managing his rakehell reputation."

She sank back on her boot heels, frowning. What did he mean by that? Something about the way he said that made suspicion prickle at the base of her spine. More lay behind what the general knew about Christopher Carlisle than he was telling.

Her chest deflated. "So there's no reason for me to avoid him?"

His gaze darted to hers. "I did *not* say that." He tapped a finger against his chair arm to punctuate his point. "Best keep your distance. As you said, he *is* a Carlisle, after all."

Well, that made her feel better. Marginally. Yet she had a feeling that despite her victory in this battle, she'd still lost the war.

"Why the sudden interest in Carlisle?"

The quiet question jarred her. Her mind raced to find an answer that wouldn't make her seem interested in the man. "No reason." *Only that I let him kiss me tonight.* "I remembered that he had an affinity for fine horses and thought perhaps he'd be interested in purchasing the colt. That's all." *Not all. Not even close.*

With a curt shake of his head, he took a sip of port and stretched out his long legs. "Garrett wants to keep the colt and train it himself."

Not if she didn't find a way to bring him home. Forcing down her guilt, she smiled. "He'll be very good at it."

"You'd be better," he muttered. Then he blew out an exasper-
ated breath. "But at least the boy will be doing *something* productive." He frowned, disappointment visible on his brow.

"He isn't a boy, general," she reminded him gently. "He's a
grown man."

"Then he'd best start behaving like it." He set down the glass
with a thud. "What kind of man lacks direction at his age? No
sense of purpose, no interest in securing any kind of respectable
living..."

Her thoughts sped back to Carlisle. What kind of man, indeed?

"When I was his age, I was already a major, with a wife, one
child, and another on the way. I had responsibilities, a steady
income, a means of proving my worth—"

Diana cringed, just as she did every time the general compared
himself to Garrett. Why couldn't her father realize what the
Morgan women had long ago come to know, that the two men
were nothing alike?

"He could have had a grand career in the military and risen
quickly through the ranks. Especially now, with the army
spreading to all corners of the empire."

"Another man like Christopher Carlisle, then?" She couldn't
help but goad him in an attempt to change the conversation, and
smiled to hide her sadness that the two men she loved most in the
world were always so disappointed in each other. "Someone
either deserving of generalship or likely to be handed over to the
enemy by his own men?"

"No." He grumbled only half teasingly into his glass of port,
"Garrett's men would have tarred and feathered him in the middle
of their own training camp before they even set eyes on the
enemy."

Her smile faded, the bitter truth of that smarting more than
she wanted to admit. She loved her brother dearly, but he

certainly hadn't lived up to what their parents—especially the general—had hoped for him. Not even close. "Some men aren't made to be soldiers, you know that. Their paths lie elsewhere." She rested her hand on his arm. "Garrett will find his."

Just as soon as she found Garrett. Unfortunately, with Carlisle's help.

"Always loyal to your brother, aren't you? To a fault."

"Loyalty is never a fault, general." She pushed herself up to her full height, then reached for his glass. "Ask any of the men who served under you."

"Perhaps not." His gaze followed her as she crossed to his desk and the silver tray where he kept his favorite liquor, the bottles and decanters all lined up with perfect military precision. "Yet no matter how much he fails, you always defend him."

She smiled as she refilled the glass. "Because I know the potential he possesses." She replaced the stopper and set the bottle down, then extended the glass as she walked back to him. "Just as I know that *you* deserved to be made field marshal."

"Bah!" He gave a dismissive wave of his hand before taking the glass from her, but he couldn't hide his expression of pride that her comment brought. "Wellesley was made field marshal, and look at what happened to him. The poor bastard was forced into politics." He took a long swallow. "I'd rather have died quickly by bullet at Waterloo than from a slow death by political debate in Westminster."

She smiled wryly at that. Knowing that answering would only mire her into another argument about how politics and the military should never mix, she put an end to the conversation by placing a kiss to his forehead. Then she poured a second glass of port for herself and settled into the chair opposite his. She'd never shied away from so-called men's drinks and had earned more of her father's respect because of it.

What haunted her, though, was that she'd disappointed him in so many other ways.

"You should be off to bed."

She eyed him over the rim of the glass. "So should you." Her gaze traveled to the memoir pages he'd been working over. Hoping to gain some insight into why the French wanted them, she asked nonchalantly, "How is your writing progressing?"

"Slowly." He let out a deep sigh. "It's taking me longer to write about the first offensive than it took to wage the entire Waterloo campaign."

A prick of hope tingled inside her as warmly as the port trickling down her throat. Perhaps the general could provide information she could use to find Garrett...or at least to convince Carlisle not to turn her in as a traitor. "Is that what you're working on now? Waterloo?"

"Nothing as exciting as that, I'm afraid. Only the meetings leading up to the campaign." He shook his head. "Paxton thinks everyone will want to read about those, so he's insisting that we go over that bit in detail. *Lots* of details." He grimaced. "Personally, I think he's wrong to give the reading public credit for having an interest in such minutiae, but he's not steered me wrong yet. Almost ten years now that he's been my aid, do you realize that? He was only a green captain when I first met him. And you, sergeant, were nothing more than a tomboy in breeches." His face shined with fatherly pride. "Now you're a fine young lady, and he's a major with solid prospects of becoming a general."

And...they were right back to where they'd started, with her father hoping she'd accept the major's suit.

She grimaced into her glass. There wasn't enough port in Portugal for that.

"That's what I was planning on doing tomorrow." He kicked out his long legs as he settled back, his glass balanced on his stomach. He waved a hand toward the papers on his desk. "Going over the entries from my diaries and making notes."

"About the time of Boney's Hundred Days?" she pressed gently. Those were the pages that the French wanted—descriptions of the events leading up to the Waterloo campaign nearly ten years ago. God only knew why. "It must have been a very important time."

"Wellington's memoirs about that period are far more interesting than mine, I assure you. While he was developing battle strategy, I was in meetings. One after another...with the Prussians, the French, the other Allies...followed by endless discussions and even more meetings." He grimaced. "Not the most thrilling of material to sell copies of a memoir."

No. So why did the French ask for them? And why on earth did they refuse them once they'd been handed over?

Her heart sank. She had no new ideas on how to free her brother. *If* he'd even been kidnapped at all. The night was ending in just as much swirling confusion as it had begun.

She bit back a groan. How had her life come to this, that the only thing saving her brother was a promise from a Carlisle?

The world had gone mad. Everything had been turned upside down, and she had absolutely no idea how to right it.

After a few more minutes of quiet conversation, Diana said good night to her father and left for her own room, only to pause in the hallway outside her door. Finally alone, safely hidden in the shadows of the silent house around her, she sank back against the wall and touched her lips.

Sweet mercy, they were still warm from Carlisle's kiss, still tingling with the feel of his mouth capturing hers. And what a feeling it had been, too...that wonderful, heavenly sensation blossoming through her of utter femininity and physical awakening, making her feel beautiful and alive. How long had it been since a man made her experience those feelings, so intensely and deeply

inside her that they were nearly overwhelming? Not just giddi-
ness over a new attraction, not even just physical lust—

But the desire to lose herself completely in another.

That's what she'd felt tonight. A longing to simply melt into
him and float away until bliss claimed her. She'd not felt that in so
very long. Not even with Robert, who had been the only man
she'd let seriously court her since returning from India. That was
one of the reasons why she wouldn't marry him, although she'd
never told him, not wanting to hurt his feelings. She knew the
passions and joys that could come from being with a man, and
despite his handsome looks, he'd not stirred those feelings
inside her.

But God help her, Christopher Carlisle had. Even now the
thought of it terrified her. Because for one desperate moment
when she'd been in his arms, she'd wanted him to do so much
more than just kiss her.

What a goose she was, to ruminate over Carlisle, of all men!
Perhaps the world hadn't gone mad. But *she* certainly had.

Pushing herself away from the wall, she hurried up the stairs
to the second floor, where she quietly opened the door to the old
nursery.

Diana paused just inside the large room where Meredith and
her nanny spent most of their days. She'd painted the nursery
herself last winter, to celebrate Meri's leaving her crib for a real
bed, creating a fairytale world of forest and flowers, with a blue
sky and white fluffy clouds sailing overhead. She'd even glued tiny
bits of colored glass and mirror to the ceiling so that, when the
lamps were put out at night, the firelight would shimmer across
them and make the mosaic sparkle like a field of stars. Toys filled
the room, from the large rocking horse to the tiny table where
Meri played at tea, along with dozens of dolls and shelves of
picture books. On the end wall, where Diana had painted a castle

so that Meri would feel like a princess when she was in the room, sat a little pink and white canopied bed.

She smiled. The little bump beneath the coverlet, nestled down among all the pillows, rose and fell with each slow and steady breath, deep in sleep.

Diana carefully sat on the edge of the bed so she wouldn't wake Meri. She peered down at the round face with its long eyelashes lowered against the tops of her cheeks and pouty pink lips parted slightly in sleep. An angel. Slowly, she reached to brush her hand through the silky chestnut curls lying across the small pillow—

A shadow moved in the doorway to the connecting room, and Diana froze guiltily. Then she took a deep breath as Meri's nanny came from her own bedroom, tying the belt of her dressing gown as she approached.

"I'm sorry if I woke you, Mrs. Davenport," she whispered. "I just wanted to look in on Meri before I went to bed."

"No apologies necessary, miss." The woman reached the side of the bed and smiled down at the little girl. "She's a sweet thing, she is. Never any trouble to speak of."

"Never," she agreed softly, unable to resist stroking a fingertip across Meri's cheek.

Hiring the kind nanny to care for Meredith when they'd arrived in England and settled in at Idlewild had been a stroke of brilliance by her mother, proven by how well the woman had cared for Meri during that awful time when Mama fell ill and died. Meri had been just old enough to know that Mama was no longer with them, and days of listening to Meri's inconsolable cries and screams for Mama had nearly destroyed Diana.

Pushing down the terrible memories, she focused on the little girl in front of her. "Did she eat dinner?"

"Aye, miss. And played well, too, 'til t'was time for bed."

Guilt pricked at her. "I'm sorry that I wasn't here to tuck her in."

"The general put her to bed, with lots of silly stories about fighting dragons." Her face beamed. "The wee one loves her father a great deal."

Her father? No. She didn't.

Diana blinked. Over the years, she'd grown used to unexpected pricks of grief like this until that was all she needed to right herself. One hard blink. But tonight, thanks to her fear for Garrett and Carlisle's intrusion into her life, it wasn't enough, and she had to turn her face away before Mrs. Davenport saw any stray emotion lingering there.

"Has she played with the new doll I gave her?" Diana forced a smile, yet worried that the sadness behind it would be visible.

"Not yet, miss. But you know how children are. She'd rather play with that raggedy old horse you gave her last year than with pretty new things." Mrs. Davenport reassuringly rested her hand on Diana's shoulder, but Diana knew it wasn't out of any deeper sympathy than for the unwanted doll. "She's lucky, that one is, to have you for her sister." Her hand fell away, and her voice quavered. "Poor duckling...what a shame that she has to grow up without a mother."

"Yes," Diana choked out in a rasping whisper through her tightening throat. "What a shame."

# CHAPTER 5

*The Next Night*
*Seven Dials, London*

The door of the brothel's upstairs room swung open to the sound of a prostitute's peeling laugh and lecherous growls from the man with her. He grabbed her around the waist to simultaneously yank her through the door and bury his face in her cleavage.

From a chair positioned directly across the room, Kit cleared his throat. "Good evening."

The bear of a man froze as the lightskirt gave a short scream of surprise. Lifting his head from the woman's bosom, he narrowed his gaze as Kit leaned back in the wooden chair, his boots kicked up upon the washstand and his hand holding a pistol pointed directly at the large Russian's chest. Nikolai Ivanov's face broke into an icy smile. His only movement was to possessively rest a hand over the woman's bottom, making no mistake that he'd purchased the ginger-haired cockney for the night.

"I did not pay for an audience," Ivanov drawled in a syrupy

aristocratic Russian accent. "And I do not need any help with what to do with this one."

He slapped her bottom so hard that she jumped.

She wheeled on him, scowling in irritation. When she began to stomp away, he grabbed her by the wrist and yanked her back to him, his other hand covering her breast. The woman stilled, knowing not to struggle. Ivanov had paid for her, and at this particular brothel that meant he could do anything he liked to her, short of maiming and murdering. Mrs. Smith's establishment provided very particular services for very particular customers. Which was why Kit had surprised Ivanov here, when the man's guard was down.

Kit coolly slid his gaze to the woman and nodded toward the door. "Jenny, would you please go downstairs and have yourself a cup of tea?"

By the astounded expression on her pretty, young face, she hadn't expected that.

"I'd like a few minutes alone with the gentleman, if you don't mind."

He tossed her a sovereign, and she snatched it out of the air, downright flabbergasted. She knew him. He'd spent enough time here chasing leads and contacts that he was familiar to all the girls. But he'd never paid one before.

"She stays," the Russian growled like an attack dog and hunched his shoulders. "You will leave. Now."

Kit calmly cocked the hammer of the flintlock. "I will kill you where you stand," he mockingly mimicked the rhythm of the man's speech. "Now."

Gritting his teeth, Ivanov grudgingly released the woman's wrist.

She jerked her arm away and retreated to the door, tucking the coin into her bodice between the tightly laced corset and her plump breasts. When she reached the safety of the doorway, she paused, her curiosity keeping her halfway in the room and half in the noisy, smoke-filled hallway behind her.

Around them, the building was alive, with music playing from the downstairs drawing room and laughter, shouts, and moans coming from the rabbit warren of rooms on the upper floors. The whole building pulsed with a crazed mix of desperation and debauchery, and over it all lingered a seedy depravity that put a bitter taste in Kit's mouth.

But such places had their benefit to him, because such places gave him access to men like Ivanov.

"Will you be here when I get back?" she asked Kit, foolishly not realizing the rash jealousy such a question would stir in the Russian. Or what she would have to do later to appease him for it.

"No." The sharpness of that blunt, dismissive answer was for her own good. If he was kind to her, Ivanov would be cruel. "Leave."

With a toss of her head and a flounce, she stepped into the hallway and closed the door behind her. Instantly the noise of the brothel was shut out, if not the musky scent of sex and the faint vibration of movement conducted through the building's beams.

Ivanov ignored the gun pointed at him and crossed to the bedside table, where a bottle of cheap port and a questionably clean glass waited for him. "So you are holding me at gunpoint." With an amused chuckle, he splashed the dark liquid into the glass. "Do you have any idea who I am?" He gestured at Kit with the bottle. "Or what I will do to you for interrupting my evening?"

"Nikolai Mikhailovich Ivanov."

The man paused, the port raised halfway to his lips.

"First Secretary to His Excellency Khristofor Andreyevich von Lieven, Russian Ambassador to London." Kit arched a brow. "And currently the man who's bedding the ambassador's wife, Dorothea."

The glass lowered as all amusement fled from Ivanov's face.

"And you won't do one damned thing to me."

Murderous rage blazed in the man's eyes for a fleeting heartbeat. Then with a laugh, it was gone, or at least hidden behind a cavalier smile. He took a long swallow of port and paused to study Kit over the rim of the glass.

"Who are you?"

"Just a man making use of a brothel." Kit sat forward in the chair, finally bringing its two front legs to the floor and resting his forearms over his knees, the end of the pistol never moving its aim from the man's broad chest. "So let's have a little chat, shall we?"

Ivanov said nothing.

"You and your men have been monitoring French communiqués between London and the Continent."

"You are mistaken. I am a diplomat, not a—"

Kit raised a hand to cut him off and repeated the statement, "You and your men have been monitoring French communiqués. Do not insult me by attempting to deny it." He lowered his hand, although every muscle remained coiled and ready to spring. The Russian said nothing. "I want to know about the movements of one of their operatives. An Englishman named Garrett Morgan."

"I do not know of him." But the flash of surprise in his eyes said otherwise.

"Think hard."

When the man said nothing, only continuing to slowly sip at his port, Kit reached beneath his overcoat to his breast pocket, to the bundle of letters tied with a pink ribbon.

"Perhaps you need something to jog your memory." He held

them up. "Correspondence between you and the lovely Dorothea von Lieven. I must say," he mused as he turned them back and forth, contemplating them, "I doubt His Excellency the Russian Ambassador wants the contents of these letters spread throughout the Court of St James's, wouldn't you agree, Secretary Ivanov?"

The man's lips twisted, as if he suddenly found the port distasteful.

"The man who wrote them might find himself sent packing from London, just in time for a long, cold Russian winter." His eyes flicked between the letters and Ivanov. "So, let's try again, shall we?" He held the letters up to the candle on the washstand beside him and let the flame singe the corner of the top letter, tempting the Russian into cooperating with the promise of destroying them. "Garrett Morgan. The past fortnight. Tell me."

Ivanov said nothing.

Kit pulled the letters away from the flame and made to put them back into his coat.

"Fine!" He bit out a string of Russian curses at being bested, then broke into laughter at Kit's audacity. "What do you want to know?"

"Garrett Morgan is working with the French." Months of tracking down leads and information had proved it to him, and now Ivanov's silent reply to that statement confirmed it. "A fortnight ago he went missing, apparently kidnapped and held for ransom."

Ivanov laughed.

Kit frowned. "Morgan isn't missing?"

"Oh, he is missing, certainly, but he was not kidnapped."

"How do you know?"

"Because if he were kidnapped, then he must be a magician to be in two places at once." He refilled his glass. "He was in London and in active communication with French agents as of three days ago."

"About what?"

Ivanov refused to answer that. Instead, he undid the first button of his bulging waistcoat and commented, "Then he went silent. That was when he disappeared, not a fortnight ago." He chuckled to himself and made a mocking toast with his glass. "Not even the French are sly enough to have a man in two places at once, or the boudoirs across Paris would be exceedingly happy places."

"Where is he now?"

"When his messages stopped coming, a few of my concerned *acquaintances*—shall we say?—decided to pay him a visit at the White Horse Inn. He was already gone."

"To where?"

"He is no longer in contact with the French." He shrugged. "He is no longer my concern."

With that, Kit knew he wouldn't coerce any more information out of the Russian about Morgan's whereabouts. So he teased the corner of the notes into the flame, letting the letters catch fire, watching the paper blacken and curl.

"One more thing." He waved out the flame, ignoring the murderous narrowing of Ivanov's eyes. "Could Morgan have fled because he double-crossed the French?" That would explain why the Frenchman didn't want the pages when Diana delivered them, if they weren't nearly as important as Morgan had led them to believe they were. Worthless, exactly as Diana had called them.

But damn the man to hell for placing his sister in danger.

"Possibly." He eyed Kit suspiciously over the rim of his glass. "Whoever you are, I am certain that you understand what it means if he did."

Yes. If Morgan wasn't dead already, he would be soon.

Ivanov smiled devilishly and slowly swirled the port. "If I were you, I would check downstream when the tide is low, and you will most likely discover where he went when he left the White Horse."

So...the Russian believed that Morgan was dead. Kit studied him closely, looking for any evidence that he was lying. And found none.

Slowly, he stood and moved to the door. He paused in the doorway to tuck his pistol back into its holster beneath his coat and tossed the singed notes onto the bed. "Thank you for your time."

The Russian snatched up the ribbon-tied bundle and held them to the candle, to burn them into ash, not realizing that they weren't love letters written by the ambassador's wife to her lover, but by Lady Bellingham to hers. "Send Jenny back to me on your way out."

*Like hell I will.*

Kit moved casually through the brothel toward the front door, as if he belonged there. As if he'd just spent the past hour in the company of a prostitute. If any of the people crammed within its thin walls recognized him, they would assume he was there for the same reason as every other gentleman who walked through the door. *Good.* Such beliefs only added to the false persona he'd cultivated as a scoundrel and younger son leeching off his earl of a brother. The more shiftless society thought him, the freer he was to hunt down Fitch's murderer.

Until tonight, when it all ended.

Ironic that it had come to this. That in the end he'd been pursuing a dead man.

Fingers clutched his arm as he strode past the main drawing room toward the entry hall, stopping him gently with a well-practiced touch.

"Leaving so soon?" A rich, feminine voice purred in his ear, followed by the warmth of her body sidling up against his from behind.

"Mrs. Smith." With a show of respect, he faced her and sketched a bow, giving her a flirtatious grin. He didn't like the woman, but he needed to stay in her good graces. "I'm afraid it's past my bedtime."

"Stay." Her red lips pursed into a pout. With her makeup and wig, it was impossible to discern her true age, but Kit supposed that she'd been selling herself and other women for at least twenty years. The hand resting on his arm certainly belonged to a woman who'd suffered a hard life, with little relief in sight for the future. "I can find someone to fit your tastes." She squeezed his arm, although Kit couldn't have said whether to keep his attention or to gratuitously feel his muscle. "In fact, I just hired a pretty little blonde thing that you're sure to find enjoyable."

"I'm afraid I have to refuse tonight." And every night.

"You never use my girls. You pay good money to *talk* to them, but you never take pleasure in them." Thankfully she kept her voice low enough not to be overheard by anyone else in the small crowd gathered in the entry hall. "Aren't they good enough for you?"

"Ah, that's the problem." He forced a forlorn expression onto his face. "I'm the one who isn't good enough for them."

She knew a line of drivel when she heard it, and her eyes flashed with dark amusement. "If it's an experienced woman you prefer, I can help you with that." She ran her hand up his arm, then down his chest. "I don't usually take on gentlemen from here, preferring not to mix business with pleasure." The look she raked over him told him in very blatant terms how much pleasure she expected to have with him. "But in your case, Mr. Carlisle, I'd be willing to make an exception."

Yes. He was certain she was. For a price. As a businesswoman, Mrs. Smith was nothing if not mercenary.

When her hand drifted down his front and cupped his manhood through his breeches, Kit sucked in a mouthful of air through clenched teeth and grabbed her wrist to stop her.

"I'm afraid not," he said gently, lifting her hand away to place a kiss in the air just above the backs of her fingers. "I wouldn't want to run the risk of not pleasing you in bed. How would I ever live that down?"

She froze for just a beat, her eyes narrowing angrily at being rejected. Then she laughed, a deep and throaty sound that eased away all the tension between them. "Is it true what I've heard about you, then, that you want to become a vicar?"

With an inscrutable expression, he answered, "My heart belongs to God."

She gave him another lingering look, this one of longing and disappointment, and drawled, "Pity."

"But I would still like to do business with you tonight, Mrs. Smith."

"Oh?" Her eyes lit up.

He reached into his coat and withdrew two sovereign coins. "I want to purchase Jenny for the night."

"No. She's already with the Russian."

"I want to purchase her *away* from the Russian," he corrected as he slid the coins into her hand. Surely far more than Ivanov had paid for the evening. "Let her have the night off, let her go to another man—anything but go back into the room with the Russian, understand?" When she closed her hand over the coins, he lowered his mouth close to her ear and threatened, "If you double-cross me on this and give Jenny to that man tonight, I will personally make certain that your brothel burns to the ground and that you find yourself on the first ship to Australia. Do you understand me?"

She blanched for a beat, then forced a saccharine smile and purred, "What Russian?"

With their self-serving friendship still intact, Kit nodded his gratitude and excused himself, sauntering out of the brothel and into the darkness.

He flipped up the collar of his overcoat to protect the back of his neck from the drizzling rain and hurried through the dark streets of Seven Dials. The only sound was the clip of his own boot heels on the cobblestones and their echo against the sides of the brick buildings edging the deserted streets, yet he reached beneath his left coat sleeve to palm the small knife he always carried there as a precaution.

He blew out a hard breath. A pretty little blonde thing. That's what Mrs. Smith had tempted him with, only for an image of Diana Morgan to pop into his head. *Christ.*

Diana was certainly beautiful—downright angelic, in fact, with her golden hair and sapphire eyes, pink lips that tasted of straw-berries and cream, warmth, softness...and in trouble up to her pretty little neck. How far could he trust her? Had she told him what she believed to be the truth, or was she simply spinning stories in order to save her own delectable skin?

He wanted to trust that she was sincere, that Ivanov was correct and Morgan was dead, that she'd been contacted in a desperate attempt by the French to secure documents that Morgan had promised but never delivered. If that were true, it would put an end to the pursuit that had been his sole focus for the past six months.

What a relief it would be to have it over. He'd finally be able to think of something other than Fitch's murder, to sleep without having nightmares of Fitch's beaten face haunting him. He could focus on his job again instead of what he'd been doing, which was ignoring Home Office duties, taking advantage of existing contacts, and ruining opportunities with future ones. Like Ivanov. He would never gain justice now—only watching Morgan swing would have done that. But Morgan's death at the hands of the French was the next best thing.

Except that too many pieces weren't fitting into the puzzle.

"Carlisle."

Kit stopped, his fingers clenching around the knife handle as a man stepped out of the shadows directly in front of him. The fog and darkness required a moment to discern his identity—

Lieutenant-General Nathaniel Grey. A hero in the wars with Napoleon, former War Office administrator, and now one of the best spymasters the Foreign Office employed. Kit knew him well and respected him, not least because the two men were distantly related by marriage through Kit's cousin Josephine.

But what the hell was he doing here?

"Odd time and place for a family gathering, don't you think?" Kit released the knife and extended his hand as Grey came forward, less in greeting than to show that he wasn't pulling a weapon on him.

Grey shook his hand. "Less mess and expense this way."

"And no fighting."

"Perhaps a little." Grey smiled, but no amusement showed in his eyes.

A warning slithered down Kit's spine. "So not a social call, then."

Grey's face was set hard in the shadows. "I know why were you at Mrs. Smith's tonight." He tugged at his leather gloves, but his attention never strayed from Kit and the damp street around them. Kit was certain that if a pin dropped two streets away Grey would note it. And react instantly. "And it wasn't to enjoy the women."

To deny it would be an insult to both men's intelligence, so Kit said nothing. And better, too, to find out exactly what Grey wanted with him.

"My men have been watching Ivanov since he arrived in London last year. As a foreign diplomat, he falls under the purview of the Foreign Office." Grey's deep voice was calm and controlled, but a cold admonishment laced through it. "The Home Office has no authority to interact with him."

"We're on English soil." Kit resisted the urge to clench his jaw and kept his face carefully inscrutable. "That puts him under Home Office jurisdiction."

"Not when it interferes with Foreign Office operations." He paused and fixed a hard stare on him. "And not when it has nothing do with official Home Office business."

An electric jolt skittered through him. Grey knew why he'd questioned Ivanov. Which meant he knew about Fitch's death. And didn't care.

"A personal vendetta brought you here tonight. One you need to give up."

*Like hell I will.* "A good agent was murdered." He paused to let that settle over Grey, just like the damp drizzle of rain seeping over the sleeping city. "Do you really expect me to believe that if one of your operatives or friends were killed that you wouldn't seek justice?"

"Of course I would. And doing so would be just as pointless as what you're attempting." Grey's eyes narrowed as they swept through the shadows around them, to make certain that they were still alone and speaking privately. "As someone who shares your allegiance to England, I'm here to warn you—stop looking into Fitch-Batten's murder. If you don't, Whitehall will notice what you've been doing, and it won't be a quiet conversation like this that they'll have with you. Your career will be over, and everything you've worked so hard to build will be destroyed."

Kit had known that from the beginning and had been willing to risk it. Still was. "He wasn't just killed," he dared to correct. "He was murdered in cold blood by a man he thought he could trust."

"Fitch-Batten was caught off-guard, and he paid the price." Grey's face was grim, with the fog and shadows only adding to the severity of his countenance. "It happens to agents, even to the good ones. That's always the risk, and we all accept it. But what you're doing now by pursuing this is causing problems for the rest of us." He looked away into the thickening fog as the icy drizzle increased to a light rain. "God only knows how much more damage you'll do if you keep chasing after a dead man like this."

His heart skipped. "Garrett Morgan's dead—you know that for a fact?"

Grey gave a quick, hard nod as his gaze swung back to Kit and pinned him with a look of cold anger. "And so did you, even before you set foot into that brothel tonight. You knew it in your gut, yet you approached Ivanov anyway and ruined months of surveillance work by my men. If I'm lucky, I can salvage most of my contacts within the Russian embassy. And if *you're* lucky"—he punctuated that with an arch of his brow—"then Whitehall won't discover what you've done."

Kit had never been that lucky. Nor did he care.

"You spoke to Ivanov," Grey continued, "and he confirmed your suspicions about Morgan.

"He told me Morgan was dead. But he didn't say why he killed Fitch."

"Let it go."

He bristled at the quiet threat disguised as a friendly warning. "Or what?"

"I can't have you interfering in Foreign Office operations." Grey straightened, his spine rigid and his presence a commanding one deserving of the rank of lieutenant-general. "I'll go to the Home Secretary myself, and he'll have no choice but to remove you from duty."

A long moment of uncomfortable silence stretched between the two men, both deadly serious as they stared at each other in the darkness. Not as friends or distant family, not as patriots in service to England, but as adversaries.

There, in the cold and darkness, with the icy rain falling over him and soaking him through to the bone, Kit made his decision—

"Then have me removed."

He strode past Grey and down the puddle-strewn street.

"Whitehall will declare that you've gone rogue," Grey called out after him. "You know what that means, what they'll do to you."

Kit halted mid-step, his heart jarring with a brutal thud in his chest. *Yes. A death sentence.*

"So be it." He walked on. He didn't look back. Didn't have to in order to know that Grey still stood there on the wet cobblestones, staring after him as he faded into the shadows and fog.

When he reached the main avenue, he waved down one of the old hackneys for hire that prowled the late-night streets and barked directions at the driver as he climbed inside. The carriage jerked to a rough start, then shook and shuddered as it rolled over the cobblestones, the springs so worn that every dip rattled his bones. He looked out the window. What he wouldn't have given to be on his way home to his rented rooms in Albany, or even to take advantage of his brother's hospitality and drop into Spalding House for the night, uninvited.

But he headed east, past the Temple and Blackfriars. To the White Horse Inn.

Grey was right, he considered, as he stared out at the city but saw only fog and darkness. He *had* gotten his confirmation tonight, because there was only one reason why Nathaniel Grey would seek him out, why he would warn Kit like that to stop his investigation.

Garrett Morgan was still alive.

# CHAPTER 6

*Three Nights Later*

*D*iana glanced around the crowded ballroom at Idlewild from behind her glass as she lifted it to her lips...and splashed champagne up her nose.

Rubbing at her nose to brush the bubbles away, she rolled her eyes at herself. *What an utter ninny!*

But that's what she deserved, she supposed, for not paying closer attention to what she was doing tonight. How could she, given the necessity to split her attention? Half of it focused on discouraging Major Paxton's attentions, the other half on keeping an eye on every guest announced upon arrival, to quickly discern how much they might know about the events of the last few weeks before Garrett went missing.

The former was easier than the latter. She was no longer under any duty as hostess to entertain the major, now that she'd danced an obligatory waltz with him to appease the general and could therefore ignore him for the rest of the party. It also helped that she had surrounded herself for most of the evening with groups of friends to serve as defensive lines to keep the enemy from advancing unseen.

Surreptitiously learning about Garrett, however, was proving much more difficult.

If Carlisle was correct and Garrett hadn't been kidnapped, then he was simply missing. So she'd been eavesdropping all night on various conversations held by anyone who seemed as if they might mention her brother. She'd occasionally even boldly asked outright if they'd recently seen him, using his absence tonight as a way to broach the topic without raising suspicions and catch word of his whereabouts. *Any* word. But so far...nothing. She knew as little now about what had happened to him as she had a fortnight ago. All she had to show for her efforts was mounting frustration and distraction.

Given that, she set down her champagne flute before she accidentally drowned herself.

"There you are!" Her friend Julia Warner sidled up to her. "Grand party, Diana." A sly smile brightened her face. "And what a coincidence that all the most eligible gentlemen in England are here."

Of course they were, she thought with a grimace. Because the general had ensured it.

She slid her gaze around the crowded ballroom. The party was supposed to have been in honor of the army regiments who had recently engaged in fighting with Burma to protect British interests in northern India, to show them that the full confidence of the empire was behind them. Which meant that Idlewild was filled with handsome young officers in their uniforms, several gentlemen who worked for the War Office or the Court of St James's, and a smattering of MPs and peers. Everyone was here to show their patriotism and unreserved support for England's soldiers.

And to be given a subtle reminder by the general that his unmarried daughter still needed a husband.

Even though she was only in her third London season, at twenty-three, she wasn't exactly young anymore. Certainly a good deal of the gossip that was going on behind flitting fans this evening involved talk of how she was already on the shelf.

She drew a deep breath and remembered the mantra her mother had repeated in times of tension to keep from being overwhelmed. "One disaster at a time," she murmured and searched the crowd once more, wondering if anyone else would be able to give her information about Garrett.

"Pardon?"

She forced a smile and pretended to repeat, slightly louder, "Everyone seems to be having a good time."

"Very much so. Lots of partners, for once. And speaking of dance partners—"

"I didn't know we were."

"I've just taken a turn about the room." Julia gestured in a circle with her fan and added conspiratorially, "Major Paxton is nowhere to be seen."

Thanks goodness. One less worry tonight. Now she could focus her attention on—

*Christopher Carlisle.* Her heart stuttered as she spied him across the room.

On second thought... She snatched up her glass of champagne and took a long swallow.

Her eyes narrowed on him over the rim of her flute as she held it to her lips. What the devil was *he* doing here?

Yet there he stood, uninvited and unannounced, having somehow slipped unnoticed into the party and looking for all the world as if he belonged here, right down to the shine of the silver buttons on his dark blue brocade waistcoat.

But of course he would. And oddly enough, striking her not as a gentleman in his evening finery that was surely crafted by the best Bond Street tailors, not as the brother of an earl, but as a chameleon who blended into his surroundings.

Was that why she hadn't noticed him at the tavern, until he'd been lying on top of her? Was that how he'd managed to so seamlessly fit into the party tonight? Because he purposefully made himself blend into the crowd? Even now, his dark blond hair was mussed just enough to give him the same rakish and slightly dangerous look as the officers around him. The rascal even had the cheek to wear a ruby pin in his cravat, that small flash of red at his neck as powerful as the full red uniforms of the soldiers scattered throughout the room.

Yet despite that inexplicable way he had of blending into the crowd, he was clearly the most dashing man in the room. There was no hiding that. Even now half the women present had their eyes on him. For heaven's sakes, Lady Sussex was practically drooling.

Julia craned her neck to see who had snagged Diana's attention. Her flitting fan stopped mid-flutter. "Isn't that—"

"Yes."

"The cousin of the man who—"

"Yes."

Her gaze trailed shamelessly over him. "Oh my."

*Oh yes.* She forced a bored little sniff. "I suppose…if you find that sort of pretension attractive."

"I do." Her fan flitted wildly now. "I definitely do." She arched a knowing brow. "And so do *you.*"

Diana choked on her champagne. "I do not! He isn't at all the type that stirs my interest."

"Handsome, charming—"

"Shiftless."

*That* he certainly was. He might have saved her that night at the tavern, might even possess the good character and competence the general claimed he saw in the man. And, drat it, she had to give him credit for that, which complicated the devil out of the changing opinion she was forming about him, that perhaps he wasn't as bad as he portrayed himself to the world to be. *Perhaps.*

But the fact remained that Carlisle had done nothing to live up to his capabilities. Instead, he'd been more than content to live off his brother's charity and eschew any attempts at a respectable living, good character or not. For that alone, she entertained no ideas about him. After all, she had to be so very careful about the men she let into her life.

Yet strange disappointment gnawed at her that he wasn't more responsible, more set on making something of himself rather than charming his way through life. That he couldn't be more like the sort of man she needed.

He stood apart at the edge of the room, lazily swirling a glass of Madeira in his palm. He let his gaze drift aimlessly over the crowd, unhurried in his perusal, as if bored with the party...

Until his gaze landed on her.

All the tiny muscles in her belly twisted into knots as her eyes locked with his. She saw the knowing glint of recognition spark in the blue depths of his eyes, the twitch of a grin at his sensuous lips, and she *knew*—

The rascal had been searching the room. For her.

His eyes trailed rakishly over her, heating every inch of skin not covered by the satin and lace of her blue dress and long white gloves. The devil was undressing her with his eyes and surely imagining what she looked like beneath, bare in the lamplight, and an unsettling sensation of feminine pleasure sparked inside her.

"Still, I would bet that he's a wonderful dance partner," Julia mused, unaware of the silent communication occurring between them. "How could he not be? I mean, *look* at him."

Diana was certainly doing just that, taking her own shameless glance over him in return, from the dark gold hair that curled at his collar down to the muscular thighs accentuated by white kerseymere trousers. So dashing and handsome... If he were anyone else—*anyone* but Christopher Carlisle—she would have found a way to wrangle a dance from him, to closet herself away with him at the side of the room or on the garden terrace where they could share a conversation in private, and perhaps let him kiss her again the way he had by the stables.

But fate never listened to her heart. Because he *was* a scapegrace second son. The worst man in the world for her.

"Then by all means," Diana mumbled, inexplicable loss panging in her chest, "you should dance with him."

"Perhaps..."

His eyes returned to hers. Holding her gaze fixed beneath his, he raised the glass of Madeira to his lips and took a long, slow swallow in what she knew was a secret toast to her. Liquid warmth splashed through her, and she couldn't help the soft catch of her breath at the heated sensation, one as palpable as if he'd skimmed his hands down the length of her bare body.

He set down his glass and ambled toward her through the crowd.

"Or perhaps he's coming for you."

The warmth he'd stirred inside her only seconds before froze instantly into trepidation. "No, he isn't. He's—"

"Headed right toward you," her friend finished as Christopher continued forward, his eyes never straying from hers. Like a man on a mission...or a wolf stalking his prey. Julia waved her fan and began to move away. "And that's my cue to leave."

She reached for Julia's arm to stop her. "You're running interference for me with the enemy tonight, remember?"

"If he's your enemy, then you know what they say...Keep your friends close." She took a glance at Christopher and murmured appreciatively, "Keep your enemies closer."

Oh, he'd already been more than close enough that night at the tavern, thank you very much. And he simply could *not* get any closer. So she refused to release Julia's arm, despite her friend's small tugs to pull it away, even when he stopped in front of her and sketched a bow to both women.

"Miss Warner...Miss Morgan." His eyes sparkled when they landed on her. "Lovely party, isn't it?"

Julia gave one more firm tug and freed her arm, and Diana was unable to grab after her without embarrassing herself. She refused to look like a goose in front of him by hiding behind her friend like a shield, even if that was exactly what she'd hoped to do.

Julia slid a glance between the two and mumbled, "Certainly interesting, at any rate."

His deep voice tickled playfully down Diana's spine. "I've come to pay my respects to the hostess."

Of course he had. And pigs flew.

She smiled tightly. "None necessary, Mr. Carlisle. Your unexpected presence here tonight is respect enough."

An amused gleam glinted in his blue eyes at her dig. *Good.* Let it serve as a reminder that she knew exactly what kind of bounder he was, especially to sneak into the party uninvited.

"But I insist. My mother taught me to always be a gentleman, and I wouldn't want to offend my late mother's memory." He flashed both women a charming grin. "If anyone is capable of boxing her son's ears from the grave, it would be her."

Julia smothered a laugh behind her fan.

"Surely you've given her no reason to scold you for your

behavior." Ignoring Julia, Diana gave him a saccharine smile. "And so need not worry about it tonight."

"Yet I do."

Frustrating devil! "Then you should give your respects to the general. The party was his idea."

"But the general isn't nearly as much fun to dance with as his daughter."

"He's spry for his age. He'll surprise you."

"His daughter keeps surprising me even more."

Julia's eyes darted between the two of them, as if watching a tennis match. Diana wanted to shake her.

It was time to end this nonsense, so she gave him a dismissive smile. "I'm afraid that I'm done dancing for the evening."

"Then I must settle for paying you other attentions." He held out his hand. "Would you favor me with a turn about the room, Miss Morgan?"

At the invitation, Julia's fan dropped away, and she gave up all pretense of not being interested in their exchange to stare at Christopher as if he were a prince.

"I'm sorry," Diana refused, not at all apologetic. "I couldn't possibly leave my friend."

Julia gaped at her as if she were a bedlamite. "Of course you can!"

Diana glowered at her. With allies like this, who needed enemies? "It wouldn't be at all polite of me to—"

"And where is your brother this evening, Miss Morgan?" he interrupted with a friendly smile.

His question jarred her, the private meaning behind it not at all friendly.

Well aware of the eavesdropping guests pressing in around them, she answered carefully, "Visiting friends in the North."

"Is he? I'd heard differently."

Her heart lodged in her throat. *That* was why he was here. He had information about Garrett.

He held out his hand again. "A turn about the room, if you'd please?"

"Of course." She placed her hand in his to be led away.

# CHAPTER 7

"You've found out something about my brother." Diana's fingers stiffened against his sleeve where her hand rested on his arm. "What have you learned?"

Aware of all the guests who were watching them, and the necessity of not bringing undue attention upon them, Kit smiled but shook his head, as if they were having a normal conversation. But just like everything else in his life, this was nothing but pretense and illusion hiding a deeper darkness.

He leaned closer to speak into her ear over the noise of the party. "Not here."

Her fingers dug into his forearm in reply.

He slid a sideways glance at her. She walked slowly beside him, the smile of a good hostess plastered into place and her head held imperially high, looking for all the world as if she were simply entertaining one of her father's guests. But beneath her composed surface simmered apprehension so intense that it seeped into him through her fingertips.

He should have been pleased that she'd so easily agreed to go off with him for a private conversation. Instead, unease stirred the little hairs at his nape that she could appear so calm on the outside that no one in the crush of partygoers suspected anything more between them than a mild attempt at flirtation on his part and the politeness of a dutiful hostess on hers. How had she learned to do that?

He was used to deception in his life. Lived it every moment of every day, in fact. But when it involved Diana, that same pretense troubled him.

"You look lovely this evening," he murmured, wanting to pry under her façade to find the real woman beneath. "Downright angelic in that dress."

"Ironic, since you're behaving like the devil come to capture my soul."

He grinned. *There* she was, the feisty creature who had fought so hard against him at the inn. He liked this bit of hellcat in her. Although—he raked a sideways glance over her—he liked the pretty society lady in her, as well. More than he should.

He hadn't lied. She did look like an angel, with her golden hair cascading over one shoulder in a riot of curls, in that blue dress of satin and lace that hugged her bosom and capped her shoulders. Just enough skin was left bare to the eye to be tempting. *Very* tempting. Even now he longed to lean over and brush his mouth over her collarbone, to discover for himself if she tasted like sweet icing that melted on the tongue or exotic spices that tingled the lips.

They reached the far end of the room. Instead of circling back along the other side, he led her into the hallway with a guiding tug of his arm. He couldn't help the spark of pleasure when she followed so trustingly. "I'm not a devil, Diana. I'm a gentleman."

"Is there a difference?"

"None I've ever discovered." He led her down the hallway and further away from the party. "But even us devils find ourselves attracted to angels every now and then."

He'd expected a soft laugh from her, a dismissive smack of her hand on his arm to remind him to behave. Instead, she surprised him with a whispered, "Please don't call me that."

"Angel, you mean?" Taken aback by her reaction, he stopped and matched her frown with one of his. Every inch of him was aware that they were alone in the hallway. "It's a compliment."

"It's an impossible standard that I can never—"

In one fluid motion, he opened the door beside them and swept her inside the room with him.

Dark and bathed with shadows, the room was lit only by the faint light of the starry night that fell through the tall French doors and giant fanlights dominating the far wall. Beyond the glass stretched the gardens, its paths lit by scattered torches and paper lanterns, an earthbound mirror of the stars overhead.

But at that moment, he saw none of it. His attention rested on only one place as he struggled to remember to breathe.

*Diana.*

A slant of moonlight fell gently over her hair and shoulders, bathing her in its silvery light and making her resemble a spirit magically cast up from the midnight shadows around them. The small pearls at her ears glistened like drops of dew, and the satin of her dress simply glowed. All of her seemed to float on the night air, delicate and ephemeral. Very much an angel. For one fantastical moment, he feared that she might vanish like the evening mist if he dared to touch her.

Completely unaware of the effect she had on him, she took a step closer. "My brother." Her soft voice spooled around him like a silk ribbon, entangling him in her spell. "What have you learned?" She placed her hand pleadingly on his upper arm, having no idea of the heat she flared inside him with that simple touch. How she utterly captivated him. "Please tell me."

He stared down at her, wanting to catch every flitting emotion crossing her beautiful face. "He's alive."

"Oh, thank God!" A deep, ragged sigh tore from her, as if she'd been holding her breath since he last saw her. Her hand on his sleeve now clutched at him, and he resisted the urge to snake his arm around her waist and pull her softness against him. "Where is he?"

He shook his head. "I traced him to the White Horse Inn. The hostlers remembered him and that he hired a post-chaise for Dover." So Kit had followed on horseback, traveling hard across the miles to arrive at the coast by the next day, only to discover that Morgan had once more vanished. The last anyone could remember of him, Morgan had purchased a ticket for the steam packet to Calais five days before, boarded the ship, and left. "He's in France."

She searched his face, but she wouldn't find any answers there, because he had no more answers to give. And he wouldn't dare share the details of how he knew even that much. Doing so would only put her into more danger than what she'd already stumbled into on her own.

"I don't understand...Calais?" Her pink lips parted slightly, drawing his attention to her mouth. "But why would he go there? Unless the French..."

Unable to make the connections, she let her voice trail off in confusion. Her fingers tightened their hold on his arm, silently pleading for his help in understanding.

He took her elbow in his hand to soften the news. "I have no idea why he's gone to France or why he lied to you about where he was going, but your brother was never kidnapped. The French made you believe it in order to obtain the general's memoirs. I don't think he knows that they even made contact with you."

"But the pages—the man at the tavern didn't want them." She shook her head, bewildered. "He refused them. You were there, you saw. Why go through all that trouble, only to refuse them?"

A damnably fine question. One he had no answer to. "Are you certain those were the pages he wanted?"

In answer, she reached a hand into the bodice of her dress. He watched, delightfully dumbstruck, as she fished out a tiny, folded note that she'd tucked there.

"Here's the ransom note." She held it out to him. "It lists the exact dates of the pages I was to provide."

Taking the note, he lifted a brow as he shamelessly contemplated her bosom. "That's an ingenious place to file your correspondence." He murmured appreciatively, "I suddenly have a newfound admiration for the Royal Mail."

"Drat you, Carlisle!" He suspected that if her face wasn't awash in a silver sheen from the moonlight he would have seen a most delicious blush pinking her cheeks. "It isn't like that, and you know it."

Ignoring her rebuke, he trailed a slow look over her from head to toe and couldn't resist baiting her by adding, "Now I'm wondering where you keep your ink set."

In aggravation, she crossed her arms over her chest, hiding her bosom from view. "After what you said the other night—about how someone inside the household might have helped the French —I didn't want to take any chances and kept that note with me at all times. I knew that eventually you would want to see it."

So he did. He read the note, the black ink legible in the moonlight.

He lifted his gaze to meet hers. "They wanted the pages about the lead-up to the Waterloo campaign."

"And that's what I brought them." But she paused, adding hesitantly, "Unless…"

"Unless?"

With a shake of her head, she took back the note and read it herself, although Kit suspected that she'd read it so many times already that she had it memorized. "I assumed they wanted the pages from the general's memoirs, because those were the pages he'd most recently been writing. But what if…" She bit her bottom lip. "What if they wanted pages of another sort?"

"What sort?"

"Diary pages." She lifted her gaze from the note, and in the silver moonlight, her blue eyes shined with otherworldly intensity. As if she could see right through him. An unsettling chill gripped him that she might be able to see who he truly was, and he simply wasn't prepared for that. "The ones he's been using to construct his memoirs. They hold all of his original notes from that time."

"But how would the French have known about the diary?"

Hope vanished visibly from her, and her hand with the note dropped to her side in defeat. "I don't know."

Kit wasn't ready to surrender just yet. Morgan's disappearance was tied to those pages somehow, he knew it. But how?

"Where is the diary now?" he pressed.

"The general keeps his memoirs in a locked cabinet in his study. I suppose the diary is in the study with them." She smiled ruefully. "I always tease him that he's afraid Wellington will break in and steal them out of jealousy because his memoirs are more interesting than the duke's."

Kit half-smiled. That was exactly how she'd tease her father, he was certain.

In that pause in the conversation, he saw the brightness fade from her countenance, replaced by a distrust that he detested seeing in her. Yet one he was certain mirrored his own. "It's all over then, isn't it? What do those pages matter now, if Garrett's alive and safe?"

"I never said safe," he corrected grimly. "I'll tell you more as soon as I discover it."

In order to make that happen, though, he needed to drive Morgan out from hiding.

"What are you going to do?" Her hand returned to his arm, as if she needed his solidity to reassure herself. The thought warmed through him.

"I'm going fishing." Which meant that he'd need the right bait. When she frowned at him, bewildered, he pressed, "How did you contact the French before, to tell them that you would bring the papers they wanted?"

"The ransom note said to leave a message at the inn, for a Mr. Overton."

Well then. Mr. Overton was about to receive another message, and through him Garrett Morgan, who would surely be in touch with his French contacts, wherever he was. "I think I can make your brother contact you, but I need the diary."

"Why?"

"Because I plan on offering it to the French."

Confusion darkened her face. "But you said Garrett hadn't been kidnapped. Why offer it to the French when they've lied to us?"

*Us.* Nothing but a slip on her part, but he liked the sound of it. They were in this together now, both of them with the same goal: to flush Morgan out from his cover. After that...well, after that, she'd hate him for what he'd do. "Because when word reaches your brother that you're offering up the real pages, he'll have no choice but to contact you to find out what's going on."

When he did, Kit would arrest him. Then watch him hang.

"The only way for Garrett to learn that would be if he were working with the French," she said, so quietly that he had to lean in to hear. "That's what you think, isn't it? That he's selling the general's documents to obtain money to pay off his gambling debts. But you're wrong." Yet her voice lacked conviction, as if she were attempting to convince herself of Morgan's innocence as much as him. "My brother might be a bit of a scapegrace, like you—"

Kit countered that inadvertent insult with a lift of his brow.

"—but he's no traitor." She waved a hand in the general direction of the ballroom. "Ask anyone here tonight. Some of them even saw him in London in the days leading up to his disappearance, and they all said the same thing, that he was playing cards and drinking and—"

*Whoring.* She censored herself, but from the flush of her cheeks, he knew that was what she was going to say.

"Behaving exactly like himself," she finished instead. "A man who's selling secrets to the enemy wouldn't behave like that."

"Know a lot of spies and traitors, do you?" he drawled in challenge.

"Do you?" she shot back.

*Dozens and dozens...* "People behave in all kinds of ways when they're under pressure." He took a step toward her and saw her breath hitch as he approached. The same way it had when he'd rescued her from the tavern, when she'd wanted him to kiss her. Did she want that now? "Some behave nervously. Others fall back into set routines. Some break down completely." A troubled thought jumped into his head, and he frowned. "How do you know what your brother had been up to? You said you hadn't seen him in over a fortnight."

"I haven't. But I've been asking people about him."

"You did *what?*" Anger flashed through him.

"I asked the guests about him, his friends, and those people who might have seen him at the clubs."

*Damnation.* The danger she'd put herself into— "Well, stop it. Let me take care of finding him, all right?"

She put her hands on her hips. "So you can turn him in and claim some sort of reward?"

"Because I don't want you to be hurt."

She froze at that honest admission, taken completely off guard by it. Yet the little minx was too proud to retreat and countered softly, "I'm not your concern."

"The general matters to me, and you matter to the general." Unable to resist, he reached up to brush a stray curl away from her cheek. In response, her arms fell gently to her sides, her warrior stance vanishing beneath his touch. "So, yes, you are my concern."

A heated shiver spilled through her at the tender caress, one he felt pulse into him through his fingertips.

"The general defended you, you know." Her gaze softened, and she looked at him now as if she were suddenly seeing him for the first time. "He said you were a good man. But I've heard stories about you, those tales of gambling, fighting, and bedding women...of all sorts."

*Christ.* "I *am* a good man," he interrupted. "Or at least as good as I can be." He was so damn tired of living this pretense! "I just wish you'd give me the chance to prove it."

Her expression melted into one of bafflement, and she bit her bottom lip as she stared at him. As if she simply couldn't fathom him.

But it was her lingering doubt about him that grated. He should be happy that the profligate reputation he'd built to hide his work was so easily believed. Yet coming from her, it rubbed him raw. He couldn't have said why it mattered what Diana Morgan thought of him, but it did. A great deal.

"So if for no other reason than that your father would be devastated if anything happened to you, let me help you, Diana. Before you get yourself hurt."

Her eyes flared with indignation. And with something else just as hot. Instead of having the sense to move away, she poked a fingertip into his chest. "You think me as helpless and fragile as that?"

"Never."

She leaned in toward him, and the finger that pressed into him softened until her palm rested against his chest. Right over his pounding heart.

"I'm a general's daughter, remember? I'm not some cake of a silly society miss who faints on a whim, or who goes into hysterics at the slightest danger."

No. Apparently, she was a woman who couldn't prevent herself from curling her fingers into his waistcoat, in an attempt to get to the man beneath. Shamelessly, he didn't try to stop her.

The same attraction from the night of the tavern sparked once more, sizzling the air between them. She was so close to him now that he could feel the heat of her body seeping into his, could lose himself in the scent of lavender that wafted around her.

"I don't sit around waiting for a man to rescue me." But that gentle chastisement emerged as a throaty and breathless protest. "Nor do I follow blindly along, passively doing as I'm told."

"Oh, I realize that," he murmured. Because there wasn't a passive bone in her body now as her hand at his chest slipped slowly upward until her fingers tangled in the hair at his nape. "I know exactly what you are, Diana."

Her gaze dropped to his mouth, and her lips parted in a tantalizing invitation to be kissed. "And what is that?"

"Trouble."

He slid his arm around her waist and pulled her up against him as his mouth came down over hers.

HER MIND SWIRLED BENEATH THE INTENSITY OF HIS KISS—NO, ALL of her swirled as he twirled her in a quick circle, then stepped her backward to press her against the wall. As if he were afraid she might slip away even now. But at that moment, leaving his arms was the last thing she wanted to do.

He feasted on her mouth as if he were a starving man who needed this kiss to survive. So much so that when he cupped his hand against her jaw to gently lift her head and guide her mouth more openly against his, his fingers trembled against her cheek.

Letting herself surrender to the moment, she wrapped her arms around his neck and lifted herself into his kiss. She wanted this as much as he did—perhaps even more—because the desire she tasted in him was a sweet ambrosia that she didn't realize she'd been craving so desperately until that moment. His hard body pressed along the length of hers, chest to chest and hips to hips, and the contact made her feel feminine and alive. Electric. And just as beautiful as he'd claimed she was.

"Christopher," she whispered against his lips, having to say his name in order to make herself believe that this was really happening.

He smiled against her mouth, then pulled back only far enough to break the kiss. When he outlined her lips with his fingertip, she closed her eyes and sighed, only to gasp when he hooked his thumb over her bottom lip and gently tugged it down, opening her lips as he once more captured her mouth beneath his. But this time, he slid his tongue inside, to take sweeping plunges and explore the depths and recesses she willingly offered to him.

When he'd plundered her kiss so thoroughly that she lost her breath, she tore her mouth away from his to gasp for air. Her arms still clutched her tightly to him, so tightly that his hard muscles flexed beneath her fingertips as she splayed her hands over his shoulders in an attempt to feel all of his strength.

His lips went to her neck and placed hot, open-mouthed kisses against her throat, and his hands swept along the sides of her body. She knew he could feel her racing pulse beating against his lips, which sent an answering throb shooting wantonly down between her legs.

From the hallway right outside the door, a woman laughed.

Diana jumped in his arms, startled. The interruption suddenly shocked her back into the reality of what she was doing. And with whom.

"We should...stop," she panted, desperate to find sense in her kiss-fogged brain. But her voice wasn't at all convincing, even to her own ears, especially when she moaned out, "Probably."

He smiled against her throat. "Why?"

*Why?* She blinked, not at all prepared for that logical question. "Because...because..." Sweet mercy, she couldn't think of a reason. Except the one she could never utter aloud. "Because it isn't at all proper."

"Oh, yes, it is." His mouth returned to hers, to tease the tip of his tongue at the corner of her lips as his fingertips now traced tantalizingly along her ribs. Goosebumps sprang up everywhere he touched. "It's a very proper little kiss."

That was the problem. Little kisses had a way of growing into so much more—especially a *proper* kiss. And how would she find the strength to resist him then? "Someone might see."

"Not behind a closed door." He nipped at her jaw, the act oddly more possessive than passionate, and all the more disorienting because of it. "And not in the darkness."

Damn him for being logical! And double damn herself that she enjoyed being in his arms and at the center of his masculine attentions, that even now her belly fluttered with excited anticipation for his hand to travel upward to her breast and tease at the nipple that had already grown taut beneath her corset. She craved his touch, the way men in the desert craved rain.

Biting down a groan as she fought the urge to surrender, she forced out, "*I'll* know, even in the darkness."

He stopped and shifted back to look down at her. "You don't like my kisses?"

Oh, so much more than *like*! "Your kisses are—" A burst of light caught the corner of her eye. "Fireworks."

He grinned with a charming arrogance that sent her heart somersaulting. "Well, I wouldn't exactly say—"

"Not you. The party." Slapping his shoulder lightly with her open hand to drag his attention away from her, she pointed at the wall of French doors that gave a perfect view of the front lawn and of the fireworks now being set off there to mark midnight. She didn't know whether to be relieved or disappointed. "The footmen are lighting the fireworks."

A predatory gleam lit his eyes. "I don't give a damn about the party." He gazed down at her with a look of such intensity and desire that she shivered. "I only want to keep kissing you."

Her belly fluttered at the sincerity of that rakish admission. Had it been at any other moment, had he held any other expression on his handsome face, she would have accused him of empty flattery. But this...

Oh, this was a grand mistake!

"You'd better care." She slipped away from him and instantly missed being in his arms. "Because everyone from the ballroom is about to come rushing in here to watch the fireworks through those windows, and we'll be caught. You have to leave before they find us together." *Before I find myself back in your arms, and this time without the willpower to stop...* "Go. Please."

He stifled a curse and ran a hand through his hair.

"Not that way!" She stopped him with a panicked grab at his arm. "Or through the French doors. Someone on the terrace might see." She gestured toward the casement window that led out to the side garden, where the light of the torches and lanterns didn't reach. "Through there."

He shot her a look of complete aggravation and loss of patience. Yet he blew out a breath as he gave in to her wishes and turned toward the open window.

"I usually sneak *in* through windows to scandalously embrace women, I'll have you know," he muttered half to himself and put his leg out the window. "This is the first time I've been forced to leave through one."

"You're planning on becoming a vicar." She refused to feel guilty about his ignominious exit, even as goosebumps still dotted her skin at the heat of his embrace. "So this won't be the last time you'll exit through windows after embracing a woman. You'll need to get used to it. Might as well start now."

He harshly muttered something beneath his breath about Russians, brothels, and Sir Robert Peel that she didn't understand and stiffly slipped out the window.

"Wait!" Impetuously, she ran to the casement and leaned out into the night. "That kiss—" She drew in a ragged breath. Doubts and longings all churned inside her, so fiercely that she couldn't find any words of explanation. Except... "I'm sorry."

He slipped his hand behind her nape and pulled her halfway through the window toward him. His mouth came down upon hers in a kiss so heated, so filled with raw desire that she whimpered.

He drawled wickedly against her lips, "I'm not."

Then he was gone, vanished into the darkness.

She stared through the open window after him, lifting her hand to her kiss-hot lips and trying futilely to sort through the riot of emotions flaming up inside her. How could it be possible that the man who uncaringly bedded society widows and foolishly gambled away his allowance could be the same one who saved her at the tavern, the same one whom the general thought so highly of? The same man who kissed her with so much tenderness yet so much longing that he set her head to spinning?

Christopher Carlisle... Who on earth *was* he?

The door opened behind her. Heavens, his departure had been close! Taking a deep breath to gather herself, she slowly lowered the sash and turned to greet the guests—

A hand clamped over her mouth. Beneath the noise of the exploding fireworks, no one heard her scream.

# CHAPTER 8

it strolled casually through the dark garden to rejoin the party, taking the long way back in order to give himself enough time in the cool air to collect himself. The *very* long way. But overhead, blue and red flashes boomed into the sky. He snapped out a curse at the fireworks, at the men who had chosen that perfectly wrong moment to set them off, and at all of China for inventing them in the first damned place.

But the flashes of light and noise reminded him of cannon fire from his days in the army, which worked wonders in tamping down his lust. So did his chagrin over kissing Diana.

Again.

Just as she'd warned, the crush of partygoers had spilled outside to watch the fireworks, along with a small army of footmen who were carrying trays of champagne for the guests to toast Britain's recent victory when the fireworks ended. They were all smiling and pointing at the sky, except for those few couples who had already used the excitement to slip away unseen into the dark recesses of the gardens for a few stolen moments.

Most likely none of them had even given the drawing room a single thought as a place to view the fireworks. Most likely that had been nothing more than an excuse by Diana to send him away.

He didn't blame her. Whenever he was around her, he behaved no better than the scoundrel he worked so hard to convince the world he was. Why she hadn't slapped him yet, he had no idea. But if she kept letting him kiss her like that, the pleasure would be well worth the pain.

Grimacing at himself for his loss of control, he strode inside through one of the open doors framing the ballroom and made his way down the hall to the front stairs that twisted in gracefully carved mahogany up toward the first floor, where the general kept his study. He knew this house well, having studied it for hours tonight through the windows before he'd slipped inside to join the party, until he knew the location of every main room and hallway, every way out, and every guest who went in. He'd planned for all contingencies tonight.

But he sure as hell hadn't planned on her.

Driven on by his frustration, he took the stairs three at a time to the first-floor landing, then hurried down the hallway toward the study. The floor was empty. *Good.* With his wits dulled by Diana's kisses, the last thing he needed right now was another distraction.

Of course, it didn't help that before he'd entered the party, he'd watched from the garden as she'd danced with one of the officers, how she'd given the man friendly smiles at his flirtations and moved gracefully in his arms. It might have been her third London season, with the gossips blathering on about how she was rapidly approaching spinsterhood, yet she was still an Incomparable, still coveted by society gentlemen across England.

He hadn't been able to fathom the sensation he'd experienced when he'd watched her dance, but now he recognized it. Jealousy. And he felt like a nodcock because of it.

*Concentrate, damn it!* He had to get into the study, get the diary, and then get the hell out. And *stop* thinking about Diana.

Replaying that mantra ceaselessly in his head, he cast a glance over his shoulder to make certain no one had followed him and opened the study door.

Inside, the room was lit by the glow of a lamp and the dying coals of a fire. Two half-filled glasses of port sitting on the desk and the lingering odor of cigar smoke told him that the room had recently been used, most likely by the general in some private conversation with one of his fellow officers. It also told him that he had to hurry so he wouldn't be caught in a room that was off-limits to guests. That—coupled with his lack of invitation in the first place—would bring down a fierce interrogation by the general that he had no intention of experiencing.

Kit scanned his eyes around the room, searching for the cabinet where the general kept his papers, where he would most likely also find the diary.

He bit back a curse. He'd arrived too late.

He crossed to the tall hutch, with its glass doors holding stacks of books on the shelves above and rows of drawers with their brass locks forming the base below. Rather, what had once been brass locks but were now broken and wrenched from the front boards, the letter opener that had been used to stab and twist at them lying discarded on the rug. The drawers had all been ripped open, and now half of them dangled, warped and splintered, from being sprung open. Books had been knocked to the floor, with sheaths of paper strewn around them. The general's manuscript pages. With all the noise and music from the party below, no one had heard the destruction.

"Damn it!" He began to open each drawer and tray, searching them all to see if the diary still remained.

"Raise your hands where I can see them."

The heavily accented voice stopped him cold. *The Frenchman.*

Every inch of him tensed instantly, ready to fight. With all of his senses on edge and his skin prickling, he slowly raised his hands as he turned to face the man. "No need for—"

He froze.

Diana stood in front of the Frenchman, a knife pressed to her throat.

DIANA TILTED BACK HER HEAD TO KEEP HER THROAT FROM PRESSING against the sharp blade and whispered, trembling with fear, "Christopher..."

Across the room, his face grew hard as every muscle in his body visibly stiffened, like a coil tightening to spring, including his hands, which drew into fists at his sides. Yet he ignored her, his icy gaze fixed over her shoulder at the Frenchman standing behind her. No emotion showed on his face, but his eyes blazed.

"I want the diary." The Frenchman jerked her back against him, eliciting a startled gasp from her as his arm clamped around her chest to hold her still. "Give it to me, or I will slit her throat."

Christopher slid a glance at the wrecked cabinet, then back to her. *Where is it?*

She could read the pleading question in his eyes, but she couldn't tell him—she didn't know!

"It was you who broke into the cabinet," Christopher directed at the Frenchman when she couldn't answer, as calmly as if he were discussing nothing more important than the weather. But every bit of him was alert and ready to lunge. The air between them crackled with tension. "So you should have found it yourself."

"It was not there." The Frenchman's breath fanned hot across her cheek, and Diana flinched, her stomach roiling. "You know where it is. Give it to me. Now!"

Christopher held up his hands in front of his chest, empty palms forward. "If it's not in the cabinet, then it's somewhere else in this room. Most likely there." He nodded toward the other side of the room. "Did you search it?"

When the Frenchman turned his head to look where he'd indicated, Christopher's hand dove beneath his jacket and pulled out a small coat pistol. He pointed it at the Frenchman and cocked back the hammer with a loud click.

"If you harm her," he threatened in a low, menacing voice, "you'll be dead before you reach the door."

With a snarl, the Frenchman grabbed Diana by the hair and yanked hard, jerking back her head and bowing her neck to press the blade against her throat. She caught her breath with a soft cry of terror.

"I might die, Englishman, but I will take her with me to hell." He made a show of sliding the knife back and forth across her throat. "And I know exactly how fond you are of her."

Sheer murder glinted in Christopher's eyes, but he didn't look at her, not even to flick her a second's glance.

"Give me the diary," the Frenchman repeated.

Christopher's jaw clenched. "Let her go."

Another yank at her hair, his fingers twisting into her locks so hard that tears of pain blurred her vision. "You are not in a position to be making demands."

"If you hurt her, you'll never get the diary."

"If you give me the diary," the Frenchman countered coldly, "I will have no need to harm her. You have my word."

*Worthless!* As worthless as the man uttering it. Only terror kept her from laughing at that.

Yet Christopher stared at the Frenchman for one long, painfully silent and still moment, then eased down the pistol's hammer and lowered the small gun to his side. "All right," he said quietly. "It's in the desk."

"No!" she cried. He couldn't—surely he *wouldn't* hand over the diary! Not when they didn't know for certain where Garrett was, not when that diary might still be the only way to find him and deliver him safely home. "You can't!"

The two men ignored her cries, with Christopher's narrowed gaze not leaving the Frenchman and the Frenchman only tightening his hold around her to keep her still, the blade pressing unyieldingly into her throat. Her eyes and nose stung as she watched Christopher pick up the letter opener from the rug and slowly cross the room to her father's large desk.

The man rotated her in a half-circle, keeping her in front of him and his eyes on Christopher. "Slowly—no sudden moves."

"Of course not," he drawled. "I wouldn't dream of doing anything that might result in you getting shot."

Placing the pistol on the desktop yet still within easy reach, he moved the chair out of the way to give him access to the center desk drawer and its small brass lock. He jammed the point of the opener into keyhole, and with a prying twist, he broke the lock with a loud snap.

He opened the drawer and reached inside, searching through the contents. Then he slowly withdrew a book.

"Is this what you want?" He flipped through the pages, scanning them, and confirmed with a decisive nod. "The general's diary."

"Bring it to me."

"No!" Diana cried out desperately, twisting futilely in the

man's grasp. "Please don't! We'll never be able to save Garrett if you—"

Christopher shot her a quelling look that ordered her to be quiet as he circled around the desk and walked slowly toward them. His eyes not leaving the Frenchman except to dip a glance at the knife still pressed to her throat, he stopped an arm's length away and held up the diary.

She could feel the man's breath stutter at her ear. With one hand still holding the knife near her throat, he grabbed for the diary with the other, snatching it out of Christopher's hand.

Christopher lunged. But instead of hitting the Frenchman, he slammed sideways into Diana, who was ripped out of the man's grasp and shoved safely away from the knife. Too startled to scream, she rolled under him as he tumbled with her onto the floor.

He sprang to his feet and put himself between her and the Frenchman. A slender blade flashed in his hand in the lamplight. The letter opener, wielded like a knife and sharp enough to stab into the man's gut—

A dull thud echoed through the room. The man spasmed violently, then dropped to one knee.

The general stood behind him, the iron poker from the fireplace in his hand.

The Frenchman bit out an enraged curse and grabbed at the poker. With his other hand, he landed a hard punch into her father's stomach.

"Papa!" she screamed.

He doubled over in pain, but summoned just enough strength to twist the poker from the Frenchman's grasp, raising it to strike again.

"*Bâtards anglais!*" The man put up his arm to fend off the glancing blow, then snatched up the diary and raced unsteadily from the room, blood dripping down his face from the cut on his scalp.

Dropping the letter opener, Christopher reached for Diana. "Are you all—"

"General!"

She pushed his hand away and climbed to her feet, to dart past him to her father's side as he crumpled against the wall, breathing hard to catch back the air knocked from his lungs and doubled-over from the pain of the punch. She sat at his side as he slid to the floor, unable to remain on his feet. *Dear God, his heart!*

"Diana, he'll be fine," Christopher said reassuringly, placing a gentle hand on her shoulder.

She shoved him away.

"This is all your fault!" she shot over her shoulder at him, then turned away to cup her father's face in her hands. His eyes were closed as he struggled to gain back his breath. She tore at his collar to loosen it, to make him as comfortable as possible. "The French, Garrett's disappearance, that damnable diary—you brought all of this down upon us!"

Her father shook his head as he opened his eyes and gazed solemnly up at her. "He's not the enemy, my girl," he rasped out hoarsely. "Far from it." Then he looked past her to stare grimly at Christopher. "Carlisle's a hero."

# CHAPTER 9

"*G*ood God," General Morgan muttered two hours later when Kit finished telling him what he knew about his son's disappearance.

*Good God, indeed,* Kit thought as he leaned back against the desk in the study.

He'd finished sharing with the general everything he could about Garrett Morgan, but he'd been careful to avoid all mention of the Home Office and to heavily censor details about Diana. If the general ever discovered what liberties he'd taken with the man's daughter, he'd be more than a rogue agent. He'd be a dead one.

Around them, the house was finally quieting down. Excuses had been made for the host's and hostess's sudden disappearances from the party, with the Duke of Hampton stepping in for the general to make the toast once the fireworks had died away. The party had ended shortly after, and the property had been cleared of all guests—and then thoroughly searched by the servants per the general's orders. The staff had been told that they were on the hunt to find any guests who might be lingering in dark corners with lovers or who had fallen asleep. In reality, they were confirming that the Frenchman had gone and the household was no longer under threat. Although Kit feared it wouldn't be for good.

The general eased himself down onto the settee beside Diana. She reached over to cover his hand with hers as he rested it on his knee. Only his fingers, drawn up into a tight fist, revealed any traces of his surprise and anger.

"Is that all?" General Morgan demanded.

All Kit planned on sharing, anyway. So he gave a cut nod and pushed himself away from the desk to cross to the card table in front of the window and the tray holding several glasses and decanters filled with liquor, put there for the party.

"You truly had no idea that your son's been missing?" Kit pulled the stopper from the decanter of whisky and splashed the golden liquid into two crystal tumblers. "Or that the French want your diary?"

And wanted it badly enough to threaten Diana's life.

At that dark thought, Kit glanced up at her. Still in her blue ball gown, she sat straight-spined next to her father, possessing the same disciplined military bearing. She'd fixed her hair, putting back into place the golden tresses that had come down in the fight, and her delicate lips and cheeks had regained their color.

Anyone who saw her would never have suspected what she'd gone through tonight. But she couldn't hide the worry that lingered on her beautiful face, or the tension that gripped her shoulders, that even now made them stiff as stone.

The general shook his head. "I came looking for Diana because it was time for the toast, and she wasn't in the ballroom. I knew she wouldn't want to miss it. That's when I found all of you in the study." His eyes grimly met Kit's as he handed the general one of the glasses. "Thank God you knew to distract him by drawing his attention to the desk so that I could grab up the fire-place poker."

Diana's gaze darted to Kit. "You did that on purpose?"

"Yes." The way she stared at him made him feel as if she'd never truly seen him before. Damn unsettling that, given the way he'd embraced her earlier.

But he didn't blame her. After all, she had no idea the man he truly was.

Yet she could also never find out. She'd already been placed into danger. To reveal any more to her would simply amplify the risk.

"I had no idea that's what you were doing," she mumbled. Her surprise over his ruse turned into visible chagrin. "You saved my life again."

"*Again?*" The general leveled a glare at Kit so fierce that it shook him to his boots.

Diana squeezed her father's hand, to draw his attention back to her. "It was my fault, general," she admitted guiltily. "I've been keeping secrets from you."

Quietly, she told her father about the ransom note and the meeting at the inn, then softened the details as she described the fight and how Kit had rushed after her, to keep her from being hurt.

Her heroic description of him only grew the guilt gnawing at his gut as he returned to his perch on the desk. The truth was that he'd have gladly strung up her brother for murder and treason if Morgan had been at the tavern in her place.

"And then Mr. Carlisle brought me safely home," she finished, thankfully avoiding the details that would have gotten him shot at dawn. But she seemed absolutely confused about him when she added, "He was a perfect gentleman."

When she met his gaze over her father's head, Kit arched a

knowing brow and mouthed, *A perfect gentleman?*

*Stop that!* she mouthed back, yet her cheeks pinked intriguingly.

Kit grinned, then coughed to cover his smile when the general glanced up at him. He quickly raised the whisky to his lips.

"You didn't trust me enough to tell me," the general scolded her gently, yet Kit suspected that the question was actually aimed at him.

"Of course, I trust you." Her voice lowered to an almost secretive whisper, and she took her own glance at Kit then, to see if he was listening. "You know how much."

"Then why didn't you tell me?"

Worry melted across her beautiful face. "I didn't want to upset you because of your heart. I planned on telling you once Garrett was safely back home, but everything spun out of control."

The general eyed Kit askance and muttered, "Apparently."

"I was wrong earlier to blame Mr. Carlisle," Diana corrected, quietly apologetic. "He's been caught up in all of this by accident, just as we were. He only wants to collect the gambling debts that Garrett owes him."

The general's eyes never left Kit. "He isn't here to collect money."

That knowing accusation sliced into Kit with a sickening jolt.

"But he is," Diana answered for him, frowning. "That's why he was at the inn when—"

Her father cut her off with a wave of his hand and sat forward on the edge of the settee, his hard gaze fixed on Kit. "Are you, Carlisle?"

There was no point in denying it. "No, sir."

"Why else would you want to find Garrett?" Diana twisted on the settee, her bewildered gaze darting between the two men. "I don't understand…"

"Tell her," the general ordered.

"I've already tried. She won't believe me." Kit took a long swallow of whisky to brace himself. "She needs to hear it from you."

"Hear what?" Her confusion changed to irritation. When the two men exchanged a silent look, she demanded, "What are you two talking about?"

"Garrett is working for the French." The general's face turned haggard. "And Carlisle knows it. That's why he was there at the tavern and most likely why he's here tonight."

"Stop saying that!" Diana shot to her feet, her hands clenched at her sides as she wheeled on Kit. "It's not true."

"Unfortunately," Kit corrected bleakly, "it is."

Her bright eyes narrowed into slits of accusation. "I've told you that my brother is not a traitor. Yet you—"

"The only way that Frenchman would have known where to look for my diary was if Garrett had told him," her father interrupted, staring grimly into his whisky. As if acknowledging it made it real, as real as if his son were already swinging by the neck for treason. "No other cabinets were disturbed in any of the other rooms, or any other cabinet in this study. He knew to go to that one, specifically, because Garrett had told him that was where I keep my papers, not knowing that I keep my diary hidden in a secret drawer inside it."

"No, you're wrong," she whispered, unable to find her voice beneath the truth about her brother. "The Frenchman *didn't* know where the diary was. That's why he came after me."

"Only after he'd searched the cabinet," Kit said quietly, raising his eyes solemnly to meet her anguished ones. "After he didn't find the diary where he was told it would be."

The color that had managed to return to her face seeped away again, and a haunted look took its place. One so distraught that it ripped through him. *Christ*, how he hated that she'd been dragged into this mess!

"But—but the Frenchman took the diary." She jabbed a finger at the desk, and at him, thrusting upon him all the anger she couldn't yet bring herself to level at her brother. "You gave it to him. I saw you."

"That wasn't my diary." General Morgan pushed himself off the settee and crossed to the ruined cabinet. "That was the household account book."

He yanked open one of the twisted drawers and reached inside to push a hidden button. The small panel at the top of the cabinet, decorated with a scallop shell, popped open to reveal a secret door. He withdrew a key from his pocket and unlocked it, then opened the tiny drawer that guarded a space not more than five inches wide and three inches deep. The compartment was perfectly hidden among the decorations, and anyone who didn't know where it was would never have found it.

He reached inside and removed a small, leather-bound pocket book. Its plain brown cover was covered in scars and stains from being carried through battle, its spine stitched with an equally plain binding that had loosened slightly from use.

"*This* is my diary." His face hardened as he brushed his hand over it. "No one knows that I keep it here. Not even your brother."

Her mouth falling open, Diana turned toward Kit, trying to absorb it all.

"I took a chance that there'd be another book inside the desk." He shrugged a shoulder. "One I could pretend was the diary. I needed to catch the Frenchman with his hands full so that he'd have no choice but to release you."

"When he did, you pushed me to the floor," she whispered, staring at him again in that odd way she'd done before, as if seeing him for the first time.

No—as if seeing right *through* him, to his soul. He knew then that he'd been correct to keep his distance from her, until this past sennight when he'd had no choice but to get close to her. Ironically, far closer than he ever should have.

"But what could the French possibly want with this diary?" the general interjected. "It contains nothing but an old soldier's stories."

"They requested specific pages in the note they sent to Diana," Kit answered quietly. "Those describing the beginning of the Waterloo campaign. They probably want to know logistics—who was where and when."

"But that was nearly ten years ago." Frustration colored her voice. "What does it matter now who the British officers were or where they'd amassed their troops?"

"Not ours," her father interrupted, returning the diary to its compartment and locking it inside. "Theirs."

Kit's gut knotted. Brilliant tactician that he was, the general was already two steps ahead. But if the French were attempting to track down the whereabouts of one of their own, then this went far beyond the jurisdiction of the Home Office. Nathaniel Grey's warning to stay away from Garrett Morgan suddenly took on a new meaning, one that had nothing to do with Russian diplomats.

General Morgan misunderstood the sudden hardening of Kit's body and shook his head in what he believed was shared frustration over the diary. "So many men came in and out of meetings then, on both sides, during the Hundred Days. How do we know which men they're interested in?"

"We don't," Kit bit out, his jaw clenched. But the Foreign Office knew, damn them. Just as they knew the French were working with Morgan. Christ—they *knew!* Which meant they'd known all along about Fitch's murder. And hadn't done a bloody thing about it.

The question now...why were they letting it play out?

"So we assume it's all important to them," Diana concluded. "What do we do?"

"We wait for them to make their next move." Kit walked back to the drink table to refill his glass. Unfortunately, there wasn't enough whisky in all of Scotland to dull the betrayal and anger now simmering inside him. "They know we've got the diary. They'll send—"

The door opened, and Kit spun around, his hand diving beneath his jacket for his pistol.

But instead of being flung wide, the door pushed open barely a foot. Just far enough for a slip of a little girl in a night rail to run inside. With wide eyes that reminded him of Diana's, a head of curly chestnut hair, and her face red from sleep, the girl cried out a loud, "Papa!" and launched herself at the general, who scooped her up into his arms and brought her down onto the settee with him.

Heedless of dirtying her skirt, Diana dropped to her knees on the floor at the general's boots. Her hand reached out to rest on the little girl's back. But the frightened child didn't notice, burying her face into the general's shoulder, her arms wrapped tightly around his neck.

Diana shot Kit a look over the girl's head, one he couldn't fathom but that reminded him of a doe startled by hunters. Not one of fear, but—*caught*. As if waiting for judgment and recrimination.

But for what? The little girl had been safely tucked away in the nursery with her nanny, Kit had made certain of it during the past two hours when he'd worked with the general to secure the house. What did Diana have to feel guilty about?

"What is it, Meri?" she leaned toward the child, her hand

rubbing circles across her small back to soothe her. "What frightened you?"

"The noise," the little girl mumbled against the general's jacket. "All the people walking up and down the stairs... I don't like it."

A soft sigh of relief escaped Diana, but even though she smiled, Kit sensed worry in her. And grief. "It's all right, darling," she assured her. "The party's over. That was just the servants putting everything back into place."

But her words and soft caresses did little to calm the child, who continued to cling to the general for dear life.

"It's all right, Meri," he told her, placing a kiss to the girl's forehead. "All the guests are gone, and the servants are all heading off to bed, exactly where you should be. Is Mrs. Davenport still in her room?"

The girl nodded. "She's snoring."

"And so should you be." He set her away from him far enough to tweak her nose, drawing a small smile from her. "So go on back to your bed, and in the morning, we'll take the dog-cart out for a drive. How about that?"

The girl nodded, appeased by that bit of bribery. "Will you tell me a story, Papa?"

"Not tonight. I have a guest." He nodded toward Kit, bringing Meri's attention to him.

Shyly, she curled up against the general's chest and eyed him uncertainly. His attempt to win her over with his most amiable grin only earned him an uneasy frown.

Apparently, his charms were failing with all the Morgan women tonight.

"Go with Diana." The general handed Meri over, but the child visibly cast a pleading glance back at her father to let her stay. "Go to bed, and I'll see you in the morning." He rose to his feet and placed a kiss to the top of her head. When he placed another one to Diana's cheek, Kit saw in him the same fleeting look of grief that had been on his daughter's face just moments before. *Odd...* "Both of you."

"Yes, general." Holding the girl protectively in her arms, she moved toward the hall. She paused in the doorway to glance back. "And the house?"

A world of meaning lingered in that quiet question.

"Footmen have been posted, so have grooms, including one on the landing outside the nursery," her father assured her. "In the morning I'll request a few men from the local guard to keep watch over the farm until all is settled."

"Thank you." Pressing the sleepy child tighter against her bosom, she nuzzled her face against Meri's hair. She inhaled a deep breath before asking, "Darling, do you want to sleep with me tonight in my room?"

"I want to sleep in my bed, with all my dolls and animals." She considered a moment, then added, "But there's room there for you, too."

Hiding her smile in Meri's curls, she rocked the little girl in her arms. From the gleam in her eyes, that small exchange had inexplicably pleased Diana more than Kit could fathom. "Up to the nursery, then."

"Diana." Kit took a step toward her, suspecting she was keeping secrets from him...*I want answers.* "Let me escort you upstairs."

"No need." When her eyes met his over Meri's head as the sleepy girl finally rested it upon Diana's shoulder, he felt a wall already being erected between them. "Goodbye, Mr. Carlisle." *Please leave me alone...* But he had no idea what he'd done to become her enemy. "Have a safe journey back to London."

Then she was gone, stepping into the hall and closing the door behind her.

Kit stared after her, resisting the urge to deny her wishes and follow after her anyway so that he could demand answers from her. And kiss her again. After tonight's revelation about the Foreign Office, he wanted nothing more than to lose himself in her soft arms and forget the world for a few blissful hours.

He slid a sideways glance at the general, who was eyeing him closely. *That* was never going to happen.

"So." General Morgan collected his glass and came up beside Kit at the drink table. He reached for the decanter to refill both glasses. "She doesn't know."

Nodding his thanks for the whisky, he lifted the glass to his lips. There was much that he'd not told Diana about her brother and his connection to the French. "Know what?"

"That you're working for the Home Office."

Kit froze, the glass halfway to his mouth. Every muscle in his body tightened. A jarring thud of his heartbeat counted off the long seconds while he returned the general's gaze over the rim of the crystal tumbler before he finished bringing it to his lips.

"No." He took a long swallow. "But apparently, you do."

"Of course I do." The general reached into the table's center drawer to remove two cigars from a specially made box of untreated Spanish cedar and offered one to Kit. "I was the one who recommended you to them."

Kit squelched his surprise as the general crossed to the fireplace. "Because you thought I was a good soldier?"

"Hell no." He removed a wood splinter from the spill vase on the mantel shelf, then crouched down to light it on the coals. Rising to his feet, he leveled a no-nonsense stare at him. "You were one of the worst soldiers who ever served beneath me. I recommended you to put you out of the ranks and away from me."

Well, *that* stung.

"You had the intelligence to be a general, but being a soldier wasn't in your character." He clamped the cigar between his teeth and lit it from the little flame dancing at the end of the spill. "You lacked all discipline and regard for the command chain."

True.

"But I've never known another man who could commit as much trouble as you yet somehow escape all punishment, who could talk a man out of all his blunt and convince him that it was his idea to give it to you."

So was that.

"You were wasting your talents by being in uniform." He tossed the splinter into the fire and puffed at the cigar until a trail of smoke curled toward the ceiling. "Especially when the Home Office could put them to better use. And did, from all I've heard."

The backs of his knees tingled. "You've been keeping watch on me?"

"Someone had to, once your father died and your brother went overseas."

That should have rankled, yet oddly enough, it didn't.

"After all, I recommended you. My reputation was as much at stake as yours." The grisly old man didn't fool him with that comment, especially when he didn't look at him as he said it, keeping the truth hidden behind a frown at his cigar as he rolled it between his fingertips. He'd kept watch because he'd been concerned.

"You have nothing to fear in that regard," Kit assured him.

"Yet you let the world believe you're nothing more than a wastrel who wants an easy living as a vicar."

When the general put it like that, one of the men he'd respected most in his life… *Damnation.* He admitted with chagrin, "It's easier that way."

"You are one of His Majesty's most decorated men."

Definitely easier than having to admit publicly to *that*. "I have to work in secret. If anyone outside the Home Office discovers what I've been doing, my career is over."

Most likely his life, right along with it. Which made his pursuit of Fitch's murderer even riskier. But he owed it to his partner for all the times that Fitch had rescued him from trouble. And because it should have been him who had his throat slit in the alleyway that night.

Pushing those grim thoughts from his head, he lit his cigar, then followed the general's lead of sinking into a leather chair positioned in front of the fire. Both men kicked out their long legs to rest their boots on the fireplace fender and quietly watched the smoke drift upward from their cigars. In the soft light of the fire and lamps, the house finally quiet around them, Kit could almost imagine that the two men often spent time together like this.

Until General Morgan studied the glowing tip of his cigar and demanded, "Is my son truly a traitor, Carlisle?"

Harsh reality came crashing back. "He's working with the French," he replied carefully, not wanting to upset the man any more than possible. "He must have a good reason."

"Revenge on me." The general grimaced into the fire. "As payment in kind for all the chiding I've done of him over the years, all the criticizing that he wasn't living up to expectations. *My* expectations for him."

"I don't believe so." Life as General Morgan's son couldn't have been easy. But sons criticized by their fathers ran away to join the navy, pursued racing or boxing, spent their days in drunken stupors in gambling hells and their nights passed out in brothels. They didn't commit treason.

"When you catch him, you'll arrest him." Not a question.

"Yes," Kit confirmed quietly.

There was no point in lying, and nothing that Kit could say to ease the general's pain at knowing his son betrayed his country and all that he'd worked so hard to defend. Nor would he insult the man by spewing any kind of placating platitudes.

So he offered the only medicine he could by pushing himself out of the chair and fetching the decanter of whisky.

"You have two beautiful and loving daughters, general." He topped off the man's glass and solemnly returned the stopper with a soft clink of crystal. "Lean on them to get through the days to come."

"My daughters," the general repeated into his glass. An odd tone colored his voice, one Kit couldn't comprehend. "You could have arrested Diana for treason at the inn. *Should* have. It was your duty as a Home Office agent, but you didn't."

He sank into his chair and stared into the fire. "No good would have come from it."

"Thank you for that."

The man's gratitude clawed at his chest. His intentions had been far less noble than that. Kit hadn't arrested her because he'd wanted to use her to find her brother. But now... *Damnation.*

"And thank you for saving her life." General Morgan threw his unwanted cigar into the fire. Then he mumbled into the flames, "I'd sacrifice everything I possess to keep Diana safe, and she'd give the same for Meri." He swirled the golden liquid in his glass. "We men do everything we can for the women we love."

"Yes, sir."

"And God help us if they ever realize that."

Kit's mouth twisted into a grin. "Yes, sir."

General Morgan looked up from his drink and pinned Kit beneath his steely gaze. The same gaze that had stared down Napoleon and other enemies across the empire. "Be careful with Diana," he warned. "She's much more fragile than you realize."

"I'll protect her with my life," he promised. And meant it.

# CHAPTER 10

*Three Days Later*
*London*

K it tossed another coin into the center of the table. "Deal."

As the cards were dealt, he leaned back in his chair and took an assessing glance around the King Street gambling hell. This place was where bluebloods came when they wanted an evening that their private clubs couldn't provide, right down to the light-skirts that were let in shamelessly through the front door, and where middle-class gentlemen could rub shoulders with aristocrats who would never have let such upstarts into their St James's Street clubs.

Tonight, he was gladly one of them. He'd already spent hours here gambling, drinking too much into his cups, carousing with chums who were always up for a good time, and flirting with the women. Even as he tossed away coin after coin on one bad hand after another, he kept grinning and shouting boisterously to the men around him at the other tables, bragging about how he planned to fleece them of their fortunes and steal their women.

In other words, behaving exactly like himself.

Or rather, exactly what society thought was the true him. How convenient that he could hide behind such an easy disguise.

Tonight, though, it was only a partial façade, because a large part of him truly longed for any way to push Diana from his head.

That he couldn't stop thinking about Diana Morgan, of all women—he nearly laughed aloud. Thaddeus "Never Surrender" Morgan's daughter, the sister of his enemy...an innocent. Pursue *her*? For God's sake, he might as well become a vicar after all.

Across the main room of the hell, Lord Stanwyck's second son, Henry Blythe, shouted out in victory as the luck of the cards finally fell to him. He rose to his feet and made a show of kissing the cards before sweeping in his winnings with both hands. The men sitting at the table with him shot him murderous looks, while others nearby scowled in annoyance. The men tolerated him only because he was the son of a marquess, generous when it came to buying rounds of drinks, wealthy enough to keep the stakes high —and a bad enough player to keep that same wealth flowing into their pockets when he lost. Which was usually every night.

That last hand was a fluke. But Kit would gladly take the opening it gave him.

"Blythe!" he shouted out, loud enough to shake the dusty chandeliers overhead. He leaned back in his chair to get a good view of the man through the crowd and rested his arm across the back of the empty chair beside him. "Did you win? Impossible!"

"Look to your own losses, Carlisle!" Blythe shot back, sending up laughter across the tables. "God knows you have enough of those to keep straight."

"Losses, you say? What are those? I wouldn't know."

Snickers, hoots, and eye rolls went up around him. *Good.* Every man in the room was used to such antics by Kit. Had come to expect them, in fact. Tonight, he wouldn't disappoint.

"But I hear you're quite familiar with losing. Heard your horse lost at the Ealing races last week. A mare, too." Kit slapped the shoulder of the gentleman sitting to his right, bringing the unfortunate man into the fray as an accident of proximity. "Just like every female in Blythe's life, the old nag gave up before she finished!"

Peals of laughter exploded around the room.

Used to Kit's barbs, Blythe shot back, "Go to hell!" He paused and gestured at the room around them. "Oh, wait—we're already there."

More laughs went up, followed this time by calls for both of them to shut up and let the men get back to their cards, booze, and women. Blythe clamped a cheroot between his teeth, nodded to the other players as he excused himself from the table, and headed toward the fireplace to stretch his legs and light his cigar.

"All kidding aside, Blythe," Kit called out to him, much more reserved this time, "I know what you can do to improve your chances at winning the races." He reached for the bottle of port that he'd spent a small fortune to purchase and refilled his glass. "But by all means, don't listen to me. After all, I'm just someone who wins every race he enters."

Unable to resist that bait, Blythe gestured at him. "Get your bragging arse over here then," he ordered. "And make it worth my time by bringing that port with you."

Grinning, Kit snatched up the bottle and a spare glass, then left the table in mid-hand, to insults and curses from the men playing with him. He sauntered up to the fireplace where Blythe was standing and set the two glasses onto the mantelpiece. No one else stood nearby who might overhear their conversation.

Blythe lit his cigar and tossed the used spill into the fire. "So you think you can tell me how to win at Ealing, do you? I doubt you've ever—"

"I don't give a damn about racing." Kit's grin belied his icy bluntness. He kept up the pretense of two old chums sharing nothing more than casual conversation by pouring the man a glass of port. "You work for the Foreign Office."

Blythe froze. Only for a beat, but it was enough to prove true the rumors about Blythe's connection to Whitehall. Recovering himself, he laughed. "You're mad!"

"You work for the Foreign Office," Kit repeated in a hard voice, one that said he would brook no dissembling. He raised his glass in a friendly toast, as if reminiscing about schoolboy adventures, but there was nothing at all friendly about the accusation he leveled. "You talk about things that you should never mention, things that only a Foreign Office operative would know." He held out the glass. "Take it and pretend to drink with me."

Blythe stared at him over the port, his jaw working so fiercely as the man contemplated what to say that the veins in his neck stood out.

*That* was why Blythe would never be more than what he was— simply an observer asked to report unusual activity among the aristocracy. A paid snitch. He would never move up in the ranks, never be trusted with important missions or information, because he could never keep his thoughts from his face. Or from his tongue.

But tonight, Kit didn't really give a damn about his old school-mate's espionage career—or lack of it. Blythe was positioned far enough inside the Foreign Office to provide answers, however limited, that would send Kit in the next direction. That was all that mattered.

"Take the glass," Kit ordered again, his grin still in place. "And it would help if you laughed."

Blythe didn't. Instead, his face remained serious as he accepted the port. "What kind of game are you playing at, Carlisle?"

*A deadly one.* "What have you heard about a French initiative to learn about military meetings in the early days of the Waterloo campaign?"

No point in asking directly about Morgan. Morgan was no more than a go-between. If Kit were to learn where the man was hiding—and why—he first needed to discover why the French wanted the diary. Then he could flush out the Frenchmen involved, and Morgan right along with them.

"Waterloo?" Blythe blinked. "Christ, man! That was seven years ago."

"Along with one dead English king and a dead French emperor. Yet here we are." Time made no difference among the ranks of kings and generals. "What do you know?"

"Nothing." He pointedly arched a brow in an attempt to intimidate him but which came off as merely juvenile. "Even if I did, I wouldn't tell you."

Kit smiled down at the port in his glass as he swirled it. "You're a low-level operative—"

"No need to be rude," Blythe countered dryly, forcefully flicking his cigar ash onto Kit's boots.

"—with zero chance of moving up in Whitehall." Especially if Blythe kept implying with inside humor to his chums about his activities. The Foreign Office didn't like people it couldn't trust. Particularly within its own ranks. "You have no way to prove your worth unless they assign you to a real mission, but they won't give you that assignment because you have no worth to them. Damned if you do…"

Blythe's jaw was clenched so tightly now that Kit didn't know how the man managed to take a swallow of port when he silently raised the glass to his lips. Amazing trick, that.

"I'm assuming that you want more from your career than simply reporting back what Baroness Habersham did on her recent trip to Italy or which Prussian prince is sleeping with Lady Godfrey...or Lord Godfrey." He tapped Blythe on the chest with his glass to emphasize his point. "But if you went to them with important information—say the name of a certain society widow who's been sending secret messages to the Habsburgs—then Whitehall would have no choice but to pay attention to you and give you the due you deserve."

Blythe's eyes gleamed at that offer for a trade. The name of a treasonous widow for information about what the Foreign Office was up to with the French. "Why do you care anything for the Foreign Office, or the French for that matter?"

"I have a personal interest." That was all the explanation he would give.

Blythe silently considered his offer for a long while. Then, making his decision, he tossed back his port and reached for the bottle to top off his glass. "I don't know specifics—as you said, I'm the lowest of the low."

"But not for long."

His lips curled at that blatantly mercenary assurance. "There are whispers floating around Whitehall regarding the French."

Not what he wanted to hear. "There are always whispers floating around Whitehall about the French," he muttered irritably against the rim of his glass as he took another sip.

"True, but this time the undersecretaries are working to quash them. Normally, they just ignore them. So there must be something special about this particular set of rumors." He puffed at his cigar and studied Kit through the cloud of smoke. "The talk concerns someone high up in the French court who's supposedly one of ours. Someone who's been sending Whitehall information for a good, long while."

"Who?"

"No idea. Could be King Louis himself, for all I know." Blythe played with the cigar in his fingers, turning it over and watching the tendril of smoke rise from its tip. "Whoever it is, he's important to Whitehall, and as a primary asset, they want to protect him. Enough to address rumors and whispers when they've never done so before." He shrugged. "No idea what any of it has to do with Waterloo, though."

But Kit did, and the realization splashed through him like ice water.

Everyone who worked for the Crown or had been part of the army in 1815 had heard stories about French generals who weren't at all happy that Bonaparte had returned and had once more sent them scrambling back into battle during the Hundred Days. They'd mistakenly pledged their loyalty to a madman and dictator and were looking for a way out that would cause the least damage to what was left of France and to themselves. Some of the stories went so far as to claim that a few of the French generals had secretly met with Allied field marshals before the Waterloo campaign began, to share what they knew about Boney's battle plans and any weaknesses in their own lines.

If one of those generals who had met with Thaddeus Morgan became a high-ranking official at the French court after the wars had ended, the Foreign Office would do anything they could to protect him. Especially if the man were still providing information to the British, now while sitting at the king's side.

And if French agents had heard the same whispers and rumors, then they would do anything *they* could to expose him. Including getting their hands on General Morgan's diary. Any way they could.

When Blythe popped his cigar back between his teeth, he clenched down hard. There was nothing friendly about the way he forced out around the cheroot, "Now tell me who this widow is so I can return to my game and lose another sizeable portion of my allowance."

"Lady Bellingham," Kit answered, with not one ounce of guilt. "She's hoping to position herself into a second marriage with an Austrian archduke and so is passing along to the Habsburgs any bits of information she overhears from her friends in the Court of St James's and the military. Mostly harmless information, yet she's doing it. Whitehall knows that even a blind pig finds an acorn now and then and will want to put a stop to it. Or use her to send false information to Vienna. Either way, they'll be impressed that you uncovered her."

As he considered Kit's information, Blythe casually flicked the ash from his cigar. "Have to admit, Carlisle, this is a damnably odd conversation to be having with you of all men." He drawled thoughtfully, "A wastrel rakehell."

Kit grinned in reply. "So you are. You know that second sons have to live by their wits to survive."

"Yes. By gambling and taking wealthy lovers to supplement their incomes." Blythe pointed the cigar accusingly at Kit. "Not by digging into Whitehall's affairs."

"By *every* means," he corrected, raising his glass in a mock toast.

Blythe wasn't amused and quietly demanded, "How do you know about the Countess of Bellingham?"

His grin faded. "She talks too much."

The underlying warning in that struck Blythe as visibly as if Kit had punched him. He tightened his jaw and narrowed his eyes to slits. Ignoring that, he muttered, "But if you know about her, then surely so does the Foreign Office."

"There are lots of things that happen on English soil that the Foreign Office doesn't know about." He'd never uttered truer words. "Even if they do, they'll still be impressed that you brought it to their attention, and they'll reward you for it."

Not enough to promote Blythe to more important secret activities, but enough for him to be given a government post. The position would be a nice accolade to add to his family's reputation and would come with a considerable salary, too. Kit believed in rewarding trust and loyalty, just as he believed in punishing those who betrayed him.

"But as long as you're working for Whitehall, in any capacity," he warned sincerely, "be careful."

Blythe smiled. As with the rest of England, he'd heard about Kit's brother, Ross, Earl of Spalding, and the charge of treason that had been falsely leveled against him. He most likely believed that this was the reason Kit had sought him out tonight, and Kit let him believe it. Lies were often easier than the truth.

"No worries there." Blythe laughed. "Even with Lady Bellingham's name, they won't give me anything exciting to do."

"No," Kit answered quietly. "I meant that they'll take your soul."

Blythe stared at him, a puzzled frown creasing his brow. But the gravity of the words hit home. *Good.* Because Kit meant every word. After all, hadn't the Home Office already claimed his?

Slapping Blythe on the back as he stepped past, Kit strode away. He swallowed down the last of his port and handed off the empty glass to a uniformed attendant standing at the door to the gaming room as he passed into the entry hall.

A former general turned high-ranking official, now positioned at the French court and handing information across the Channel to the old enemy—the secret of that man's identity lay within the pages of the diary. He knew now why the French wanted it so badly, and badly enough to turn one of the Morgans' household staff against them, to convince Diana that her brother was being held for ransom.

Yet he had no idea how Garrett Morgan fit into all of this, or why Nathaniel Grey had tried to convince him to cease his hunt for Fitch's killer.

But he was damned well going to find out.

"Carlisle!" one of the men from the growing crush inside the hell called out to him as he collected his coat, hat, and gloves from the attendant manning the door. "Leaving so soon?"

"But it's barely midnight!" Another gentleman joined in, chiding him.

"Lost all your money already?"

"Better ask Spalding to raise your allowance!"

That last barb irritated the hell out of him, considering that his government salary was more than enough to provide a fine West End London living.

But all he could do was flash a bored expression and send a jaded glance around him. "Plenty of hours left before dawn. Why waste them here with the likes of you?"

Hoots and howls went up from the room in reply.

Kit slipped on his coat and walked out the door and into the damp air. Since the day he joined the Home Office, he'd let the world think whatever they wanted to about him. Cultivated that scoundrel persona, in fact. But he'd taken comfort in knowing the truth about himself. That had always been enough.

Until now.

Now, the pretense grated, and he had no idea how much longer he'd be able to continue this act.

He tossed a coin to a groom waiting on the footpath. "Fetch my horse."

It was time to pay the Morgans another visit.

# CHAPTER 11

"*H*ello there."

The deep voice played down Diana's spine like seeking fingers. She didn't have to look up from her book to know—

"Christopher."

Not daring to glance up from where she sat on a blanket spread across the lawn near the old dovecot, from where she could watch Meri as she played, she felt him approach and stop just behind her. He was near enough that she was certain she would feel his boots against her back if she simply leaned backward.

With a bored sniff belying the way her body tingled at his presence, she turned the page in her book and refused to look over her shoulder at him.

"If you spend any more time here at Idlewild," she warned, "we'll have to start charging you rent."

She heard the rustle of fabric and the faint creak of his leather boots as he squatted down behind her. "I'd make a fine tenant farmer, I'll have you know."

"And *I'd* wager that you don't know the first thing about farming."

She could almost feel his grin against her nape as he leaned closer to look over her shoulder at her book. "But I know a great deal about farmers' daughters."

She rolled her eyes and volleyed, "And *I* think you—"

"But not so much about generals' daughters."

Her heart stuttered. Then it turned somersaults against her ribs when he eased down to sit behind her on the edge of the blanket.

"Well, you're in luck then," she said coolly, "because there's not much to learn."

But her comment only caused him to chuckle in reply.

She grimaced. The man had been a downright nuisance lately. When he hadn't been popping in for unannounced visits since the party to speak to the general, he'd been on her mind as she'd replayed all of their stolen kisses in her head. And dared to dream about doing more with him than mere kissing. Even when she'd been awake, the rascal had given her no peace, sending little gifts for apparently no reason...flowers for her, toys for Meri. She wasn't certain if they were meant to be an apology or an attempt to charm her into his good graces so she'd more easily share whatever new information she might discover about her brother.

But it was the gift to her father that had made her speechless. Christopher had purchased a cabinet to replace the one that the Frenchman had smashed and had it delivered to the general, complete with a secret compartment.

When she thanked him by sending a note to his rooms at Albany in London, he replied in typical Christopher Carlisle fashion by sending her a second piece of furniture—a little wooden step stool. The attached message claimed that it might be of use the next time fireworks were shot off at a party and windows had to be used instead of perfectly good doors. She nearly chopped it into firewood right there in the front hall.

She could just see him from the corner of her eye, not daring to look fully at the devil, as he surely wanted. His leg was bent, his forearm resting across his knee. He must have come straight from the stables because he still wore his riding gloves, smelled deliciously of leather and horse, and the knee of his tan breeches was dusty from the road. Curiosity pricked at her to see if he wore a hat or if his dark blond hair was messed by the wind, his cheeks colored from the fresh air and sunshine. But she didn't dare give him the satisfaction of turning to look.

The rascal leaned closer, bringing his mouth close to her ear. "Something tells me that there's a lot more to you than what you're sharing."

Her breath hitched, yet she kept her gaze glued on the book, although she couldn't have repeated a word of what she read. He was far too close for comfort, and in more ways than just his physical presence.

He'd saved her life—twice—and she knew now that he wasn't the selfish bounder the gossips claimed him to be, that the stories about the women, cards, and wild behavior had been wrong. Even the general held a favorable opinion of him. All of that worked together with that dashing smile of his, with his crisp wit and sharp intelligence, to attract her in a way she hadn't felt in years.

Yet she couldn't let herself be drawn in by his charms. Even if he was a good man at heart, he was still a shiftless second son, one without prospects or a clear path for his future, and so still needed to be kept at arm's length because of it.

"I've told you everything I know about the French and my brother's whereabouts." Tamping down the trembling in her fingers, she turned the page and lifted the book straight up before her face. "So please leave me in peace to read."

But the rascal didn't follow her orders and leaned in even closer to look over her shoulder at the book. "What are you reading?"

"Nothing you'd be interested in."

That show of pique only earned her another grin. "But I'm interested in lots of things." Then he turned his head to gaze up at her, his cheek resting far too familiarly on her shoulder. If he meant to unsettle her, he was doing a fine job of it. "You, for one."

"Ah! Fiction, I see."

A low laugh rumbled from him and seeped into her, sending a little shiver down into her breasts. With him sitting so close like this, it was impossible not to remember how it had felt to have his mouth on hers, his hands caressing her body. Most likely the scoundrel knew it, too.

"What are you reading? Tell me. Something so scandalously shocking that you can't share it? One of those Gothic novels that women have been secretly passing around? *The Monk? The Dark Prince?*" Before she could stop him, he took the book out of her hand and snapped it closed to read the cover. He paused. Surprise filled his voice. "*Housekeeping and Husbandry in the Southern Counties?*"

She snatched it away. With an angry scowl, she finally turned to face him, only to find his mouth mere inches from hers. She couldn't help dropping her gaze to his sensuous lips. Or longing to kiss him. She forced her eyes up to his. "What's wrong with a woman who wants to improve her mind?"

"And her sheep," he muttered, which earned him a light slap on the shoulder with the book. "Nothing's wrong with it. But it *is* a surprise for a society miss, you have to admit."

"I'm not a typical society miss."

His gaze moved slowly over her, taking her in as she sat there on the blanket in her pale blue day dress, her cashmere shawl draped over her shoulders. "Oh, I've certainly come to realize that," he murmured. "You're a general's daughter, in every way."

Pride flared warmly inside her, even though he most likely didn't mean that as a compliment. "And speaking of the general, he's in his study." She opened the book again and stuck it up between them, hiding her face behind it. "You can find him there."

"I'm not looking for the general." He placed his finger on the book and slowly pushed it down. "I was looking for you."

"Stop that." She dismissed him by raising the book again. Hopefully, this time, he would accept the hint and go away.

Instead, he took the book completely out of her hand and tossed it away to the edge of the blanket, out of her reach.

Before she could give him the tongue lashing he deserved, he tugged off his glove and caressed his bare knuckles across her cheek.

She squeezed her eyes shut against the shuddering temptation of his touch and rasped out, with far less conviction than before, "Stop that."

He slowly dropped his hand away.

Opening her eyes, she stared at him and blinked hard, trying to fathom this man and her inexplicable attraction to him. She should have been happy that he'd stopped caressing her. Instead, she felt the loss of his touch as physically as she did her shawl when it slipped off her shoulders and puddled around her on the blanket.

Her belly tightened. She didn't play at courtships and flirtations the way some society misses did, instead viewing them as a serious path toward finding a husband. After all, she had to be careful with the men she chose to bring into her life. *Very* careful. There was no room for error. Certainly not when it came to the man that she would eventually marry. Whoever that man would be, he had to be dependable, trustworthy, and honorable. He couldn't be a man who refused all responsibility in favor of a life of merrymaking.

He couldn't be Christopher Carlisle.

But, frustratingly, knowing that did nothing to squelch her attraction to him.

"Why are you here?" she demanded, and drat her voice for being far too breathless.

"To see you." Christopher reached down for the shawl and chivalrously placed it back over her shoulders. He tenderly—and opportunistically—tucked a stray curl behind her ear before he sat back.

Her cheeks heated in response, and she looked away. "Now you've seen me. So you can go."

Refusing to look at him, she gazed down the lawn to the edge of the chestnut plantation where Meri played with a host of dolls and stuffed animals that they'd carried down in a big basket from the nursery. Mrs. Davenport had gone into the village for the day, as she did every Saturday, leaving Meri in Diana's care until dinner.

But Meri never looked up to notice that Christopher was there. Most likely, she wouldn't have cared anyway. There were always men arriving at Idlewild—soldiers there to see the general, friends of her brother wanting to cajole him into misbehaving with them, and their handful of tenants coming and going. What was one more visitor? For that, at least, Diana was thankful. Because Meri hadn't noticed that since the night of the party the general had placed guards around the farm to keep watch.

"I don't want to go," Christopher murmured in what she was certain was his most flirtatious drawl. "I want to stay right here and get to know you better."

Goosebumps broke out traitorously across her arms. "You'll be rather disappointed, I'm afraid."

"Highly unlikely, based upon what I've glimpsed so far." He paused for one perfectly timed rakish beat. "Which sadly isn't at all enough." Before she could utter the perfect biting reply to that, he added, "You're keeping secrets."

An electric jolt pierced her. Only for one fleeting heartbeat, but with the force of a lightning bolt.

She kept her face carefully still and her gaze straight ahead on Meri as the little girl picked up a red ball and tossed it high into the air. *Impossible.* He couldn't know. No one knew, except for the general and Garrett.

"You've found me out," she said dryly, hiding the truth behind more truths. "I *am* keeping secrets. I told Susannah Gresham that her bonnet was pretty when it was the most hideous thing I've seen all season, and just this morning at breakfast, I told Major Paxton to have a good day when I couldn't have cared less if he did, then stole a second sticky bun when the butler's back was turned."

"Not those kinds of secrets."

She watched Meri throw the ball across the lawn toward the house and then run to fetch it. "Well, apparently, I've also been committing treason by attempting to give information to the French."

"*That* secret I know about." Instead of being discouraged, the man seemed more determined than ever and pressed, "What I want to know is the other secret you're keeping." He leaned in and brought his mouth to her ear, close enough that the warmth of his breath tickled her earlobe. "The one that puts a guilty expression on your face when you think no one is looking. The one that makes you seem sad even when you're smiling."

"You're mistaken," she countered, unsettled that he'd noticed so much about her. But then, hadn't she noted nearly everything about him, as well? Right down to the little scar at his right brow that gave him a bit of a dangerous appearance.

"Unfortunately, I don't think I am."

She tore her gaze away from Meri, surprised by the somberness with which he said that. She stared at him, all the thoughts in her head about him roiling in a twisted knot that she couldn't untangle and her heart doing absolutely nothing to help. *That foolish thing* wanted to confide everything in him, then beg to be given the solace she knew she'd find in his arms.

Only when the ball bounced across the lawn toward her and stopped at the end of the blanket did she finally tear her eyes away from him.

"And what secrets are *you* keeping?" She picked up the ball and tossed it back to Meri. "After all, you can't expect me to reveal all of mine as long as you're hiding your own."

There. *That* should silence him for a while. God only knew what he and the general had been discussing since the party.

"I don't want to be a vicar."

His confession made her smile, and she threw his words back at him. "That secret I know about."

Meri tossed the ball toward them again.

"Then how about that I find myself inexplicably drawn to you?"

She turned around to gape at him. The ball went bouncing past, rolling down the lawn and disappearing behind the old dovecot at the edge of the plantation.

When she finally found her voice, she repeated his words, this time in little more than a rasp, "Not those kinds of secrets."

She scrambled to her feet. She needed to move. *Now.* And move away from him.

"I'll fetch the ball!" she called out to Meri, who had already forgotten about it and picked up an armful of dolls, to carry them into the trees to enact her favorite fairytale. But Diana needed air and space. Suddenly being outdoors on the blanket didn't provide nearly enough, not when Christopher kept stealing it.

Hitching up her skirt, she left him sitting on the blanket and hurried away. Share secrets? She simply couldn't. *Especially* that kind. And especially not with him.

The little red ball had landed in the weeds near the abandoned outbuilding, which her family had never used except for storage, and hadn't even used for that in so long that she couldn't remember the last time. But they hadn't had the heart to tear down the pretty little brick building that matched the stables and old dairy barn, and now Diana was glad of it, if only to have it there to hide behind while she caught her breath before having to deal with Christopher again. Meri was playing and would be fine without her for a few minutes, during which time perhaps he would go to the house to speak to the general and leave her alone.

He was so very attractive, she'd admit, and not just physically. *All* of him was alluring in a way she hadn't noticed in a man in a very long time. One that sent her heart racing and her body aching to be in his arms, to be kissed and caressed in all kinds of delicious ways.

But if he kept pushing her to reveal her secrets, he'd also prove dangerous.

She knelt down to reach for the ball. A large hand snatched it from her fingertips. *Christopher.*

Oh, that man! She wheeled on him, the curse that fell from her lips only the first volley in the tongue-lashing the frustrating devil deserved. "Why won't you—"

Then his mouth was on hers, kissing her hungrily, and all thoughts of secrets and of denying herself his attentions fled. She whimpered beneath his kiss in capitulation.

His left arm slipped around her waist to pull her against him, while the right shoved open the narrow wooden door of the dove-cot. Without protest, she willingly allowed him to walk her backwards inside the dusty building, his lips never leaving hers. He kicked the door closed behind them.

"Christopher." As the long-sleeping feminine need awoke inside her, her arms wrapped around his neck, and she kissed him back, matching his hunger with her own.

The kiss grew even more heated and greedy, until he cupped her face with his hand and held her head still while he plunged his tongue between her lips in relentless but sensuous strokes. He tasted of man and whisky, with a hint of wildness that was simply heady, and she shamelessly drank him in.

His hand slid slowly down the side of her body, and she instinctively arched into the caress, like a cat being petted. Fitting, because when he brushed over her bottom, she was certain she purred.

By the time he finished ravishing her mouth and moved his lips away from hers to place hot, open-mouthed kisses down her neck, she'd given over to the joy of being in his arms and had melted against him, her soft front pressing against his hard chest. Her fingers played in the silky hair curling at his collar as his hands journeyed over her, as if he were trying to feel every inch of her.

"Why," she asked breathlessly, then gasped when his hands brushed the sides of her breasts, "do you...keep doing...this to me?"

He laughed as he nuzzled his face against her hair, and the deep sound rumbled into her. "Kissing you?"

"Yes." The single word emerged not as an answer but as a moan of permission. One he accepted by placing a kiss to the swells of her breasts topping her bodice.

"Because I want to." Another kiss to her breasts, this one

lingering long enough for the tip of his tongue to dip into the valley between them. "Why do you keep letting me?"

"I'm not."

In pantomime, he feigned mock confusion as he straightened just enough to cast sideways glances at her arms as they continued to enwrap his shoulders. Just to make his point, he squeezed her bottom, then grinned in victory when a moan fell from her lips.

She slapped at his shoulder, feigning irritation when what she truly wanted was for him to do that again. "*I meant* why do you keep attempting to seduce me?"

"A beautiful and soft woman in the warm, afternoon sunlight —what kind of rakehell would I be if I didn't try?"

"But it's not true, is it? You're not at all a rake—"

"Shh. Don't tell." He slid his hands up to cup her breasts from beneath. "After all, I have a reputation to uphold."

"Christopher." But the scolding on her tongue turned into a low moan when he began to massage her fullness against his palms.

She melted into him. Such a wonderful sensation, warming her all the way down to her toes, including that aching spot at her core. His fingers teased at her nipples through her clothing, and she arched herself into him to beg him with her body to increase the pleasure he was giving.

Accepting her unspoken invitation, he slipped his hand inside her bodice, to free a single breast from her corset and chemise. The cool air inside the dovecot caressed her, and her nipple drew up into a hard nub, aching for him to place his hot mouth on it.

"I'm kissing you, Diana," he murmured distractedly, his attention focused on her nipple as he slowly circled it with his fingertip, "because I very much want to. And no other reason." He looked down into her eyes as he repeated, "Why are you letting me?"

"Because I very much want you to," she answered, the raw truth tearing breathlessly from her.

With a wicked grin, he dipped his head to her breast, to trace the tip of his tongue teasingly around her nipple the way he'd just done with his finger.

She shivered at the torturous caress, so close to giving her the pleasure she craved yet still impossibly far away. She dug her fingers into his hair to pull his head tighter to her breast.

With a groan, he closed his lips over her, laving her with his tongue and sucking softly. Oh, the sensation was divine! His mouth on her breast twisted all the tiny muscles in her lower belly into an achingly tight knot.

As if worshipping her, he suckled at her, slowly but intensely, drawing her breast deep into his mouth as his hands caressed over her hips. She couldn't fight back the moan of pleasure rising from her lips. It had been such a long time since a man had kissed her like this, had made all those wantonly delicious sensations spiral inside her. So very long...

"Seduction," he rasped huskily, naming the wicked thing he was doing to her with his mouth. "What do you know of it, a sweet angel like you?"

*More than you know.* But she could never tell him. Certainly not now, when his hands at her hips were guiding her backward to a rough worktable placed against the wall, even as his mouth never left her breast. Not when he sent such pleasures rippling through her that she could do little more than cling to him, yet welcome every touch and kiss he gave her.

"Don't call me that," she panted out.

Leaning into her, he shifted her onto the table, until half of her bottom rested on the edge. Her hip was propped at such an angle that one leg lifted scandalously off the ground.

"But you are an angel," he murmured, trailing kisses along her jaw. "Absolutely beautiful and lovely…heavenly."

He had her off-balance now, both physically and emotionally. She clutched at his shoulders to keep from falling away as his hand strayed down her leg to her ankle and calf, exposed by the skirt hitched up beneath her. As if he simply couldn't resist touching her. But then, she understood his desire, because she couldn't resist the pleasure of his touch.

His hand brushed up her leg and pushed her hem up to her knee. "You have no idea, do you, the effect you have on men? How much every man who sees you longs to have your attention, your touch, even your sharp wit, focused only on him?"

He stroked his hand behind her knee in featherlight tracings, not daring to go any higher. Yet he teased his fingers playfully at the top of her stocking, as if contemplating removing it and baring her leg completely. If he did, would he place his mouth there the same way he'd done to her bared breast, to give her yet another kind of wonderful kiss? She trembled at the temptation of it.

He murmured yearningly against her lips, "You're the angel every devil wants to possess."

"*No.*"

He froze at that single word, his hand stilling immediately against her leg. But she could feel the tension inside him, the longing to keep touching her—and more—even as he slowly lifted his head to stare down at her in surprise.

"I mean—" Heat flushed through her cheeks. "That's not—"

Flustered, she tightened her hold on his shoulders to keep him from moving away, only to bite back a groan when she felt his muscles flex so invitingly beneath her touch. If she had any sense at all, she would shove him away and hurry back to her blanket and book where she belonged.

But she simply couldn't bring herself to leave his arms. He truly was well on his way to seducing her, and he didn't even realize it.

A wanton and reckless thought sparked inside her...*What if I let him?*

How wonderful it would be to lose herself in his strong arms, if only to temporarily push away all the worry, pain, and fear, all the horrible sadness and grief she carried inside her that sometimes flared up so intensely that she thought it might just devour her. For a few precious moments, he could make her forget. She could lose herself in him, and he would never ask for more. Not him. A man like him would never ask to court her, would never want to marry her...would never ask for a future she couldn't give.

She could never have him completely, but she could claim these few moments of harmless kissing and touching that would never lead to anything more.

"I'm not an angel." Closing her eyes against the bittersweetness of the moment, she reached for his hand and guided it up between her thighs.

His breath hitched. "Diana," he murmured in pleased surprise against her temple.

"Touch me," she whispered, then heard him groan softly at the invitation she offered as his hand slid up to tenderly caress her.

She closed her eyes against the stinging emotions rising inside her and let the wave of pleasure consume her.

He teased lightly at her, as if afraid she might yet stop him. But doing that would simply end her. With subtly increasing pressure, his caresses grew firmer and deeper, making her squirm beneath him with both pleasure and longing for more. There was no point in denying her desire for him, not when he could surely feel it. Her sex grew slick and slippery beneath his fingers as he caressed her— No, he was *exploring* her, taking all kinds of gentle, little caresses to discover her most intimate place, to learn where to touch her to bring her the most pleasure.

Tears of emotion watered her lashes at his thoughtfulness, and she brushed her lips over his cheek, unable to put into words her gratitude for making her feel so feminine and beautiful. So desired. He would never know how much this encounter meant to her, nor could she ever tell him. But she could show him, and with a trembling sigh, she parted her thighs as wide as her skirt allowed.

With her name nothing more than a rasping murmur, he gently sank a finger fully into her tight warmth. She gasped at the wonderful new sensation, and he kissed her to drink up the sound of mixed surprise and pleasure on her lips.

He stroked slowly inside her as he continued to kiss her. The feeling was simply exquisite, somehow both exciting and comforting at the same time. Each sinking caress came as a smooth and gliding stroke, each retreat a swirling tease, and every movement grew the throbbing ache at his fingertips.

Unable to stop the trembling that overtook her, she buried her face against his neck. A second finger joined the first, stretching her intimate lips wider and eliciting a throaty whimper of pleasure from her at being filled so deliciously. Her arms tightened their hold around his shoulders, and she pressed into his hand, shamelessly begging for more. It had been so long since she'd felt this feminine, this wanted...*too* long, and now that it was happening again, she didn't want it to stop. She forced from her mind all the gossip she'd ever heard about Christopher, the fear over her brother's disappearance, even her own grief and pain, and simply let go.

His thumb delved down into her folds to strum over the little nub at her core, and her hips bucked against the edge of the table. "Christopher!"

With whispered assurances her desire-fogged brain couldn't comprehend, he teased at the little bead again. All the muscles inside her clenched down tightly around his fingers, drawing a growl of appreciation from him. He stroked her there again, and a shuddering cry tore from her, followed immediately by a wave of coursing heat and light. Her body clenched hard around him, only to release a heartbeat later in undulating pulses of pleasure that sped out to her fingers and toes. She clung helplessly to him, the bliss he'd given her overwhelming.

In the stillness that followed, the silence between them was broken only by the sound of her breath as she fought to regain both it and her balance. She kept her face buried in his neck. She was too overcome—and inexplicably too shy—by what they'd just done to look at him.

As if he realized the confusion inside her, he kept her close within the circle of his arms and rested his lips against her temple. "Are you all right?"

She nodded against his shoulder, then bit her lip to keep from crying out in protest as he slowly slipped his hand away from her.

"I hadn't intended—" He stopped himself, then paused, as if searching for the right words, before admitting, "But I don't regret it."

"Nor do I," she whispered, unable to speak any louder for fear that her voice would crack and reveal how confusion warred with pleasure inside her.

He smiled against her temple. "Thank God."

To hide the seriousness of what she felt, she forced out a teasing, "Because you don't want to face down the general at the end of a dueling pistol?"

When he loosened his hold around her and shifted back far

enough to stare down at her, the expression of desire and deter-mination on his handsome face stole her breath away. "Because I very much want to do it again."

Her heart stopped with a brutal thud.

Of all the things to say... He had no idea of the cut he'd just sliced into her chest. The impossibility of what he was asking. He waited for her reply, but she couldn't make that promise. No matter that she wanted more—so very much more! And with *him*, a man who was beginning to mean more to her than she would admit.

But too much was at risk. Too much that could be ruined forever.

He touched her chin, holding her face still as his eyes locked with hers. "When all of this with your brother is over, then you and I will—"

"Then it's over," she whispered, interrupting before he could say anything that would break her heart. Because there was no future with him. Absolutely none.

She somehow managed to find the strength to not crumple beneath the surprised flare in the blue depths of his eyes, a flare that instantly dulled to resentment. Another stab to her heart, yet it couldn't be helped. She had to keep him away.

She hadn't lied to him. She didn't regret what had just happened. How could she, when it had been simply wonderful, and only because of him? But she also could never let it happen again.

Unable to give him the explanation he deserved, she slipped from his arms to put the length of the dovecot between them. Her hands shook as she pushed her skirt back into place and readjusted her bodice, aware of his eyes on her the entire time.

"Diana, we need to talk."

She ignored that and hurried toward the door. "I have to get back to Meri."

"Meri will be fine for a few more minutes."

Yes, but *she* wouldn't be. Not here in this small space, not when the scent of him still clung to her and she still pulsed with the pleasure he'd brought her. Not when her desire for him beckoned her to surrender completely, in every way, to the sheer bliss she knew he would give her.

And not when he was still determined to learn her secrets.

"She gets into so much trouble, you have no idea." She opened the door before he could stop her and charged out into the bright sunshine, rapidly blinking her eyes but only partly because of the light. Christopher didn't immediately follow, but based on the bulging state of his breeches, she hadn't expected him to.

She hurried back to the blanket and gazed down the lawn, then turned in a circle to look everywhere around her. Meri was nowhere to be seen. As usual.

With a grimace of aggravation, she hurried toward the trees, calling out the little girl's name. Of all times for her to run off—

"Meri! Where are you?"

She loved playing in the trees, taking her dolls and stuffed animals there to reenact whatever story the general had most recently read to her from the big book of fairytales she kept at her bedside. But today was *not* the day for hiding in the thicket.

"Meredith!" Her calls grew angry despite her attempts to keep her frustrated exasperation from showing, especially if Christopher happened to stroll out of the dovecot and see her. Oh, the last thing she needed was for him to know the true effect he had on her! "Meri, answer me!"

But only the sound of the breeze in the leaves and the chirps of the birds replied.

She walked to the edge of the plantation and tried to peer

through the trees but couldn't see very far. The plot hadn't been harvested for wood since before her family had bought the farm, and the underbrush had been allowed to grow unchecked.

She stood still and listened—nothing.

"Meri, answer me this instant!" With a harsh sigh, she started down the narrow dirt path that the girl had worn through the trees from all of her play. "If you don't answer me right now, you won't get any pudding with your dinner."

No sound, no movement... An icy chill of worry began to creep down her spine. Hunting through the undergrowth, she stepped further into the thicket, then froze.

Meri's favorite doll lay discarded on the ground in the weeds.

Panic seized her chest as she ran to it and snatched it up, then wheeled around in a circle, now frantically screaming for Meri. She would *never* have left this doll behind!

"Meredith!" she yelled, all of her shaking with fear.

Christopher hurried through the trees to her and took her arm to stop her from dashing frantically through the brambly bushes, which had already snagged at her dress and bit bloody scratches into her arms and legs. "What is it? What's wrong?"

"I can't find Meri!" She desperately grabbed at his lapels to keep her knees from buckling beneath her. "She's missing." The fears of her worst nightmare tore from her in a hoarse cry, "She's been taken!"

$\mathcal{K}$it slowly stalked the perimeter of the overgrown chestnut plantation, his eyes searching the ground and underbrush for any sign of what had happened to the little girl.

In the hours since Meri went missing, while everyone in the household had split into pairs and taken a different section of the property to search, the afternoon sun had slowly drifted toward the horizon. Now, it was sinking below, and darkness was coming. They would have to call a halt to the search soon, and Kit dreaded the anguished expression he'd see on Diana's face when he told her that they had to stop for the night.

The countryside around the old manor house seemed alive as the servants moved slowly over the property, looking for any trace of Meri. Kit had quickly organized them, after taking a distraught Diana back to the house and putting her into the housekeeper's care. In her upset state, the last thing he wanted was her running frantically across the property, putting herself in danger. Each servant had strict orders about what to do if they found anything—to stop right where they were, immediately send up a hue and cry, and not touch anything. He wanted to see everything for himself, to discover any clues that might be there about who took Diana's sister.

Only the general and Major Paxton insisted on riding out on horseback to the far edges of the property. She wouldn't be there, Kit knew. She would either still be close to the house or completely gone from the property by now. But he didn't stop the two men, wanting them as far out of his hair as possible while he searched the more likely places she would be. His attention had been glued to the ground, and his eyes had never stopped moving, never lifting from the first two feet of undergrowth where a child of Meri's height would have disturbed it.

Nothing.

And now, unable to see clearly because of the falling dusk, he had no choice but to stop. He bit out a viscous curse and turned back toward the house.

With every step he took, he became more convinced that whoever had taken Meri was the same person who had tricked Diana into believing that her brother had been kidnapped. And that person worked inside the general's household. Which was why Kit had insisted that the servants search in pairs.

True, someone could have sneaked onto the estate by foot without being seen. He or she could have gotten close enough to the house to wait within the cover of the woods for the right moment to take the little girl. But there was no sign of a struggle, and at three years old, Meri was big enough to have put up a fight if a stranger approached her, would have known to scream for help.

That meant whoever took her wasn't a stranger and had simply been waiting for the right opportunity.

Guilt ate at his gut. *He'd* been the reason that Diana hadn't been watching over her sister as she should have been.

He raked a furious hand through his hair. Bad enough that his pursuit of Morgan was interfering with his Home Office duties, but he was letting himself be distracted by Diana, in all kinds of ways. Now a little girl's life hung in the balance. If anything happened to her, Diana would never forgive him.

He'd never be able to forgive himself.

What the hell had he been thinking? The worst woman in the world for him to have an assignation with, for many, *many* reasons. Not the least of which was that her brother was a traitor and murderer, the same man he was determined to hunt down and watch swing. Or that her father was General Thaddeus Morgan, a deadly shot and not at all a man Kit wanted to face across a dueling field. Or that she'd been courted by his cousin Robert—*why* on God's earth had Robert let her get away? His wife, Mariah, was a wonderful woman, Kit would admit, but Diana...

She was right. She wasn't an angel.

"The blasted woman's a goddess," he muttered.

*What* had he been thinking? He hadn't. He'd temporarily lost his mind. When she'd been in his arms, he'd completely forgotten the reason he'd come to Idlewild in the first place. There'd been no revenge, no treason, no duty to fulfill. There had been only her, with the softness of her flesh beneath his hands, her lavender scent engulfing him, her wit making him laugh even as he wanted to ravish her.

For one delicious moment, he hadn't cared about justice for Fitch. He'd simply wanted to make love to her.

"Carlisle!"

As he approached the front portico, General Morgan hurried across the lawn toward him from the stables, tugging off his gloves as he approached. He appeared haggard, with worry putting a crease between his brows and deepening the lines around his mouth and eyes.

"Any word?"

Kit grimly shook his head. After hours of searching, with no sign of the man's daughter yet found and most likely none now to be uncovered, he couldn't bring himself to say what he knew in his gut—that they would hear of her only when the kidnapper contacted them.

"They took her because of the diary, didn't they?" Despite keeping his nerve through some of the bloodiest battles in English history, the general now couldn't keep his voice from shaking.

"I believe so. Which means they won't harm her." To reassure him, Kit explained, keeping his voice low to prevent being over-heard by any of the servants, "Most likely she's still within a five-mile radius of the estate, and they'll turn her over when we give them the diary."

The general looked away to keep Kit from seeing any stray emotion on his face. "I'll give them whatever they want to keep my family safe, and the bastards know it, too." He looked at the ground, then voiced the thought that had surely been eating at him all afternoon. "Garrett told the French where to find the diary in my study. Did he tell them to come after Meri, as well?"

"No." That much Kit was certain about. He quietly admitted the nagging suspicion that had been plaguing him since the night at the tavern, "I don't think your son has anything to do with the diary."

"But you said he was working with the French."

"He is." Nothing about how the French were attempting to gain possession of the diary implicated Garrett Morgan. Especially taking the child. "But if he wanted the French to have the diary, he could have simply given it to them. He wouldn't have had to fake his own kidnapping to convince Diana to hand it over, or encourage the French to take Meri hostage for it."

But that information brought the man little comfort. "If anything happens to—"

A shout went up from the dark field to the south. A horse galloped at breakneck speed through the shadows toward the house. As it drew nearer, its rider shouted again.

*Paxton.*

At the commotion, Diana rushed outside. She ran down the steps and stopped beside them in the glow of the oil lamp hanging over the door.

"What's the matter?" She clutched at the general's arm. "Is it Meri?"

Before her father could answer, Paxton's horse slid to a stop beside them. He jumped to the ground and let his horse trot away toward the stable. He panted as hard as his mount as he strode up to them, a piece of paper clenched in his outstretched hand.

Diana frantically rushed forward. "Did you find Meri?"

The major gave a sharp shake of his head. "I found this." He breathlessly reached past her to give the note to the general. "It was pinned to the door of one of the abandoned cottages down by the old stone bridge."

Kit's eyes narrowed on the man as he far too familiarly put his arm around Diana to comfort her. But her attention was riveted to the note, and she couldn't seem to have cared less what Paxton did. While Kit wanted to break the man's arm.

General Morgan stepped onto the porch and held the note up to the lamp to read it. "It's what we thought." He kept his face carefully inscrutable, most likely to prevent upsetting Diana any further. "They've taken Meri. They're demanding the diary for her return."

Diana paled, the whiteness of her face visible even in the shadows. "Then we give it to them. Now."

"Not so fast," Kit warned calmly. "We need to discuss this."

She wheeled on him, a look of such burning betrayal on her face that it sucked the air from his lungs. "I want her back here—with me. I don't care what I have to do to make that happen."

"Diana," Paxton assured her, the pointed use of her given name prickling at Kit, "we will get her back safely and as soon as possible."

She stared defiantly at Kit, waiting for him to make the same promise. But he remained silent. No good could come of false hope.

"Carlisle's correct," her father told her quietly, aware of the servants who were walking back to the house now that darkness had made their search impossible. "Let's go inside, take a moment to gather ourselves, and plan out what to do next. We don't want to rush into this."

"What's to rush into?" Diana challenged in exasperation. "They have Meri and want the diary, so we give it to them and get her back. That's all we need to worry about."

"Not all." Kit exchanged a concerned glance with the general. "Who took Meri and left that note? No one came on or off the property—"

"You think it was someone from Idlewild?" Paxton spat out in disbelief.

He knew it was. And based on the quality of the plain linen paper on which the printed message was written, a senior member of the household staff at that. The note that had been left for Diana before could have been arranged by anyone, right down to the stable boy. But not this one.

From the way she stepped back from Paxton and folded her

arms protectively over her chest like a shield, she realized that, too.

"I think," Kit answered, "that we have to consider all possibilities."

Paxton snorted.

The general raised a hand to silence his aide. "Carlisle and I will discus this, and you will be consulted, major, when decisions have been made."

At her father's marked defense of him, Diana looked at Kit with a bewildered expression he couldn't fathom. Was an understanding of his true identity finally beginning to seep into her?

"She *will* be safely returned," Kit assured her, doing his damnedest to ignore the way Paxton remained at her side, his arm once more wrapping possessively around her shoulders. "They won't harm her."

"You don't know that," she whispered, her eyes glistening in the lamplight.

"I do. They have nothing to gain in harming her and everything to lose," he told her quietly, wishing he could reach for her, to console her in his arms. "Take comfort in that."

Despite her nod, he knew she found no solace in his assurances.

"We'll deliver the diary as instructed." General Morgan said that to Kit, now ignoring the major completely. "And hope that the person who took her has enough honor to follow through with his promise to return her safely."

Kit nodded grimly. "We need to go inside and discuss our options."

"Options?" Paxton parroted, clearly irritated to be left out of the conversation, and to have the general trusting in Kit more than in him. "What do you know about situations like this? No offense, Carlisle, but I'm a decorated officer in His Majesty's army." His lips curled up territorially. "You're a vicar in training."

Kit smiled icily. He wanted to smash his fist into the man's face.

General Morgan's grim gaze never left Kit. "Paxton, go home."

Infuriated at being dismissed, the major gestured at Kit. "You would accept his help over mine? I know every inch of Idlewild—"

"Go home, major." The iciness of the order reverberated through the air.

Paxton clenched his jaw. "Yes, general."

Kit took Diana's arm and led her inside, aware the entire way of the major's enraged gaze on his back.

# CHAPTER 13

*D*iana sat stiffly on the settee in the drawing room, staring down into the untouched cup of tea that her father had insisted she take, although tea was the last thing she wanted at that moment. All she wanted was Meri back in her arms, safe, where she belonged. Alternating between flashes of numbness and blinding anguish, she forced herself to sit still, somehow choking back the scream building at the back of her throat.

"The instructions in the note say to take the diary to Bradwell-on-Sea within two days' time," the general said quietly as he stood at the fireplace while Christopher paced the room. But Papa's concerned gaze never left her, which only made the pain inside her grow even more intolerable. So did Christopher's relentless pacing.

"That makes sense," he replied between strides. "The French will want to leave English soil as soon as they have the diary. They won't risk losing it again." He halted and faced the general. "We *will* get Meri back unharmed. They'll return her here as soon as word reaches the kidnappers that their operatives have the diary."

Diana's gaze darted up to him. "You mean—they won't release her to us in Bradwell when we give them the diary?"

His eyes softened with sympathy. He was attempting to reassure her, but his somber expression only made dread pang hollowly in her chest. "Most likely, she's still within five miles of Idlewild. And that's exactly where they plan on keeping her until they get the diary."

Suspicion pricked at the back of her knees. "How do you know that?"

"She's a little girl with a big voice. They won't risk that someone will see them carrying her away or that she'll scream out and bring attention to them. Better to find a hiding place nearby and tuck her away there. And they certainly won't risk taking her halfway across England for the exchange."

"*How* do you know that?" she repeated, anger beginning to rise inside her and replace the fear. She leveled a hard look at him. "What do you know about things like this? Kidnappings, ransom notes, the French—you, of all people?"

He didn't move, not even a tensing of muscles. Not even to utter a single word of explanation or defense.

She slowly rose to her feet, unable to keep seated a heartbeat longer. "The major called you a vicar in training. He wasn't far from wrong. You've been out of the army now—for what?—ten years? And Papa said you were under his command, which means you were part of the infantry. Not in any kind of espionage work."

Her eyes locked onto his, but she couldn't read anything in those dark blue depths. For once, the inscrutable mask he wore was impenetrable to her.

"So *how* do you know all these things?"

"Diana," her father scolded, while Christopher said nothing to explain himself. "You need to trust him."

"*Trust him?*" Fear and worry pulsed inside her. How on earth was she supposed to place her trust—and Meri's life—into his hands? "A man who spends more time in gambling hells than in pursuing a productive living, who has never attained success at anything in his—"

"Carlisle is a colonel in His Majesty's army and an agent for the Crown," Papa interrupted, his own anger and frustration at the situation visible in the tired lines etched into his face. He grimaced, his mouth turning hard as he gazed past her at Christopher. "He's one of the most lauded men in Whitehall."

"A *colonel*?" Bewilderment shot through her. "But—but you said that he was a terrible soldier."

"I was." When she wheeled to face Christopher, he shrugged. "But they keep promoting me anyway."

"Because you deserve it," the general commented, seeming not at all pleased to be revealing these secrets. He nodded at Christopher and told her, "He's a Home Office secret operative. Has been all these years, ever since he left my command."

Christopher added with an uncomfortable smile that did nothing to ease the confusion spiking inside her, "Although I'd appreciate it a great deal if you didn't tell anyone."

"But that's—that's not..." The ground fell away beneath her, and she sank back down onto the settee before she slipped to the floor. Her brother Garrett, now Christopher Carlisle—was anything in her life the way she thought it to be?

"That's not the scoundrel you assumed me to be?" he finished, his expression sobering. Despite the harsh accusations she'd just unleashed, there was no anger in him. Simply grudging acceptance. "That's what I want the world to believe. My job is a lot easier if everyone thinks I'm inconsequential."

She pressed her hand to her forehead as the room began to spin. Dear God, she was going to be sick!

As she pulled in deep, even breaths to calm herself, she struggled to sort through everything she thought she knew about him. She couldn't reconcile what they were both telling her with the stories she'd heard about his behavior from his cousin Robert, the gossip she'd heard about him from behind flitting fans at society soirees, and what she'd seen of him over the years with her own eyes, including when he saved her life. And now, when he was helping to save Meri's.

He began carefully, "I know it's a bit of shock—"

A strangled laugh fell from her lips. Oh, he had no idea!

"—but you need to trust that I can help you with your sister." He slowly approached her, then knelt down beside the settee, his troubled eyes fixed on hers. "I am very well trained when it comes to situations like this." He rested his hand reassuringly on her knee, and his voice roughened as he promised, "I will bring her back to you."

Holding her breath as his face blurred beneath her gathering tears, she nodded, unable to choke out any words.

"I'll deliver the diary," the general interrupted quietly. But his shoulders sagged, and at that moment, he looked older than she'd ever seen him. "I'll take my saddle horse and leave at dawn for the coast."

"You can't," Christopher countered grimly, setting the note onto the tea table in front of her. "They want Diana to deliver it."

Her heart stuttered, so forcefully that she winced. Steeling herself, she took the note in her trembling hand and quickly read it. With every word, the fear and dread bubbling inside her only boiled harder.

"Of course." She set down the note. But even as she whispered her agreement, she felt the blood drain from her face. "Whatever they want."

"No." Her father strode toward her. "Absolutely *not*."

"They want me to deliver it, so I will deliver it. And Meri will be safely back here with you by the time I return." She set down her tea before her shaking hand could spill it. Dear God, what she wanted was whisky! A bottle of the stuff, until she was numb to her soul.

"You are not leaving this farm," the general ordered. "I will not let you put yourself into danger."

Exasperation poured through her. "General, we don't have a choice! They have Meredith." Her voice quavered, although she couldn't have said whether from fear or rage. "And I will do *anything* they ask of me to bring her back unharmed. I will not put her life at risk by not doing what they want."

Unable to win the argument against her, her father turned toward Christopher. "But why ask for Diana? Why not me or one of the servants?"

"Not one of the servants because that would give away who's been working with the French." Pulling himself to his full height, Christopher took the note and read it again, frowning deeply as he scoured the message, as if hoping to find overlooked answers. "Not you because you're a former soldier who knows how to fight and defend himself." He grimly looked down at her. "But Diana is a small, young woman whom they can easily intimidate and over-power physically and who is willing to do anything to save her sister."

"They don't know me very well," she reminded him, a tight smile curling at her lips. "I'm much fiercer than they give me credit for." Ignoring the admiration shining in Christopher's eyes at her declaration, she turned toward her father. "General, would you please fetch the diary? I'm leaving in the morning for Bradwell."

For a long moment, her father stood still, unmoving. Then he finally acquiesced. "All right." His expression softened on her with love. And sympathy. "But you need to tell Carlisle the truth. It's time."

The electric jolt that shot through her came so fiercely that she flinched.

"I can't," she whispered pleadingly, climbing to her feet because it was impossible to sit still. She blinked hard to clear her eyes of the stinging tears that instantly heated them. "You know that."

"He's putting himself in danger to help us. He deserves to know." He came forward and took her shoulders in his hands, then placed a reassuring kiss to her forehead to temper his order. "Tell him, sergeant."

But the old, endearing nickname only constricted her chest until she couldn't breathe.

"You can trust him with your life." He took her chin and tilted up her face, until she couldn't ignore what he was asking of her. But, oh God, how much panic swirled inside her at the idea! Her hand pressed against her belly as her stomach pitched sickeningly. "And with Meri's."

Then he left the room and closed the door, sealing her inside with Christopher.

Silence stretched between them, and she kept her gaze firmly pinned to the carpet in front of her. But she could feel the heat of his gaze, patiently waiting for the explanation she'd *never* wanted to give him.

"You don't have to do this, Diana. We'll find another way." His deep voice twined through her as he came up slowly behind her and took her upper arms in his hands. "I know how hard this is for you. I'd do anything to protect my own brother. But you don't need to risk your life like this for your sister."

"Yes, I do," she breathed out. "Because she isn't my sister." A tear finally broke free and slid down her cheek. "Meri's my child."

# CHAPTER 14

$\mathcal{K}$it froze. He couldn't have possibly heard correctly. Her...*child?*

But when she drew in a shaking breath and turned to face him, the raw anguish in her blue eyes told him the truth.

*Good God. He'd had no idea...*

"That's what the general meant." She lowered her gaze to his chest and fixed it there, as if afraid to look him directly in the eyes for fear of what accusations she might see. "What he wanted me to tell you." Her voice emerged so softly from her trembling lips that he had to lean in closer to hear her. "Meri is my daughter."

Before he could fully fathom the enormity of that, she stepped away from him. He knew to let her go, even when she began to pace, the overwhelming emotion visible as it bubbled up inside her.

"I was nineteen." She wrung her hands with every step, still refusing to look at him. "We were living in India at the time, just outside Calcutta. The general had been posted there to work as a liaison with the East India Company's private army, although he seemed to be there mostly just to remind the Company that the

Crown actually rules the empire and that the Company only exists at the pleasure of the king and Parliament."

Kit could well believe that, knowing how the War Department worked.

"One of the Company's officers was less than willing to accept my father's input at first. It took the general months of entreaty to win the man over." She paused. "It took me far less time to win his heart."

She stopped in front of the fireplace. As if needing to keep herself busy, she reached to run her trembling fingers across a small music box sitting on the mantelpiece.

"He was handsome and dedicated, with so much ambition and character... How could I not fall in love with him? No one saw it coming, especially not us." Her head was turned just enough that he could see a sad smile tugging at her lips. "But we did, and my parents approved of him. He was a soldier, after all, with a bright future with the Company. Exactly the kind of man a general's daughter is meant for. We became engaged and planned to marry the following spring." Then her smile faded into grief, and she blinked hard. Once. "But he was killed that winter in an accident."

Kit said nothing, even as his chest tightened in sympathy. And with something else that took him several jarring heartbeats to recognize, because he'd never before been jealous of a dead man.

She whispered, "Six weeks later, I discovered that I was with child."

She opened the lid of the music box and gazed inside at the delicate brass mechanism, but Kit knew she wasn't seeing it. She was lost, four years ago and half a world away.

"I didn't know who to grieve for—John, me, or the baby who would grow up without a father. A baby I could never claim as my own."

*Jesus.* The hell that must have descended upon her... To have gone through that and survived—

She was the strongest woman he'd ever met.

"I could never have given my baby to relatives or strangers to raise. Other women have, and I would never criticize their choice to do what they think is best for themselves and their babies. But I couldn't. I just *couldn't.* To lose both John and my baby..." Her voice trailed off, and she inhaled a deep breath to find the resolve to continue. "It would have ended me."

He ached to reach for her, to pull her into his arms and soothe away the pain and grief. But he knew better. She had to move through this on her own. And when she was finished, he would be right here for her, with open arms.

"Can you understand?" Finally, she looked over her shoulder at him. She met his gaze for only a moment before turning away again, but the anguish he saw in her eyes sliced into him like a blade. "Every day of my life would have been spent wondering how she was, what games she liked to play, if she looked like me or John...But raising her as my own child would have ruined my father's career and reputation, destroyed all he'd worked a lifetime to achieve. I could never have done that to him."

No, she wouldn't. If there was one thing he knew about her for certain, it was how fiercely Diana protected her family.

He said quietly, "So you pretended that Meri was your sister."

She nodded and reached up to the music box to trace a fingertip delicately over the little brass plate. "We all agreed...the general, Mama, even Garrett. We would keep secret what happened and raise Meri within our family. They all protected me." She blinked rapidly, not daring to look at him now. "So many sacrifices! Including the general's career."

Four years ago... "That was why the general retired so suddenly." No one had expected it. He was a man at the height of his career, who could have given another decade of service to England.

"We had to act quickly, you see, before it became apparent that I was increasing. Because I was still grieving for John, Mama and Papa didn't want to send me away, and where would I have gone? We were in India. Every bit of the place was watched by Company men, all of them looking for any opportunity to shame the general and, by extension, the army. Mama and I couldn't simply travel to the coast and return with a babe in arms. Everyone would have known that I..." She turned to face him, with a plea in her eyes for sympathy and understanding. "But if Papa resigned his post—well, we were fortunate, because the trip home from India can take up to six months if you go by sea, because ships have to go all the way around the tip of Africa at the Cape of Good Hope." For a moment, she found the strength to smile in black amusement, before it faded and the grief returned. "The trip was filled with anything but that."

She reached trembling fingers for the tiny brass key at the back of the music box and gave it a slow twist to wind it. She could just as well been twisting his gut, so viscerally did Kit feel it.

"So we sailed. My growing waist was hidden beneath loose-fitting dresses, and any illness due to the baby was blamed on seasickness." She lowered her face and placed her hands over her belly, as if feeling for the babe she'd once carried there. "When the baby couldn't be hidden anymore, we stopped at one of the last ports in Morocco and left the ship, where we rented a little house. And where I gave birth."

The metallic notes dinged softly and slowly from the music box, one by one, beneath the turning disc.

"When the baby and I were well enough to travel on, we boarded a ship for London. My mother carried the baby in her arms from our rented house to the docks and up the gangway, and just like that, my child had become hers."

The pain in her voice pierced him, and he fought back the increasing urge to reach for her.

"Everyone believed the baby was hers. Why wouldn't they? My parents had a loving marriage, one that would make a pregnancy believable, and my mother was the general's second wife, much younger than he was. At thirty-seven, she was still young enough to have a child. And because it had been over six months since we'd left Delhi, that was plenty of time for people to believe that she'd discovered en route that she was expecting a surprise baby and then gave birth before arriving in England. No one would ever know the truth." Her voice cracked. "Not even Meri."

"Diana," he whispered hoarsely, breaking his silence.

"I insisted that I would name her. *I* would give my daughter her name, even though Mama and Papa didn't want me to." Her hands drew up into little fists that she jabbed toward the floor in grief and anguish, unintentionally emphasizing the struggle she'd gone through. "I *insisted*—so that she would be named after her father...Captain John Meredith."

She clenched and unclenched her fists now at her sides, and Kit resisted the urge to grasp her hands and hold them tightly in his.

"She would never know who her real father was, but at least I could give both of them that gift, no matter how small. The world would never know, but—" She choked off, and she swiped a trembling hand at her eyes. "But the angels in heaven know," she continued, her quavering voice no louder than a whisper, "which means that John knows. And he knows how much I love her, even if I can never show her."

With that anguished whisper of loss, he lost the battle to keep away and stepped forward to encircle her in his arms.

He murmured her name and pulled her against him, holding her close. Each tremble and shudder that swept through her as she struggled not to cry swept into him like a tidal wave. He squeezed his eyes closed and whispered soft words of reassurance, although he couldn't have consciously said what he was murmuring to her, except that he wanted to give her solace. His own heart grieved for her and all she'd lost, burning painfully in his chest.

"From the moment Meri was born," she continued in a soft whisper against his shoulder, needing to exorcise the desolation inside her by telling him everything, "we referred to her as my sister, with my mother and the general as her mama and papa, Garrett as her brother. We've never told anyone the truth."

"Until now," he murmured, nuzzling his cheek against her hair. The enormity of the trust she and the general were placing in him made him tremble. "Your secret is safe with me."

"And yours with me." She slipped her arms around his waist and rose up onto her tiptoes to touch her lips to his. In that kiss, she softly sought absolution and understanding. When she lowered away from him, her expression was one of pure vulnerability. And unqualified trust. "The general and I will leave for Bradwell in the morning, but I cannot tell you how grateful I am that you're helping us."

Not nearly enough.

Guilt gnawed at his gut. He could do more. He could take the diary to Bradwell himself. In the end, the French wouldn't give a damn how they received the diary as long as they got it, Meri would be released, and Diana would be safe.

Yet if he did that, if he handed secrets over to the French, his life would be over. Whitehall wouldn't give a damn that he'd done it to save a little girl's life. They would view what he did as a double-cross and declare him a rogue agent. He would be dead before Diana returned to her daughter.

But if he didn't go with her, if he let Diana and her father walk into danger with Meri's life hanging in the balance... *For God's sake!* A society miss and an old man, being sent to face down the French—

"I'll deliver it," he rasped out.

Surprise flared in her eyes, but so did relief. The sight ripped into his heart. Because she trusted him, because she wanted him there with her.

Because he knew then that he would give his life to protect her and her daughter.

"The French will accept the diary from me. They want it badly enough to risk kidnapping a little girl right from her home. They won't care how they get it as long as they do." He paused, saying so quietly that he suspected she might not hear him, "Even if it means I'm the one who gives it to them."

"Enough people I care about are in danger. I won't put you at risk, too." She punctuated that soft admission of affection with a tender touch to his cheek.

He kept his face carefully inscrutable as the darkness that had been chasing him for months finally consumed him.

He steeled himself as he made his decision. He placed his lips to her forehead, squeezed his eyes shut, and lied, "I'll be perfectly fine."

# CHAPTER 15

$\mathcal{T}$he mail coach stopped with a rocking jerk in front of the posting inn. "Bradwell-on-Sea!"

Diana heaved out a long breath. *Thank God.* After full two days of traveling, including moving through the night to avoid the risks that might come of stopping at an inn, she'd finally arrived just as the sun was sinking behind the horizon. And not a moment too soon. If she were left alone with her thoughts and fears for a minute longer, she might very well go mad.

She'd had nothing to do since leaving Idlewild but stare out the window and try to let the passing scenery distract her. Once darkness fell, she couldn't even do that because it was impossible to see beyond the glass. All she could do was count the passing miles and worry about Meri.

Thinking about Christopher didn't help. *That* man could drive her to distraction, certainly, but thoughts of who he truly was only worked to make her uneasy.

How had she been so wrong about him? How had he managed to hide a secret life from the world, in which he wasn't at all the scoundrel second son she'd thought him to be but a man dedicated to Crown and country, a government operative who commanded the respect of men like her father? A colonel, for heaven's sake! She could barely fathom it. Only now, after almost two days of churning it over and over in her head was she able to begin to reconcile the two men.

But the outcome was so much worse than before, when he was merely a scapegrace. Because now she knew him to be dependable, successful, even admirable. Because now he knew the truth about Meri and neither condemned her nor pitied her for it, instead insisting on helping her bring her daughter safely home. Because now she had no good reason to keep him at arm's length.

But she also had no possible future with him.

One of the coachmen flung open the door as he hurried past on his way to help unload the trunks and bags. As Diana left the compartment, pins and needles shot up her leg, which had been asleep from the last hour's cramped ride, and it buckled beneath her. She lost her balance and stumbled forward.

Strong arms caught her. They lifted her into the air and swung her in a circle before lowering her lightly to the ground. The front of her body brushed down the hard planes of a man's chest, the accidental contact electrifying. She knew even without seeing the face hidden beneath the brim of the beaver hat—

"Christopher," she whispered.

In the deepening shadows of the sunset, he grinned at her. "Throwing yourself into my arms already?" He tsked his tongue disapprovingly. "Please, darling, control yourself."

Her mouth fell open in shock. Then it snapped closed. Oh, that arrogant—

"Normally, I'm all for holding you in my arms." Although he teased, and most likely only to distract her from her worries about Meri, a darker preoccupation colored his voice. "But watch yourself, will you? I already have one Morgan miss to worry about. I don't need a second."

Before she could give him the set-down he deserved, he snatched up her bag, took her arm, and led her away, out of the coaching yard and down the plank footpath lining the street. Night was falling quickly, and lamps were being lit across the little port village. Yet lots of people still strolled through the streets, and they weaved their way through them down High Street in the direction of the docks.

"Have you been here long?" she asked quietly, careful not to be overheard by anyone.

"Since this morning." He'd ridden his saddle horse, and so had made better time than she.

Her chest tightened with dread, and she forced herself to ask, fearing the answer, "Any word about Meri?"

"It's still too early for the French to make contact. But I'm certain she's safe." He squeezed her arm to reassure her, then swiftly changed topics. "I secured a room for us at the hotel. Since we don't know how long we'll be here, it seemed better to have the comfort and privacy of a hotel rather than a shared room with five others in the coaching inn."

Appreciation at his thoughtfulness warmed her chest. "I'm glad you're here," she admitted.

He smiled down at her. "You, too."

Well, that was a lie, if ever she heard one. If he'd had his way, she'd be locked up in Idlewild, and he'd be here alone to hand over the diary.

He hadn't been pleased that she'd insisted on coming here, or with the story they'd had to concoct for the servants and tenants to explain her sudden departure. That Christopher had brought a message from Garrett, claiming that her brother had gone to the seaside to visit friends and invited her to join him. That knowing all the demands of planning and hosting the party she would be exhausted and could use a bit of rest by the sea. But then Meri had gone missing, and he'd stayed to help in the search. They'd told the household that Meri had been found after midnight, after wandering away and becoming lost. That Diana had left to collect the girl and take her on to their family physician in London, then would send Meri back to Idlewild while she continued onward to meet up with Garrett at the seaside. And because of the suddenness of all that had happened, she wouldn't be taking her maid with her.

The story was a good one, though, she had to admit. That pretense helped to protect her even here, halfway across the country. There wouldn't be anyone she knew in Bradwell, of that she was certain. But if anyone *did* happen to see her with Christopher when she was supposed to have been with Garrett, thanks to their story she could claim that the person was mistaken, that she truly was with her brother, even if all her thoughts about Christopher were far from sisterly.

"How was your trip?" he asked.

"Long." She pulled in a deep, steadying breath. "And the diary?"

"Safely stowed in my breast pocket."

When she darted a glance to his chest, he grinned at her.

She rolled her eyes. "You did that on purpose."

"To have a beautiful woman look at my chest? You bet I did."

*Imp.* Despite her fatigue and fears over Meri, a small smile curled at her lips. He was attempting to distract her from worrying about her daughter, if only temporarily. His plan wasn't working—she wouldn't feel better until she knew Meri was safe—yet she appreciated the attempt.

A thought struck her. "How do the French know that I don't have it? Why didn't they try to stop me on the way here to take it?"

"Because they know that I would never endanger you by letting you carry it." There was absolutely *no* teasing in that.

All the tiny muscles in her belly had been a tangled mess since Meri was taken, and his comment only cinched the knot tighter. She murmured, "I was simply hoping that they didn't know where I was."

"Believe me, they know where you've been every minute of the past three days, and they've watched you every step of the way from Idlewild." He smiled grimly and casually glanced around the dark street, the shadows long as the last red streaks of sunset faded in the west. "They're watching us even now."

A chill swirled down her spine. "They're watching us?"

"If you wanted documents so important that men were willing to kill for them, wouldn't you be watching the people you've tasked with delivering them?" Another squeeze of her arm, but this one did little to comfort her. "Don't worry, Diana. We *will* bring Meri home safely, I promise you."

Blinking hard, she gave a sharp nod and looked away.

"Our plan is to wait here until they decide to contact us. Then we'll follow their instructions and deliver the diary. She'll be waiting at Idlewild for you when you return. They won't harm her."

But his assurances didn't put her at ease. Her baby had been kidnapped and was being held God only knew where, most likely terrified and alone, crying out inconsolably for her... A shudder of anguish raced through her, and she forced down the pain and fresh tears by sheer force of will.

"Why would they keep their word?" She wanted to rip them apart with her bare hands! "They're kidnappers, for God's sake! They have no decency."

"Because they know who I am."

She choked back a strangled laugh. "You're awfully sure of yourself."

"I am." He smiled tightly, but she caught a glimpse of something darker inside him, something dreadful, and she shivered. "But I'm even more certain that they realize the repercussions of double-crossing me."

Before she could question him further, he led her across the hard-packed dirt street and between passing wagons loaded with crates and barrels. They were only a hundred yards from the docks. The scent of saltwater teased at her nose, and between the warehouses and shipping offices lining the waterfront, she caught glimpses of boats of all sizes docked at the wharves and sitting anchored farther out in the bay.

"If the French don't keep their word, no one connected to Whitehall will ever trust their agents again." His voice developed a hard edge. "They'll never be able to negotiate for information or favors after that."

"Honor among thieves?"

"Dishonor among spies," he corrected. "But it works the same way in the end. You can't trust the information you've been given if you can't trust the person who gives it, and they have no reason to destroy all the trust they've garnered with the English by double-crossing us. The court of King Louis won't allow it." His mouth tightened. "In short, they won't harm Meri because their own government will kill them if they do."

She wished she could believe that.

"Here's our hotel." He opened the front door and escorted her inside. "Welcome to the Mermaid."

With fears and worries surrounding Meri engulfing her, she barely noticed the hotel around her or the crowd of guests filling the lobby. She glanced blankly into the adjacent dining room as they passed, where people gathered around small tables and several more waited for a place to sit. The hotel was full to overflowing, and half a dozen more people were lined up at the counter in the lobby, where the hotel manager patiently shook his head at every request and referred them down the street to the coaching inn to find a room.

Christopher guided her up the stairs to a room on the second floor, took out a key from his breast pocket, and unlocked the door. Then he lit a candle on the hallway sconce and led her inside.

She took a deep breath to force down her rising anxiousness and attempted to focus on the room, lit softly by the glow of the candle. A dresser, a washbasin with a pitcher, towels, and soap, and very little else in the room—except for the bed. A perfectly good bed by all standards, clean and comfortable, with a lace canopy stretching over its four posters and lots of thick, down bedding for cool nights by the seaside. Yet her pulse spiked at the sight of it.

Christopher closed the door behind them and set her bag onto a wooden chair in the corner. He noticed her hesitancy as he lit a small lamp on the beside table, then shook out the candle stub to extinguish it. "Is something wrong with the room?"

"There's only one bed."

"There is."

"And no trundle."

"There is not."

She slid him a sideways glance. "And no rug on the floor for you to sleep on while I'm tucked into bed."

He flashed her a rakish grin and drawled, "There certainly is *not.*"

She scowled at him, irritated. How could he still be attempting to distract her? Hadn't he realized yet that she was too upset, that all she could think about was Meri and whether she was all right?

And to distract her like *this*, of all ways… "Christopher Carlisle, if you think for one moment that you will—"

"That I will take one of the extra blankets from the bed and sleep on the floor in front of the fireplace?" he interrupted. "Yes, that is exactly what I think." He paused with an exaggerated expression of shock. "Unless *you* were thinking something entirely different, that you and I would— For shame, Miss Morgan!" The devil had the gall to look affronted by the suggestion. "What kind of creature do you take me to be?"

Not falling for that for one second, she crossed her arms over her chest. "Certainly not a vicar."

He laughed and placed a chaste kiss to her forehead before stepping away.

"I am sorry about the sleeping arrangements—and so is my back," he muttered. "Or it will be after a night on that floor. But this was the last private room left in the village." He moved around the space, checking to make certain that it was ready for her, including inspecting the pitcher on the washbasin for water. "Tomorrow is the village's festival of St Brendan, the patron saint of sailors and seamen, and apparently, everyone in southeast England comes to Bradwell to celebrate. *Everyone.*" He frowned into the box by the fireplace to check if there was enough fuel there to keep them warm through the night. "Which is probably why the French picked this place. With all the people coming into town for the festivities, no one will notice us or them among the crowds, and they can sail away on one of the boats in the harbor as soon as the exchange is over. Which reminds me." He reached beneath his jacket, withdrew the diary, and extended it out toward her. "You have to carry this from now on."

With a firm shake of her head, she pushed it away. "You keep it."

"The French won't take it from you by force. We don't know

when they'll ask for it, or how, just that you have to be the one to hand it over. And when they do, you have to give it to them without struggle, understand?"

She eyed it warily. "But to just hand it over like that, without seeing Meri to know if she's all right—if we give it to them, we'll lose our only bit of leverage."

"That's how it has to be. Right now, they hold all the power, and they know it. We have to do as they say and trust that they'll keep their word."

Not having any other choice, she accepted the diary. She stared at it in her hands, as if it were a snake ready to strike.

"It won't work," she softly voiced her fear.

"It will. You need to trust in that."

She gave a sharp nod that wasn't at all convincing.

Before he could see more doubt darken her face, she crossed to the window. She peered out across the bay with all its boats silhouetted against the black sea in the rising moonlight and the festival tents and booths erected just to the side of the wharves, all lit by lanterns and torches. So many people... She wrung her hands. How would they ever find the French to give over the diary in this crush?

"Relax, Diana," he said quietly as he approached her from behind and took her shoulders in his hands. "She'll be fine, and so will you."

He released her and stepped back. Immediately, she missed his closeness and the comfort he brought.

"In a few days, you'll have everything you want. You'll be back home with Meri, going on with your lives as if none of this ever happened."

Including without him. Because he would have no reason to continue to see her once Meri was safe, once her brother's guilt was disproved, as she knew it would be. Already she felt the loss of him as palpably as the loss of his hands on her arms.

She turned to face him, tilting her head as she stared at him. Now that she knew the truth, she was learning to see through the mask he wore, to read him to the point that she could almost see the thoughts spinning through his head.

*Almost.* Because he still kept part of himself from her.

"And you, Christopher?" she pressed gently. "What do *you* want?"

HIS HEART SKIPPED. SHE DIDN'T MEAN THAT AS AN OFFER OF intimacy, not when she was so distressed about her child that she shook with it, even now. Yet his gut reflexively tightened at the temptation she posed, at the answer a dark part of his heart wanted to give. Because he wanted so very much, more than he deserved—justice, a future...Diana.

Now, he could never have it.

"I know you want to arrest Garrett," she said quietly, misunderstanding his hesitation.

"That's where you're wrong. I don't want to arrest him. I wish to God that I didn't have to, that he hasn't done the things he has." How much he wished that! She had no idea.

"Then save yourself the trouble and don't arrest him."

He curled his lips into a patient smile. "I can't do that." *Not even for you.*

She stepped closer, making the suddenly small room as tiny as a doll's house. "Because you're dedicated to England."

"Yes." *And to Fitch.* At the cost of all else. Including his life.

She lifted her chin in faint challenge. "Will you accept it when Garrett's proven innocent?"

"Will you accept it when he's proven guilty?"

"No, because he won't be."

He bit back a frustrated laugh. "You're awfully certain of your brother's innocence."

"I'm certain of the character of all the men I care about."

A hollow pang corkscrewed itself deep into his gut, because he knew she didn't include him in that group. But God help him, he wanted her to.

When she moved to step away, he stopped her with a gentle touch to her elbow.

"Now that we're here in Bradwell," he warned, "you'll have to do exactly as I say at every step. Understand?"

The little minx had the audacity to appear offended. "When have I ever not?"

Knowing better than to answer truthfully, he said instead, "You can trust me with your life." He prayed to God that she did. Now that he'd come to the end of the fight, what Diana thought of him mattered. A great deal. He took her hand and lifted it to his lips, to place a kiss to her palm. "Forget everything you've heard about me. Trust only what you've seen with your own eyes and know with your heart to be true."

She nodded. Only a small, jerking movement. But relief rumbled through him. Unable to resist bringing them both a moment's solace, he leaned down to kiss her.

"So not a vicar, then?"

He stopped, his mouth only a hairsbreadth from hers. "Alas, no."

"Pity. I should have enjoyed listening to you deliver a sermon on the merits of chastity." Despite the grim worry that exuded from her, a lightness teased in her voice. She was desperately trying for normalcy when her world had been tilted on its axis, and his heart ached for her. "It would have been greatly amusing."

"And short."

When a faint smile pulled at her lips through her worry, he knew then that everything would be all right. That she possessed the strength and determination needed to rescue her daughter and thrive, long after he was gone.

She stood so close now that he could feel the heat of her along his front, could smell the lavender scent that surrounded her like a cloud. "No one truly believes that you want to become a vicar, you know. So why do you tell everyone you do?"

"To irritate my brother." *Sweet Lucifer.* He called on all his restraint not to sweep her up in his arms and carry her to the bed, to make love to her the way he'd wanted to do since that night at the tavern. And to ease her pain, if only for a few hours.

"Is it working?"

"Beautifully, in fact." His smile faded, and he let his gaze linger on her, far more longingly than he should have. "Beautiful."

She caught her breath, the soft sound pulsing into him.

He'd wanted to distract her. Well, *that* had certainly done the trick. For both of them.

He cleared his throat, then took a long step away from her. There was safety in distance, no matter how frustrating. And other ways to distract her. Ways that were far more proper, if far less pleasurable.

"You've been cramped up in coaches for the past two days," he told her, grasping onto any excuse to leave the room. And to get far away from that bed. "Why don't you take a few minutes to finish settling in and then meet me downstairs? We'll explore the village and festival, and you can stretch your legs and take in some fresh air."

"And after?"

She was asking about the French, but he didn't want to steer the conversation back there any sooner than he had to. So he dodged. "After, we'll come back here, where I'll pay an exorbitant amount of money to have a dinner tray and hot bath brought up for you, and then we'll get a good night's sleep." He grimaced. "With me on the floor. All right?"

She shook her head. "I just want to stay here, in the room, until I have to deliver the diary." She wrung her hands in front of her and began to pace the small room. "I couldn't—not while Meri's being held. I can't think about anything else except how frightened she must be, if she's being cared for, or—"

Her voice choked off, unable to bring herself to say it. After all, speak of the devil…

"I understand." Truly, he did. But then, hadn't he spent a decade depending upon such coping mechanisms himself? After all, that was how he'd gotten through the world. One lie at a time. Until he was forced together with Diana. Now he wanted nothing more than for all the lies to stop. "Which is exactly why we have to go out. We have to make ourselves visible to the French, to let them know it's safe to approach us. The sooner they find us, the sooner you can return to Meri."

And perhaps give her an hour of thinking about anything else but her child. If he could. He'd certainly do his damnedest in trying. Because she would be no good to Meri or anyone if she went into the exchange as nothing more than a ball of churning emotions.

He reached for her arm, to stop her pacing. "Understand?"

"Yes." But the nervous word was barely louder than a breath.

"I'll be right by your side the entire time." He tenderly tucked a curl behind her ear. "And most likely, the French won't make contact until tomorrow morning."

She gave a jerking nod.

His chest tightened with her pain. Despite a voice inside his head screaming that he was a damned fool, he pulled her into his arms and held her against him. He wanted only to protect her, to soothe her fears and bring her comfort, however small.

When she slipped her arms around his waist to snuggle herself deeper into his arms and find comfort there, a warmth swelled inside him unlike any he'd ever known. Any lingering doubts he had about doing this for her vanished like morning fog.

He lowered his mouth to her ear and, as if sharing a secret, murmured, "You are one of the most capable women I have ever met, Diana. You're strong and beautiful...so very resilient. You will survive this, and you will come out even stronger for it."

Reluctantly, he released her from his arms and stepped away. Then he turned to leave the room, to find enough distance from her to clear his head and keep his focus on what was coming for them.

"You never answered my question," she called after him. "About what you want for yourself?"

He paused in the doorway. What she was asking for—*the impossible.* She wanted him to consider a different future for himself than the one he knew was coming, because he had no future. Once he handed over the diary to save Meri, Whitehall would end him.

"I know," he answered quietly. Then he stepped into the hall and closed the door.

# CHAPTER 16

"*L*ook there!" Christopher pointed across the aisle at one of the fair booths. "I was hoping someone would be selling those."

Amid the crowded festival, Diana turned to watch as Christopher tossed a coin to a woman beside a griddle that lay across the coals of an open fire at the edge of the fairgrounds. She scooped up a large spoonful of whatever it was that she was frying and deposited it into a paper cone, then handed it to him.

Beside him, Diana rose up onto her tiptoes to see what he'd bought. He was trying very hard to distract her tonight by taking her to the festival, and she was trying very hard to play along. The attempt was endearing, and drat the rascal for making her feel even more special when she was with him. But worried thoughts of Meri still hovered at the forefront of her mind.

Yet curiosity got the better of her, and she couldn't keep herself from peering into the cone. Tiny fried bits about the size of small grapes with a briny, fishy scent… "Cod pieces?"

As he led her away from the fire and back toward the heart of the night-time fair, he popped one into his mouth. "Periwinkles."

Around them, the festival of St Brendan was in full swing, and the little village had come alive with everyone enjoying themselves in preparation for tomorrow's more solemn holy day when they celebrated the saint's feast. That afternoon, a parade of fishermen, sailors, wives, and children had marched from the parish church through the town and down to the water, where the local priest performed the annual blessing of the boats and unofficially began the more raucous celebrations of drinking, eating, gaming, and dancing that would go long into the night.

Rows of vendor stalls and tents crossed the sloping field just above the wharves, and a crush of people filled the space between as they bought food, shopped for trinkets, and drank far more than they should have out of their rented tankards and mugs. Bonfires and torches lit the night. Music drifted from bands scattered across the fairgrounds, punctuated by shouts from the musicians as they encouraged people to dance. Cheers went up around various games from the winners, followed by jeers from the losers. People wearing costumes and masks dotted the crowd, with many dressed up like pirates and mermaids. All of them were having a rollicking good time.

All except Diana.

She was trying. She *truly* was trying—for Christopher's sake, if not for her own, because it mattered so much to him that she think about something other than Meri tonight. That for a few hours, at least, she might forget about the French and their threats and simply experience the fair, as if they were any other couple who had come to town for the festival.

So she forced a smile and played along. "What are periwinkles?"

"You've never had periwinkles?" Positioning himself beside her so that she wouldn't accidentally be jostled by the crush of people pressing in around them, he offered her the cone. "They're mollusks that grow along the coast." He popped another into his mouth and made a soft sound of appreciation at the taste, clearly exaggerating to prick her interest. "The locals scrape them off the rocks, pluck them from their shells, and then cook them up with some garlic, pepper, and lots of butter." When she only stared at him, speechless, he stopped in mid-chew. "They're delicious."

She screwed up her nose. "They're snails!"

"Sort of." He waved the cone temptingly in front of her. "But less French."

"No, thank you."

"Where's your loyalty to England?"

She pushed the cone away. "Snails are snails, regardless of nationality."

"Try one." His eyes gleamed, daring her to take one. "You'll like it, I promise."

She gestured toward one of the stalls across the way. "I'd rather have the roasted chestnuts they're selling over there."

He looked aghast. "Where's the adventure in that?" Yet he took her arm and escorted her through the crowd in the direction she'd pointed.

She slid him a sideways glance of recrimination. "I have enough adventure in my life right now, thank you very much."

That mutter earned her a concerned glance from him. In an attempt to focus her thoughts elsewhere, he popped another couple of periwinkles into his mouth and asked between chews, "How did you grow up in so many different places and not develop a fondness for exotic dishes?"

"Or at least a willingness to try unusual ones, you mean?" She stayed close to his side as they continued through the fair, having to lean in to be heard over the music.

"That, too." He offered the cone again, only for her to push it away with a scowl at his persistence.

"Lots of places, yes, but always on or near British army posts, none of which are known for their daring cuisine." She gave an exaggerated sigh that drew a smile from him. "You were in the army. You know how it is. In one hand, they give you your uniform, and in the other, a pot of boiled beef and leeks."

He winced. "Don't remind me."

She couldn't help the smile that pulled at her lips, despite the heaviness that still weighed upon her, and he rewarded her for it by a touch to the small of her back. A familiar and affectionate caress. They had no future, but Diana was grateful to be given this bit of him, no matter how small. For a few precious hours, she could lean on his strength.

He ate the last of the periwinkles, crumpled the cone in his hand, and tossed it away.

"But you're no longer a soldier," she reminded him.

No, he was a servant of a different kind to the Crown, yet his life wasn't so very different from that of her father and Major Paxton. His uniform might be invisible, but he was still obliged to follow orders, still required to do whatever Whitehall wanted from him and go wherever they assigned him.

"What will you do?" Feeling the distance creeping in upon them already, she wrapped her arm around his to keep close to his side. "You can't pretend forever to be waiting for a living in the Church."

"No, I can't," he agreed somberly. From the way he said that, she suspected that something else weighed on his mind.

And damn the foolish hope that sprung up inside her chest that he might want a life away from service, that made her ask far too breathlessly, "What will you do then?"

He dismissed the question with a stilted shrug. Then, he threw it back at her. "What do you want to do with your life, Diana?"

She froze, surprised at his question. No man had ever asked

her that before. They'd just assumed that she wanted the same as all other society misses—dresses, parties, a pretty little townhouse she could waste her time decorating between afternoon calls and teas. But Christopher genuinely wanted to know, and for once, she realized, not because he wanted to distract her.

She pulled in a deep breath and placed her trust in him as she shared, "I want to start a charity that will teach boys how to work with horses, so they can find good positions as trainers, drivers, and grooms. Maybe even secure positions in the cavalry."

"That's ambitious."

"I suppose." Always before, with her father and the major, she'd dropped the subject at this point. But with Christopher, she felt emboldened and seized the chance to explain. "But the stables and paddocks at Idlewild are already the largest in the county, with plenty of room to expand. We have good grooms and drivers in place now—men who served with the general in the army, who can teach apprentices and stable boys the proper way to work with horses from the very start. They'll pass down all their knowledge, and the boys will use that to improve their lives. And not just their lives, but their families' situations as well. Too many charities help children but do nothing for the families. My charity wouldn't be like that. We'd help everyone."

"Including the horses."

"You think I'm being silly." She didn't dare look at him. She didn't want to see the same expression of patronizing sympathy she'd seen from her father and the major when she'd told them of her dreams.

"When I think of you, Diana," he murmured, leading her onward in a winding path toward the roasted chestnuts, "silly isn't at all a word that comes to mind."

His husky words curled through her, warming her as they went.

Yet he cast her a dubious glance. "But I thought you'd want a husband, with a family and house of your own. Someone to help you raise Meri."

"I do want that, too. It's just..." She'd confided in him so far. There was no need to hold back now, so she admitted, "Finding a husband isn't that simple."

They reached the man who was stirring hot chestnuts over a small fire, and Christopher tossed him in a coin in exchange for a scoop. "Why not? You're a special woman, Diana." He nodded his thanks, then handed her the nuts wrapped in their scrap of paper and led her onward. "You could have your choice of eligible gentlemen."

"It's so much harder than that." She frowned down at the chestnuts, not having an appetite for them. "I have to be certain that the man I marry loves me enough that I can trust in him about Meri *before* we're wed, a man who will love her as much as the other children we might have together." Unable to look at him, she fussed with the nuts as she added, "A man who can provide the stable life that a little girl like Meri needs."

"And her mother."

She stiffened, catching that comment as a gentle accusation. But he wasn't wrong. "After a life spent constantly relocating to new places around the world every few years, is it wrong to want that?"

"Not at all. But my cousin Robert would have provided all of that for you." He snatched up one of the chestnuts and popped it into his mouth. She couldn't be certain through the chewing, but she thought she heard jealousy in his voice. "Why didn't you marry him?"

"Robert is a good man, but I wasn't absolutely certain that he would accept Meri as my child." There was relief in being able to share these worries with him, when she'd never been able to speak of them to anyone before. Not even to Garrett. "Not completely. Not when his reputation is central to his business ventures. Meri and I would only have put that in jeopardy."

"And Major Paxton?" He took her by the arm and led her through the pressing crowd. "He seems very interested in you."

"His interests are not returned." She handed him the sack, unable to eat another nut. She hadn't eaten much more than a few bites during the past two days since Meri was taken, and even now, her stomach churned at the thought of food. "I assure you of that, despite what the general hopes will happen."

He stiffened, but his face remained an unreadable mask. "He's picked Paxton for you, then?"

"He wants me to be happily married and thinks that the major would give me that."

"But you don't want Paxton." Not a question, she noted. She didn't have time to ponder that before he asked, "Why not? He seems like a good man with a solid future."

"In the army," she added, following him deeper into the fairgrounds. "And that's the problem. I can't be a soldier's wife. That life is too difficult." *Too insecure, too unstable*...all the things she never wanted to subject Meri to.

"I'm trying hard not to take that as a personal insult." He tossed the unwanted nuts away. "Technically, I'm still a soldier, too, you know."

She knew that, and it ate a hole in her heart. Yet she tried to sound as unaffected as possible when she replied, "Then it's a good thing you're not interested in marrying me."

He gave a stilted and self-conscious laugh. One that was forced.

She didn't want to talk about this anymore. Not with him. "What life do you want for yourself, Christopher? You can tell me." Her lips twisted wryly. "I'm quite good at keeping secrets."

He laughed, and she felt his defenses lowering. Yet the mask he wore to hide himself from the world still remained firmly in place. Would she ever be able to see completely beneath it?

"I can't answer that," he said, but he didn't glance down at her, his gaze focused on the crowd around them. She knew he was scanning it for the French.

"Why not?"

"My future is not my own." When she frowned at that cryptic answer, suspecting that he was keeping the truth from her even now, he added, "Nothing is certain beyond what's happening at this very moment, and that I'm doing everything I can to protect you and your family."

Her eyes and nose stung with emotion. When he said things like that... How on earth could she have ever thought him nothing but a shiftless scoundrel?

When she looked at him now, she could see right through that charade, as clearly as if he were wearing a costume. Just as she could see the flaws in the stories she'd heard about him, those clues that now appeared as bright as day. Now when she looked at him and saw exactly how dashing, strong, and daring he actually was, she also saw how wholly competent, capable, and successful.

How impossible for her.

No matter that he'd proven himself to be a hero and that the general respected him. No matter that she had come to trust him with her life—and now, in saving Meri, with her heart. His life was not his own. Not as long as he remained in service to the Crown. He could be sent away wherever and whenever Whitehall needed him. How could she live with the uncertainty of never knowing when he would come home...or if? Of the constant upheaval his work would bring to her life and Meri's?

There was no future for her and Christopher. Fate ended all hope of that before any chance at a life together had even begun.

But knowing that didn't stop her from wanting him. Or prevent her foolish heart from loving him.

She stopped and faced him, her hands clutching at his waistcoat to emphasize how much he meant to her, how much faith she had in him. "You could have everything you want, if you let yourself."

Before she could lose her courage, she rose onto her tiptoes and kissed him.

KIT DIDN'T MOVE, TAKEN COMPLETELY BY SURPRISE. HE LET HER KISS him, her lips soft and delicate as they moved entreatingly against his. Almost imploringly. As if she could convince him through her kiss of how much faith she held in him.

He wanted nothing more than to believe her. Yet he knew the truth. He had no future.

"Diana, stop." Her name was a plea for mercy as his shoulders sagged, as the full effect of her hit him like a brick—the desire and longing to possess her in ways that were more than merely physical, to be with her not just for tonight but the rest of his life.

Something deep inside him shattered, and as the pieces of his heart fell away like shards of glass, he saw fully for the first time all that he could never have.

The loss of her was excruciating.

Clutching her shoulders in his hands, he rasped out, "I can't be the man you need."

"I don't want you to be anything but yourself."

The irony pierced him. Ten years of living a lie, of pretending to be someone he wasn't...until Diana. Until it was too late.

His hands dropped to his sides. "I can't be that either."

Her eyes glistened in the lamplight. But she couldn't find the words either of them needed to gain solace in the double-cross fate had played on them.

"We should go back to the hotel." He looked away, before she could see the grief on his face. "We could both use some rest."

She hesitated, and for a moment, he held his breath, fearing that she would press for answers, and what the hell was he supposed to tell her if she did? That he loved her, and loved her enough to sacrifice everything to keep her and her daughter safe?

But thank God she could sense that he didn't want to discuss this and acquiesced quietly, "All right."

He took her arm to lead her out of the festival.

They were pushed together because of the crush of bodies that filled the fairgrounds and pressed in on them from all sides. She walked beside him, close enough that her skirt brushed against his legs, and she occasionally bumped against him when the crowd jostled them.

But she felt a thousand miles away, completely out of his reach, and the gulf stretching between them grew wider with every panging heartbeat. Yet he tightened his hold on her elbow. He wouldn't abandon her until he was forced to.

She halted suddenly, her eyes growing wide and her mouth falling open as she stared ahead into the crowd.

"Garrett?" She shook off his hand and took a tentative step forward, as if she couldn't believe her eyes. Then relief melted over her face, and she cried out hoarsely as she started forward, "Garrett!"

"Diana, wait!" But she slipped through Kit's fingers as he grabbed for her arm and dashed forward into the crowd before he could stop her, disappearing among the sea of bodies.

## CHAPTER 17

*H*er heart leapt into her throat. *Garrett.* He was here!

Diana pushed through the throng of people crowding between the rows of stalls and tents. But after every step she took, the crush closed in around her and she couldn't see more than a few feet in front of her. The sea of people made searching the crowd of faces even more difficult. But her brother was here. She *knew* it!

Not a trick of her eyes, not an illusion—she'd recognize Garrett anywhere. Even here.

She hurried across the fairgrounds, glancing around her in every direction for any glimpse of him. Her heart pounded so hard that she could barely take a breath between the fierce beats that ricocheted in her chest. Dear God, where *was* he? But he was safe and alive, and she desperately wanted to hug him to her in relief. And then throttle him for making them all worry so much.

But she couldn't find him. Nowhere. Not a flash of him to be seen.

Doubt jolted through her, and she stopped, her hands falling helplessly to her sides even as the people bumped into her from all directions.

Had she truly seen him? Her throat tightened. Maybe she'd only seen another man and so desperately wanted to find her brother that she believed—

Farther ahead in the crowd, a man turned to look back at her. Their gazes met... *Garrett.*

Then he stepped between the wooden booths and disappeared into the shadows.

She ran after him, practically shoving people out of her way as she stumbled forward. She reached the narrow gap between the stalls where she'd last glimpsed him and slipped into the darkness.

Someone grabbed her arm, and she was yanked inside the stall. The narrow plank door slammed shut behind her. A hand came down over her mouth before she could scream.

"You're safe."

Her heart lurched into her throat, and she mumbled against the man's palm. "Garrett?"

"You've always been the more responsible sibling." His hand slipped away. "You're supposed to be saving me from trouble, not the other way around."

In the darkness of the shuttered stall, with the only light coming in through small gaps between the boards, she could just barely make out—

"Garrett!" She threw her arms around his neck and hugged him. "I knew it was you!"

"It's me," he murmured, holding her just as tightly.

She pulled away from him to cup his face between her palms and turn his head this way and that, searching for any sign of injury. "Are you all right? Are you hurt?" The questions poured out of her, so did a wave of relief. "Where have you been? I was told that you'd been kidnapped, that you were giving information to—"

"We don't have much time. We only have a few moments before the French realize that they've lost sight of you and come searching."

A chill swirled down her spine. "A few moments for what?"

"Give me the general's diary," he ordered. When she hesitated, he pressed, "I know you have it with you."

Her dread turned to betrayal as the sickening truth washed over her.

What Christopher had told her was true. There was only one reason why her brother would want the diary, only one way that he could possibly know that she was in Bradwell and had it with her.

"You're working for the French," she whispered, too sad and angry at him to find her voice. She drew her hands into fists at her sides. "*Why?* Why are you doing this?"

"Nothing is as you believe it to be." In the shadows, his eyes gleamed brightly as he held out his hand. "Give it to me, Diana."

Anger roiled inside her until she didn't know what to believe about him. Except— "You took Meri to get the diary," she seethed, now tangling her fists in her skirt to keep from attacking him. She wanted to scratch his eyes out! "It was you…"

"*Never.*" The force behind that struck her like a blow. "I am working to keep everyone safe, including you and Meri."

"Safe?" The word choked from her in furious disbelief. "She's been kidnapped!"

"She's fine," he said calmly. "She's on a farm near Idlewild, being cared for by a kind old couple who are most likely spoiling her rotten."

Her heart couldn't believe that. "You're lying."

"I'm not. The person who took her placed her on that farm, to keep her out of sight until you give them the diary. My men have the farm surrounded and are watching over her every moment to ensure that she's safe."

"Men?" she repeated, bewildered. "You have *men*?" How on earth was her brother in a position to command anyone? Her world had not only turned upside down, but also inside out.

"Lots of them, all ready to move in at a moment's notice." In the shadows, his mouth twisted into a wry smile. "The worst that will happen to her is a scratch by one of the barn cats."

"Don't tease."

"I'm not."

She blinked rapidly to keep back tears of rage. "If you knew where she was, then you'd free her. You'd send word to the general, and he'd—"

"She can't come home just yet. But you have to trust me with her safety. You know that I would *never* harm her and that I would never lie to you about her."

She rasped out, desperate to believe him, "She's safe?"

"Perfectly fine."

*Thank God... Oh thank you, God!* A ragged breath seared her lungs as she gulped for air, and she grabbed for him to keep her knees from buckling beneath her in relief.

"My men won't let anything happen to her, I promise you. But she can't go home until the French have the diary. We have to play this out, all the way to the end." He gently took her upper arms in a plea for cooperation. "Trust me, Diana. I would never lead you astray."

She didn't fight him when he reached into her pocket to take the diary.

As he turned his back to her in the shadows to hold it up to the torchlight slanting between the boards, he flipped through it, searching for a specific entry. He found the page he wanted and scanned over it, then he lowered it back into the shadows, where she couldn't quite see what he was doing with it. Not that it mattered. Meri was safe, and in a few hours, the French would have the damned thing and she'd never have to think about it again.

He turned around and held it out to her. "Take it."

"You're giving it back?" Confusion fell over her. If Christopher was correct, and her brother was working for the French, then he shouldn't be handing it back. He should be giving it to the French himself. *This* should have been the exchange they'd been waiting for. "Why would you—"

"You're going to hand this to the French," he answered, ignoring her question. "They'll approach you tonight, most likely before you leave the festival. Give it to them when they ask for it. They won't harm you if you don't fight them. And Meri will be waiting for you at Idlewild when you return."

"Won't you be there for the exchange?"

"No. They can't know I'm here. You *cannot* tell them, understand?" He offered the diary to her again, this time making certain she took it and placed it back into her pocket. "Give this to them when they ask for it, and by dawn, you'll be on your way home. So will Meri."

Her heart lurched into her throat. "And where will you be?"

The flash of uncertainty in his eyes told her the truth. At least he didn't insult her by lying to her. "You can tell the general that I'm safe and will be home as soon as possible."

She clung to what few tendrils of hope she had left. "Can I also tell him that his son isn't working for the French?"

He gave her a tight, chastising smile, then abruptly changed the topic, dashing all of her hopes that he wasn't a traitor. "So I hear that you're staying at the Mermaid. With Christopher Carlisle."

She glared at him, offended by his prying and refusing to answer. Why should she answer his questions if he wouldn't answer hers?

"Be careful with Carlisle, Diana. He isn't what he seems."

She didn't bother attempting to hide her pain. "Neither are you."

His smile faded.

"I know exactly what Christopher is." And so did Garrett, obviously. "He told me that he's working for the Home Office."

"He's keeping more secrets than that."

Her heart stuttered. No, he'd told her everything… But suspicion made her whisper, "What secrets?"

"Ask him yourself." He retreated toward the door. "Tell no one that you saw me."

"Why can't I—"

He slipped through the door and closed it before she could chase after him, wedging it shut so that she couldn't open it.

"Garrett!" She pounded her fist against the planks. "Come back! I need to know—come back!"

The boards rattled beneath her pounding, but the sound was lost under the noise of the festival. With a fierce curse, she grabbed onto the door with both hands and yanked with all her strength, wrenching it open.

She ran from the stall and out into the fairgrounds, turning in a circle to search in every direction, but Garrett was gone, vanished into the mulling crowd. A cry of frustration and anger rose on her lips. She scanned the fairgrounds around her —*nothing*. Not a single glimpse of him.

Gone. As if he hadn't been there at all.

The sea of bodies, the smoke from the torches and lanterns, all the odors, the noise—it pressed in upon her until it threatened to suffocate her. She had to leave this place. *Now*.

She shoved her way through the crowd, desperate for space and air. She had no idea where she was going, no idea what direction would take her back to the hotel, and back to where Christopher would know to find her. So she headed down a row of stalls that she'd wandered past earlier and hoped would lead her out of the shifting maze that the fairgrounds had turned into.

She stopped. An icy chill pricked at the base of her spine.

Someone was watching her.

Slowly, she turned to scan the crowd. Everyone was milling about, talking and laughing, drinking and eating. A few couples were dancing randomly in the walkways. People in masks and costumes now outnumbered those in regular dress, and all of the crowd moved in undulating waves like the sea...

Except for two young men wearing seamen's clothes, who slipped through the crowd directly toward her. Their gazes were fixed on her, ignoring the festival around them.

*The French.* Were they coming after the diary now? Garrett had said they'd approach her before she left the festival. But fear raced through her veins. She couldn't do this, not without Christopher at her side, and retreated slowly backward through the jostling crowd.

They increased their strides.

Diana turned and ran. Her heart pounded as she shoved her way through the crowd, not caring who she pushed aside or the angry shouts and curses that went up at her. Run! No glimpse of Garrett, no sign of Christopher— *Run!* She didn't dare slow her strides to look behind, but with every step, she sensed the two young sailors drawing closer.

A stitch in her side shot pain through her abdomen. Stumbling onward, she pressed her hand against her waist to physically push down the pain and keep going.

Her fingers brushed against the hard edge of the diary in her skirt pocket. Knowing she couldn't outrun them, she halted in her steps. With a frustrated cry of surrender, she wheeled around to face them, pulling the little book out of her pocket and brandishing it like a weapon.

They stopped less than ten paces away and stared at her, like dogs cornering a rabbit.

"You want this?" She shook it in the air, drawing the attention of the crowd around them as she yelled the question again, this time in French.

She didn't give a damn who saw her now, who overhead what was happening. Her family was in danger, and curse them all for making her fear for the ones she loved!

One of the men pointed at the diary and nodded. Then he held out his hand to beckon her to come to him.

*No way in hell.* "If you want this, then take it," she bit out, all of her shaking with fury and fear. "And leave my family alone!"

Then she threw the diary at the two men as hard as she could.

She spun around and broke once more into a run. From the corner of her eye, she saw the two men dive into the sea of bodies after the book. Victory surged through her, but not enough to drive away the fear.

Not stopping to look back, she ran on.

She changed directions and headed toward the edge of the fairgrounds near the wharves, where the light from the festival's torches and fires didn't reach. Safety lay in the darkness, and she was desperate to flee. Helpless and vulnerable, she stumbled onward toward the black bay.

A man stepped in front of her without warning. She ran into him, knocking hard against his chest. She staggered back a step, and his arms went around her to steady her.

With a small gasp, she darted her gaze up to his face. Then nearly broke down with relief. "Christopher!"

"This way." Grabbing her hand, he pulled her with him as he ran toward the dock.

She stumbled beside him as she struggled to keep up with his long strides. But he didn't slow.

"The French have the diary," she panted out. "I saw Garrett— Meri's safe. He knows where she is. She's safe!"

"Good." He glanced back through the darkness toward the festival. "But we're not."

He led her at a near run down the wooden pier that stretched between the docked boats and into the shadows. She followed, putting her complete trust and her life once more into his hands.

When they reached the end of the pier, he jumped onto a little boat tied to the dock and pulled her up with him on the small aft deck. He cut the rope with a flick of a knife and shoved the boat away from the dock to let it drift out into the dark bay. Then he kicked open the little door to the tiny cabin below and pushed her inside.

She landed on her back with a soft bounce on a thin mattress that covered every inch of the cabin's narrow floor, only to gasp when he followed after her and slid his tall, broad body over hers.

His mouth came down against hers. The kiss possessed a single, determined purpose to pour into her the relief he felt that she was back with him, safely delivered into his arms. But it also worked to make her melt helplessly into a puddle beneath him.

When he finally lifted his head to break the kiss so they could recapture their breaths, she stared up at him in the darkness. The worry and affection for her that she saw on his face made her heart stutter beneath the enormity of it.

"Christopher." Her fingers trembled as they traced his widening smile, then matched it with one of her own. Happiness unlike any she'd ever known filled her to her soul. For the first time since Garrett went missing she had faith that everything would be fine. "It's all over, and we—"

"Shh." He touched his lips to hers to silence her, then lowered his mouth to murmur into her ear. "We don't want anyone to hear us. We just want to float away with the tide, like a boat that broke away from its mooring."

But being overheard was the last concern on her mind when his mouth returned to hers. The slow and sultry kiss he gave her tasted of comfort and solace, of heat and yearning.

She wrapped her arms around his neck and arched herself invitingly into him, lost in the joy of knowing Meri was safe and in the deliciousness of being in his arms, of having his weight pressing down upon her and his strength pulsing into her with every heartbeat. Her fingers sifted through the soft curls at his nape in silent encouragement to deepen the kiss, and he did just that, teasing at the seam of her lips with the tip of his tongue until she opened to him.

With a soft groan, he plunged his tongue inside and took exploring sweeps into her mouth, tasting and plundering in equal measure. She shivered hotly when he stroked his tongue seductively along the length of hers, to tease her into responding. When she did, tentatively circling her tongue around his, a growl sounded from the back of his throat. He shoved his hand into her hair, to hold her head still as he began to thrust wickedly between her lips in a relentless rhythm that left her trembling.

But this was only a kiss, and she yearned for so much more. She wanted the peace and reassurance she knew she would find in his arms, a few hours of selfish pleasure when she could forget all her troubles and simply feel warm, feminine...wanted.

She tore her mouth away from his and slid her lips back to his ear, her arms tightening their hold around him. With her cheek pressed against his like this, his heavy body lying over hers, she could feel his quickening breath and the pounding of his heart. It wasn't from being chased.

"Please," she breathed into his ear. That single word swept through him with a masculine shudder, a tensing of muscles, and a hardening of his limbs as they lay tangled up in hers. "Meri's safe, and so are we. And for right now, we're together." She placed an entreating kiss to his earlobe, and he inhaled sharply in response. "Make love to me."

He squeezed his eyes shut, regret gripping his face. "You deserve better than one night. But that's all it can be—one night of physical pleasure, nothing else. Certainly no future. And in the morning, you'll hate me."

"No," she breathed out, her whisper nearly lost beneath the soft lapping of the water against the hull of the boat. "I would never—"

"You'll hate me," he repeated firmly. "Because I will gladly take everything you offer, but I can give nothing back. I *cannot*." He rested his forehead against hers, her mouth so close that the warmth of his breath tickled over her lips. "Dear God, Diana... Don't you understand? I can't give you the security and stability that you're seeking. I can't give you any kind of future beyond dawn."

"I know that we have only tonight, that everything will change in the morning." When he began to argue, she leaned up to capture his mouth with hers and kiss away all his doubts, the way they'd all vanished inside her. The brutal truth tore from her— "But I'd rather have one night with you than none at all."

A pained expression gripped his face, his head slumping with a faint shake. "I don't want you to ever go through again what you went through with John Meredith."

For once, the mention of John's name didn't pierce her with grief. Sadness still lingered inside her, and always would. But she no longer mourned. The past held no sway over her. Now, there was only this moment and the joy that this night with Christopher would bring.

Touched by his concern, she reached trembling fingers to brush through the hair at his temple. "I won't get with child tonight."

He hesitated, as if he'd meant something else. But for the life of her, she couldn't imagine what. Then he said quietly, "You deserve so much better."

Better than the man who rescued her tonight and made certain that she was safe in the darkness? The man who was here in Bradwell only to help her rescue her daughter when he didn't have to, who could have taken the diary and used it for his own gain, abandoning her family when they were in need?

Better than making love to a man who was a true hero?

"No, I don't," she whispered, capturing his face between her hands and turning him toward her to kiss him. She murmured against his lips, "Make love to me, Christopher."

This time, his hard-won restraint snapped. He pulled her into his arms and rolled over onto his back beneath her before she could catch her breath.

# CHAPTER 18

it flipped her over to bring her on top of him. Her ripe mouth formed an *O* of surprise.

With trembling fingers, he reached up to caress her cheek. Dear God, she was beautiful. She lay along the length of his body, with her breasts pressed against him and her skirt and legs tangled around his. She clutched at his shoulder to steady herself. Beneath her fingers, his muscle tensed, revealing exactly how much he wanted her. So did the hardening bulge in his trousers that now pressed indelicately into her lower belly.

"Tell me to stop," he warned, his voice a husky rasp, "and I will."

"No," she breathed out, as soft as the night surrounding them. Her fingers trembled as they curled into his jacket to keep him close. "I won't say that."

*Thank God.* Because wild horses couldn't have pulled her out of his arms.

He reached up to remove the pins from her hair and threw them away. They pinged softly against the end wall of the tiny cabin. His eyes never left hers as he ran his hands through her hair and spread it over her shoulders, until the ends fell forward and tickled his chest.

"If you change your mind, I can sleep outside on the deck," he teased flirtatiously.

"No, you won't."

Her breath turned shallow and fast as his hands slid down her back to the row of tiny buttons. His fingers slipped them free, one by one, until her bodice sagged loose around her bosom. "I'll take one of the blankets, curl up under it, and be fine. You'll have this whole bed to yourself."

"No, you won't." She inhaled sharply when he tugged at the lace zigzagging through her short corset, tangling it around his fingers as he pulled it free.

He couldn't help grinning at her. Or stop the tingle that tickled at the backs of his knees and slowly crept its way upward, heating everywhere her body touched his. "Then I'll just sit out there in my coat."

"You won't do that either."

The tingle reached his groin and turned into a pulsating ache. *Never* had a woman refused her way into his arms before.

But then, no other woman was Diana Morgan.

"Then what will we do if I stay right here, hmm? What pleasures can I give you?" When the corset slipped free, he slid his hand into her bodice and beneath her shift, to capture her breast against his palm. "What can I do to make you scream?"

She leaned into his hand to press him harder against her and panted out, "Anything...you'd like."

When he toyed with her nipple, a moan escaped her, and the erotic sound sparked a burning inside him. "You're awfully sure about this."

She opened her eyes and stared into his. He couldn't prevent the tightening of his chest at her expression, so delicate and vulnerable. So much affection. For him. His grin vanished beneath the intensity of it.

"I'm awfully sure about you," she whispered. Then she cupped his face between her hands and leaned down to kiss him.

A fierce yearning unlike any he'd ever experienced before overcame him, along with acute anguish to know that they would only have these few precious hours. But he needed her— No, so much more than that. His *soul* ached for her, the way that deserts ached for rain.

He reached to remove her dress.

"Christopher, wait."

He froze, fearing she'd changed her mind after all.

A soft plea for understanding glistened in her eyes. "I know who you really are now—how kind and courageous—and that's the man I want to give myself to tonight." She touched her lips to his and whispered so longingly that the soft sound made his heart stutter. "I've never been more certain of anything in my life."

What she wanted washed over him with an electrifying jolt. For over ten years he'd played the part of a rogue and rake, never letting his true self be revealed to any woman, not even when he was buried inside her. He'd kept his heart distant. Always.

But Diana wanted so much more than just his body. She wanted to strip away every pretense right along with the layers of clothing, until he was exposed in every way. The enormity of it terrified him.

When she reached inside her bodice to cover his hand with hers, squeezing his fingers in a reassuring gesture, all of his doubts vanished until there was only certainty that tonight was good and right. Until there was only her.

"I want you, Christopher." She caressed a thumb over his bottom lip. "I want to make love to *you*."

His eyes stung, and he couldn't stop the tremble that shook him.

"So let me," she whispered, so softly that the words were barely more than a breath.

Her eyes never leaving his in the shadows, she reached down to take her hem in her hands and slowly peeled her dress up her body.

DIANA LIFTED HER ARMS AS SHE PULLED THE DRESS OVER HER HEAD and off, then dropped it unwanted at the side of the mattress. The corset fell away next, leaving her only in her thin cotton shift and stockings.

She sat on his lap, still straddling him, yet shamelessly so, even with his growing erection pressing against her inner thigh. When a tremble shivered through her, it wasn't from nervousness but need. He had no idea how much she wanted this. But she planned to show him exactly that.

She slowly untied his neckcloth and let it fall to the mattress. Then she took his jacket lapels and pulled them over his shoulders and down his arms. At that moment, with his arms behind him, imprisoned in the jacket sleeves, she gave a throaty laugh. Why not tease him the way he'd done to her?

She leaned forward to place a lingering kiss against his bare neck and mused, "I think I like you like this."

He grimaced. "Helpless?"

She smiled wickedly and dared to take a slow lick across his flesh. Good Lord, he tasted divine. "My prisoner."

He laughed, and the deep sound rumbled deliciously into her. It was a small reminder of how connected they were, and how much more fully joined they would be in only a few moments. The growing ache between her legs flared at the thought.

"I'd suggest you grab a length of rope from the deck and tie me up properly," he mumbled, "but..."

"But you're afraid I'd think you a rake?"

He arched a brow. "I'm afraid you'd actually do it."

"Never." She finished removing his jacket and purred, "I want your hands free."

Understanding what she meant, he slipped his hands beneath her shift and caressed slowly up and down her outer thighs.

She drew in a long, deep breath and closed her eyes, letting the sensations of his warm hands on her bare legs sweep over her. Intoxicated by the taste and touch of him, she barely realized when she removed his waistcoat and braces, when he slipped his shirt up over his head and off.

But she was well aware when his chest was bare beneath her hands as she ran them over his front. The hard muscles flexed and trembled beneath her seeking fingertips, and his breath grew just as shallow and rapid as hers. When she scraped her fingernail over his flat male nipple, he inhaled sharply.

"I'm sorry," she whispered.

"No, it's not—" His voice became a deep groan when she placed her mouth over it, to kiss it apologetically. "Diana."

Emboldened by his reaction, she took his shoulders and gently pushed him down onto his back, so she could place kisses across his chest and tease at his nipples with her fingers and tongue, the way he'd done before to hers. His skin was warm and soft, with a dusting of hair that trailed down toward his bellybutton and lower. She followed, tracing the ridges of his abdomen with the tip of her tongue. His hands tightened their hold on her upper arms in response, but he didn't stop her, not even when his body tensed beneath her.

When she reached the waistband of his trousers, she hesitated. She'd only been with one man before tonight, and so long ago. What they'd shared had been sweet and gentle, and she'd never dared to have her mouth on him like this. But now, with Kit, the sweetness of affection she felt for him was accompanied with a physical longing to take pleasure from him and give it in return, one she knew he sensed with the same mounting intensity that gripped her.

He stroked her cheek. "You don't have to—"

She silenced him with a swirl of her tongue into his belly button, one that shivered through him. Before he could recover from the theft of his breath, her trembling fingers had unbuttoned his fall and reached inside, to free him from his trousers.

Spellbound at the sight of him, she traced a trembling fingertip down his thick length as his erection rested against his thigh. He flexed beneath her touch, which only made her want to more boldly explore him with slow caresses of her fingers.

"But I want to," she whispered as she took him in her palm to hold him still, then lowered her mouth. Her lips brushed against his round tip with each word. "You taste too good not to."

When she pulled back to lick her lips and claim the flavor of him lingering there, she wasn't prepared for the groan that tore from him. Her gaze jumped up to his, to find him staring at her mouth with an intensity she'd never seen from a man before in her life.

Wantonness heated deliciously inside her. Letting him look his fill, she boldly lowered her head and placed a sultry kiss directly to his tip. There was no shame in kissing him like this, no reason to deny either of them this pleasure or her this wonderful new experience. This was the man she wanted to give herself to, and this part of him was his masculine core. How could she not show him what he meant to her? And selfishly, how could she deny herself?

So she opened her mouth and slowly took him between her lips.

"Dear God," he groaned and shoved his fingers into her hair.

She closed her eyes and let the sensations flood over her...the soft skin over steely hardness between her lips, the salty-sweet taste on her tongue, the strength of his fingers as they curled against her scalp. Inside her, the long-sleeping feminine desire and need fully woke, and her body came alive, in a thousand electric tingles.

When she swirled her tongue over his round head and tasted a drop of the essence that had formed there at the tiny slit, she moaned softly. Hot tears formed in her eyes, and she shivered, overwhelmed by him.

"Diana," he rasped out huskily as his other hand slid down her body, caressing at her breasts through her chemise. Her hard nipples had already drawn into tight points, but his fingers made them ache and throb in time with the growing desire between her thighs.

When his hand slipped between her legs and caressed her bare folds, her heart slammed against her ribs so hard that she knew he could feel it. But he didn't hesitate as he stroked against her, his caresses growing deeper with each hard suck she gave to his erection, until he slipped two fingers inside her.

Startled, she lost control, and her teeth scraped against his sensitive tip. His length flexed against her tongue.

"Jesus," he exclaimed softly in pleasure, yet disbelief colored his husky voice that this was actually happening. As he stroked into her, his fingers giving a teasing swirl with each plunge and retreat that had her shaking, he warned, "If you keep that up—"

"What?" she countered, not only scraping her teeth against

him again but now daring to take small bites down his length. Inside her, all the tiny muscles clenched around his fingers in an attempt to take him deeper of their own volition, and she moaned softly as the first tingles of release began to lap at her toes. She panted out, "You'll do what?"

Biting back a curse, he pulled her into his arms and rolled her onto her back. He pulled her chemise up to her waist and spread her legs wide beneath him as he settled into the cradle of her thighs. His eyes never left hers as he grabbed his length and guided it to her core, then shoved his hips forward and plunged into her tight warmth in one smooth motion.

"I'll make love to you," he answered, then began to move inside her in long, powerful, and possessive strokes that ripped her breath away.

"Christopher!" With a soft cry of happiness, she wrapped her arms and legs around him and held on tightly.

Oh, it was wonderful! *He* was wonderful. She reveled in the deliciousness of being finally filled by him, of having his weight pressing down upon her, of being so closely joined that she couldn't say where she ended and he began. Every hard plunge came with a low groan from the back of his throat as he let all control vanish. Every retreat came with a teasing swirl of his hips that tore a whimper of loss from her lips and made her desperate to have him fully inside her again to the hilt.

"That's...that's so..." She moaned and arched herself against him, her feet now planted on the mattress to push herself up to meet each downward pump of his body into hers.

"Nice?" he rasped out, breathless in his exerted attempts to bury himself inside her.

"Very," she panted out, her hands clutching at his biceps.

"And this?" He looped her left leg over his shoulder, opening her wide beneath him in a new and delicious angle.

When he plunged into her, he went so deep that her breath left her throat in a strangled cry of pleasure. "Yes! Oh, yes…"

She shuddered as liquid heat began to pool between her legs, right where their bodies joined, and threatened to consume her. A tingle tickled at her toes, still in her stockings because they hadn't stopped to fully undress. Even now she could feel the scrape of his trousers against her inner thighs, the rough tops of his boots when she ran her foot down the back of his calf to shift positions and linger on this side of release for as long as she could.

But it wouldn't be long, not if he kept rubbing his pelvis against her clitoris like this. Every thrust against it shot electricity out to the ends of her fingers and toes, and she couldn't stop the wave swelling up inside her, couldn't stop the pool of liquid heat at her core from spilling over—

She cried out as a deep shudder swept through her, and pleasure overtook her. Her body spasmed around his, tightening and releasing in waves, and she clung to him as she flew over the edge into sweet release.

He stilled his movements, despite his erection still being hard and thick inside her, and let her pleasure lap over him like the waves hitting gently against the boat around them.

When she'd regained her breath, he began to move again. This time, not with the uncontrolled passion of before, but with slow, careful slides into her wet warmth as she tightly encircled him. This time, he kept her wrapped within the circle of his arms, and she realized that he was no longer having sex with her—

He was making love.

Tears formed at her lashes, and she squeezed her eyes shut. With every ounce of her being, she wanted to imprint this moment into her mind, his body onto hers, so she would never forget it.

"Diana," he murmured, his cheek pressed against hers, his

mouth at her ear and his body never stopping its slow rocking into hers. He whispered so softly that she couldn't hear, but her heart understood every word... *Beautiful Diana...goddess...angel...*

"Christopher," she whispered back, placing a kiss to his cheek and tightening her arms and legs around him. "My Christopher."

A single tear slipped free, unseen in the darkness. It wasn't sadness that gripped her but overwhelming joy. Never before in her life had she felt this happy, this safe...and loved.

He clenched his teeth to keep his control even as he brought her to release a second time, not with a cry from her lips like before but a soft whisper of his name. This time, the pleasure that overtook her was sheer bliss, and she held her breath, waiting for him to follow after, to pour himself into her—

Suddenly, he reached between them and yanked himself out of her tight warmth. His arms went around her like steel bands and held her tightly to him, belly to belly. His hips jerked, and with a groan, he shuddered violently as a deep breath tore from him. A wet warmth spilled across her abdomen.

He remained still for a few moments. Then he rolled on his side and gathered her into his arms, fighting for breath as he buried his mouth in her hair. Warmth licked at her toes and swelled inside her. She wrapped her arm around his waist, her legs tangled in his, never wanting to let go.

She rested her cheek against his shoulder and felt the rapid tattoo of his heartbeat. A long, satisfied sigh escaped her when he brushed his fingers through her hair and let it cascade over his chest.

He placed a kiss to her temple. "Are you all right?"

She was disappointed, she couldn't deny it, that he had withdrawn and denied her that special end of this precious act. But she also knew that he was protecting her, and her chest swelled with even greater affection for him. And yes, with love. There was no point denying it any longer. "I'm wonderful."

He gave a playful growl and tugged at the neckline of her chemise, to place a kiss to the top swells of her breasts. "Yes, you certainly are."

Happiness bubbled through her, and she laughed. She placed her hand over his, weaving their fingers together, then placed both of their hands onto his chest. Right over his heart.

Not knowing what to say, not knowing what territory was safe to venture into after this new intimacy between them, she retreated into lighthearted teasing. For now. "Looks like you made me scream after all."

He pulled her over on top of him and grinned wickedly at her. "Want to see if I can make you do it again?"

"No." When his brow creased with a bewildered frown of disappointment, she leaned down and kissed him with such wanton intent that he groaned beneath her lips. "I want to make you."

# CHAPTER 19

it stared up into the darkness at the short ceiling
of the tiny cabin and heard nothing but the soft
sound of Diana's breathing and the lapping of water against the
hull. On any other night, a warm woman's arms and the gentle
rocking of a boat would have been enough to lull him into deep
sleep. But there'd be no sleeping tonight. Dawn was coming soon.
God only knew what would happen after that, and he didn't want
to waste one precious moment with her.

He shifted her naked body closer in his arms and placed a kiss
to her forehead. They'd finally paused after making love a second
time to remove what few pieces of clothing they'd still been
wearing and now lay bare under the warm blankets. He'd left her
only long enough to anchor the boat, which had drawn peals of
laughter from her at the sight of a naked man climbing onto the
deck and mutters from him about generals' daughters having no
appreciation for the sailors of His Majesty's navy.

Nestled into the hollow beneath his shoulder as she lay beside
him, she made a soft sound of appreciation and brushed her hand
over his chest. Then she pulled up the edge of the curtain covering

the small window and glanced out at the night. There was nothing to see. Around them, the bay was dark, silent, and still, and for now, he could selfishly let himself believe that the rest of the world didn't exist and that dawn would never come.

"Where are we?" she asked.

"Lost." He'd never uttered a truer word in his life.

She gave him a chastising purse of her lips.

"Safe," he amended, nuzzling his face against her neck and breathing in her sweetness, that intoxicating perfume of lavender now mixed with the musky scent of sex. "You're safe."

"*We're* safe, you mean."

He grimaced. Leave it to that sharp mind of hers to realize that he'd excluded himself in that declaration. Now that the French had the diary, the Crown would consider him a rogue agent for handing it over, and that's what he would let them believe—that it had been his idea from the beginning, that Diana and her father had nothing to do with it. He would protect them. But he never would be safe again. "No one will hurt you, love." That endearment fell far too easily from his lips. "They won't come after you or the ones you care about ever again. I promise you."

She traced an *X* over his bare chest. "Cross your heart?"

*And hope to die.* But speak of the devil... So he changed topics. "You'll leave in the morning, on the first coach headed toward London."

Her face darkened in the silver moonlight that slanted into the tiny cabin through the hatchway that he'd left open, so he could hear if anyone rowed up upon them in the darkness. "And you'll continue to pursue Garrett."

"Yes." As long as Whitehall allowed him to breathe. Which most likely wouldn't be long.

But Morgan was here in Bradwell, and Kit wouldn't let this last opportunity for justice to slip through his fingers.

With a frustrated sigh, she rolled away from him and onto her back beside him, somehow managing not to touch him at all on the narrow bed. He felt the loss of her like a chill seeping through his bones, and he fought with himself not to grab her back into his arms.

"Why won't you realize that Garrett isn't a traitor?" she said into the darkness. "He's been protecting Meri and keeping her safe. He was watching over me tonight at the festival when the exchange happened." In her mounting frustration, she fisted the sheet at her side. "For God's sake! He had the diary in his hands tonight. If he was working for the French, why would he give it back? Why not just take it from me?"

The chill turned into an electric jolt. He rolled over on top of her, pinning her beneath him.

"He had the diary?" He searched her face for any clues in the shadows. "You gave it to him?"

"Not exactly." When she tried to wiggle free, he held her still, and she glowered up at him in frustration. "I saw him before the exchange. He told me that the French would be contacting me soon, that Meri was safe and his men were guarding her. He took the diary from me, flipped through the pages, and then gave it back."

His heart skipped with dread. "He tore pages out of it?"

"No. He just handed it back, said to give it to the French when they asked for it." Her frown deepened. "What does any of that matter? The French have it now."

But they didn't. That realization stood his hair on end. What her brother had done—

He stared down into her confused face as all the pieces of the puzzle finally fell into place, each one fitting into the other like Russian nesting dolls... Why her brother concocted that story about visiting friends before he went missing, why the Foreign

Office knew of Morgan's connection to Fitch-Batten's murder and didn't care, why Nathaniel Grey had ordered Kit to stop chasing Morgan.

Her brother *was* working for the French. But with England's blessing.

Yet Morgan had known all along where the diary was hidden and could have given it to the Foreign Office at any point. So why work in secret? Why murder Fitch? And if Morgan had nothing to do with his own fake kidnapping or Meri's real one, then who did?

That was the question now...*who?*

Another player had entered the field.

"Garrett didn't take it when he had the chance," she protested gently, not knowing what information she'd just revealed. "Surely that proves he's not a traitor."

His mind whirled, and distracted, he mumbled, "Your brother isn't what he seems."

"He said the same about you."

Of course he did. If Morgan was working for the Foreign Office, then he would have been told about Kit's manufactured identity. He smiled tightly. "But you already knew that."

"He didn't mean the Home Office. He meant that you were keeping other secrets." She stiffened beneath him as his smile faded. "What secrets?"

She moved again to free herself, and this time, he let her slide out from beneath him.

Clutching the blanket to her front, she sat up. "I think I deserve to be told the truth now, don't you?" She placed her hand over his. "*All* the truth. From the beginning."

"That's a lot of truth," he warned, attempting to inject a hint of teasing to lighten the sudden tension between them.

And failing, when she grimly countered, "I think I'm strong enough to handle it."

She was the strongest woman he knew. But this... He blew out a harsh breath, relenting. "It started six months ago."

He rolled onto his back and stared up at the ceiling again, wishing to God that he had a bottle of whisky to help him get through this. She wanted the truth, so he would give it. He only hoped she'd understand when he finished.

"I had a partner who worked with me on Home Office assignments. We were even at Peterloo together, but three streets away when the massacre occurred. The Home Office wanted us there to help keep the peace, but we decided that we'd rather be in a tavern than in the field listening to people talk about not having the vote."

"Peterloo?" she whispered.

He gave a curt nod. Guilt for not being there still ate at his gut. It was slaughter at the hands of the cavalry, condoned by the Home Office, and the event that had started him doubting his unqualified allegiance to Crown and country.

"Fitch and I often went our own way on assignments, both from what the Home Office wanted from us and from each other. That time, it had been a mistake." But it wouldn't be the last. "We might have been able to save some of the protesters if we'd been there."

Her hand tightened over his. "Fitch?"

"James Fitch-Batten. The son of a canal builder from Lincolnshire who saw his father work himself to death making other men rich and so wanted a better life for himself. We would never have been friends if we weren't thrown together by the Home Office." He smiled wistfully. "Dear God, could that man drink! I've never seen anyone go deeper into his cups than Fitch, yet still be stone-cold sober enough to hit a bull's-eye with a pistol from twenty paces."

"He sounds like a remarkable man."

"He was." *Was.* The word lay bitter on his tongue. "One of the best operatives the Home Office ever produced."

"Next to you, of course."

At that soft compliment, he lifted her hand to his lips and placed a kiss to her palm. Instead of releasing it, he placed it on his chest.

"Your friend's no longer an operative, then?"

He paused. She'd asked for the truth... "He's no longer anything."

When she stiffened and tried to pull her hand away, he tightened his fingers around hers and kept it in place, right over his heart.

"Last winter, Fitch and I were investigating communications between the French and their operatives here in England. A standard assignment. We'd done work like that dozens of times. So we scheduled a meeting with one of our assets, a man we'd worked with before and trusted."

As if sensing the tightening knot of guilt and fury inside him, she lay down in the hollow between his arm and his chest and nestled herself against him, providing comfort with her presence.

"It was routine work, and I didn't want to give up my evening for it. Given a choice between being in a woman's bed or walking through the cold London rain at midnight just to confirm what we already knew, I'd have been a damned fool to go."

She stiffened against him but said nothing, yet he knew that revelation upset her. She'd asked for the truth—*all* the truth—and he was giving her exactly that.

"I didn't go to the meeting." Didn't *want* to go. Not to do work for the Home Office when it was becoming harder and harder to believe in his work, when he was sick and tired of letting White-hall dictate his personal life. For once, he'd simply wanted to be *normal*. "I let Fitch go without me." He paused. "By three in the morning, when he hadn't yet tracked me down to tell me how the meeting went, I become worried. So I went looking for him. I found his body in an alley."

So softly that barely any sound at all crossed her lips, she breathed, "He was murdered?"

"Yes." He paused to keep his voice from cracking with emotion. "And I wasn't there to stop it."

He lifted his arm from around her and sat up, dropping his legs into the small space beside the edge of the mattress. He yanked open the curtain covering the tiny cabin window but could see nothing in the darkness except moonlight teasing across the black water. No stars, no other boats—not even the land edging the bay. An illusion of being utterly alone in the world, but not even adrift.

The irony of that pierced him. Being adrift meant the possibility of eventually washing up onto shore, in a new place, with a new chance. But this, sitting here simply waiting in his own private purgatory, waiting for the end... *Hell.*

And damn the world that fate should finally deliver a woman like Diana Morgan to him! Now, of all times. Dangling in front of him the possibility of a happy, secure future with a woman who was his match in every way, only to cruelly snatch it away.

She sat up behind him, her hand touching his bare back. "What did you do?"

"I went on the hunt." His eyes still scanned the darkness of the bay, but what he saw were flashes of Fitch's dead body, so badly beaten that his face was almost unrecognizable, his left shoulder dislocated and his right arm broken, his kneecaps smashed. The cut at his throat so deep and vicious that it had nearly severed completely through his neck. He'd died neither easily nor quickly, in an act of unchecked brutality and viciousness that Kit hadn't seen since Peterloo, when defenseless men, women, and children had been sliced open with sabers and trampled beneath horses. "I tracked down every clue, every lead. That's all I've been doing since then. Hunting down the man who did it."

Leaving carnage and scorched earth in his wake, destroying relationships and contacts that took years to establish, turning his back completely on the Crown and its offices. Until it all brought him here.

"And I won't stop until Fitch has justice." Or until he drew his last breath.

"That's why you're after Garrett," she whispered. Not a question, but a confirmation. "You think he's the man who murdered your friend."

He looked over his shoulder at her, and his dark expression made her gasp. "I know he did."

⁓

THE HAUNTED LOOK IN HIS EYES CHILLED HER DOWN TO HER SOUL, and she shuddered. "No," she breathed out, stunned. "That's... that's not possible. Garrett would never—*could* never..."

But his gaze didn't soften. A gleam of certainty remained in his eyes.

When he didn't reply, she admitted painfully, "My brother has been a failure his entire life. He has been successful at nothing. Not the army, not university, not any kind of business venture. *Nothing.*" Her voice rose with mounting alarm. Garrett was nearby in Bradwell. If Kit was this determined to find him, to hang him for treason and murder, if she couldn't find a way to convince him — "For God's sake! He's never won a single fight in his life. He's lost every bout of fisticuffs, every fencing match, every race. You *know* my brother. You truly think he has the wherewithal to be able to physically overpower a trained agent and murder him?"

"Morgan was there that night. A witness saw him go into the alley and come out with blood on his hands. Footprints in the mud matched your brother's. So did a footprint on the stone. One imprinted in Fitch's blood."

"That means nothing." Yet doubt began to gnaw at her belly. "Lots of men have the same size foot."

"But men don't wear down their boots in the same way. That's what showed up in the footprints. That's what matched your brother's boots."

"You—you had Garrett's boots?" Her mouth fell open as her mind whirled to fathom what he was telling her. "How?"

"I bribed one of your servants to bring them to me. I had them resoled and kept the originals, and within two hours, the servant put them back right where he'd found them. Your brother didn't know they were ever gone." When the blood drained from her face, he lifted a brow. "You said you wanted the truth. Here it is, Diana, warts and all."

"I did. I just—" *Good God.*

"So I had his soles, the imprint in blood that I'd pressed onto a sheet of paper, and the drawings I took of the other footprints in the alley, right down to how deep each place on the shoe pressed into the dirt. I matched the wear of Morgan's boot soles to the prints. A perfect match. That, and the witness's physical description of the man he saw enter the alley conclusively put him there."

"But that doesn't mean Garrett murdered Fitch." She clung to straws now. *Anything* to convince him! "People are murdered in London at night all the time, straying someplace they shouldn't. Just because Garrett was in that same alley doesn't mean that he was responsible."

"I investigated your brother and learned that he'd been in contact with the French, through those same communication channels that Fitch and I were sent to confirm. Most likely, he waited until Fitch met with our asset, then followed him until the right moment presented itself. Better to silence Fitch than let Morgan's name get back to the Home Office as a traitor."

No—no, this was all wrong! She slapped her hand on the mattress in fear and frustration. "My brother doesn't possess that kind of cunning!"

"Your brother had a copy of your father's diary made and then switched it out tonight when you handed it to him. What you gave to the French tonight was a fake." His eyes softened then, not with understanding but pity. "He possesses *exactly* that kind of cunning."

She pressed her fist against her squeezing chest as she replayed that moment from tonight in her mind. How Garrett had demanded the diary and flipped through it, to make certain that it was the original and still contained the information the French wanted. How he had angered her on purpose, then turned his back, to distract her while the diary was temporarily out of her sight in the shadows, so he could switch books and hand her the copy. *Oh good Lord.*

"Why?" she forced out breathlessly, her mind spinning. "*Why* would he do that?"

"I don't know. And to be honest, I don't care." With a bleak expression, he reached up to stroke her cheek, but for once she found little comfort in his touch. "You and Meri are safe. That's all that matters now, not who has the diary or why."

"But it does." She grabbed his hand and held it tightly. "If Garrett kept the real diary from going to the French, then he's not a traitor. The exact opposite, in fact."

She eagerly searched his face for any traces of the same

conclusion that she'd made, any signs that he could give up his hunt for her brother. But the grim expression never lifted from his face, and she *knew*—

"You don't care." Icy dread flared out to her fingertips, turning all of her numb. "You don't care that he's not a traitor. You still think him a murderer. That's why you're still planning on chasing after him, isn't it?"

"Yes."

That single word reverberated through her like cannon fire. "My brother didn't murder your friend. But whoever did—"

"Diana—"

She repeated forcefully, "*Whoever* did is also capable of doing the same to you. You know that, yet you're risking your life anyway."

His bleak silence answered her.

"*Why*, Christopher?"

"Because Fitch deserves justice."

"Not at the cost of your life."

"If that's what it takes," he admitted. Yet something told her that he was answering for far more than her brother. But what?

He shoved himself up from the mattress. But there was no room to pace, with only two feet between the end of the makeshift bed and the short ladder that led up to the deck. He crouched by the ladder, unable to straighten to his full height in the tiny cabin, and stared silently out into the dark night through the open hatch.

"Christopher, you're wrong." Fear for his safety swelled inside her. She couldn't bear to lose him now. "What happened to Fitch was terrible, but nothing you do can ever bring him back. *Nothing*."

He stiffened, but didn't turn to face her or crawl back into bed with her, where he belonged.

"I know what it's like to lose someone you love to such a senseless act." Her eyes stung as fresh grief swelled inside her. "I know how wrenching it is, how you would do anything to bring them back, how you would offer anything—including yourself." She inhaled a long, jagged breath. "When John died, I spent days praying, bargaining, telling God to take me instead and make it all be some kind of terrible mistake, to let—" She choked. "To let me die, too. *Any* kind of sacrifice I could make to bring him back."

"It's not the same."

"Grief is grief," she corrected gently. "It's always hell."

A grisly laugh strangled in his throat. "Then I'm in a special kind of hell."

"Yes." With trembling fingers, she reached for his hand as it dangled at his side. Around the knot of grief in her throat, she whispered, "But you're not alone."

Her fingers tightened around his, and he shuddered. Yet he didn't pull his hand away, and she foolishly took hope in that.

"You didn't know what was going to happen that night. There was no possible way for you to have stopped…"

The icy realization for why he was so determined to risk his own life froze her blood, and her heart stopped. When it began to beat again a moment later, each beat pounded a brutal thud through her.

"That's it, isn't it?" With a tug to his hand, she pulled him around to face her. "That's why you've been hunting Garrett all these months, why you went to the lengths you did—why you're willing to risk your life." She rose up onto her knees on the edge of the mattress. "Because you blame yourself. Because you think that you could have stopped it."

"I don't think it," he bit out. "I know it."

"It's not your fault that—"

"I should have been there!" He grabbed her by the shoulders.

"This wasn't an accident. He was *murdered*, and I should have been there to stop it. For Christ's sake!" His fingers dug into her arms. The anguish pulsating from him was palpable, the pain visible on his face. "He was my partner, and I wasn't there when he needed me."

"Christopher—"

"Instead of going with Fitch to Covent Garden, I went to Mayfair to spend the night tupping Lady Bellingham."

He dropped his hands away, as if he couldn't bare to touch her as he admitted this. As if he didn't deserve to.

"*That's* why I wasn't at my partner's side that night as I should have been. Because I preferred being between the countess's thighs to doing my duty. And Fitch was murdered because of it."

The self-recrimination on his face sliced into her like a knife twisting into her belly.

"So *don't* tell me that we're all grieving for lost loved ones or that you understand the hell I've gone through—the hell I am *still* going through. That we all want to make deals and sacrifices to bring them back." A bitter laugh fell darkly from his lips. "Risk my life to get justice for Fitch? I shouldn't have a life! It should have been *me* in that alley, *my* throat that was slit."

He lowered his face until his eyes were level with hers, his mouth so close that she could feel the warmth of his lips shadowing hers. Fear that she was already losing him ripped her breath away.

"So you tell me, Diana. What sacrifice do I offer when I should already be dead?"

# CHAPTER 20

*K*it sat at the stern of the little sailboat, leaning against the short cabin wall and resting his forearm over one bent knee. He wore only his trousers, but even otherwise bare to the air, he felt none of the cold. He'd turned numb before he left the cabin, from the way Diana had stared at him when he'd finished confessing everything. As if he were once again no more to her than a stranger.

On the eastern horizon, the sky was beginning to lighten as dawn approached. Finally. He had no idea how long he'd been out here, waiting for daylight to come so he could sail the boat back to the wharf. But long enough that the waves had picked up and were now rocking the boat side-to-side in a slow, steady motion in anticipation of the breaking day.

Time had run out.

He would take her back to shore, put her onto the first coach headed west, and then leave. Just as he'd planned. She'd forget him soon enough. After all, she was the beautiful, intelligent daughter of one of England's most respected generals, and she would find a husband who would cherish her and love Meri as his own. The husband she deserved.

Kit would forget her, too, eventually. But not until the day he died.

Beside him, the little hatchway opened with a soft click. Wrapped in a blanket around her shoulders, Diana climbed carefully up onto the small deck. Then wordlessly, she knelt down beside him.

Her blue eyes were as deep as the eastern sky behind her, holding the same radiance as the dawn. His gut clenched when those eyes stared into his, when she reached up to touch his cheek.

*Leave me alone...I can never be the man you need me to be.* But he couldn't find the strength to utter the words that would send her away.

When she brushed her thumb across his lips, then leaned in to kiss him, the tenderness nearly undid him. It wasn't passion he tasted on her lips but understanding and forgiveness.

Silently, she slipped over his legs to straddle him, the entire time deepening her kiss, until she entreatingly coaxed him into opening his mouth to her so that she could claim what lay inside. The tip of her tongue slid over his inner lip to taste the sweetness there, then twirled slowly around his tongue, drawing it out until she could close her lips around it. Her gentle suck coiled through him, right down to the tip of his cock.

She sat away from him. With her eyes never leaving his, she pushed the blanket from her shoulders. It slid down her back and bared her completely, both to his eyes and the dawn.

*Sweet Lucifer.*

Her pale skin was awash in the sapphire and midnight blues of the sky. Only the dusky pink of her nipples contrasted the cool, cobalt light falling upon her as the last vestiges of night gave way to morning. Unable to resist her siren song, he traced a fingertip lightly over each ripe bud, watching as they grew even more taut beneath his attentions.

He leaned forward and took one between his lips.

Her breath caught, then she relaxed against him as he suckled at her. He drew her deep into his mouth, and when she arched her back toward him, he rewarded her with a gentle nip and hot lave of his tongue. Then he moved to give the same sweet torture to her other breast.

So sweet and tempting...a goddess.

Her bare flesh was warm and smooth beneath his hands as he trailed them across her back beneath the silky curtain of her hair, then down to cup her buttocks in his palms. When he squeezed them, an insensible moan of pleasure spilled from her lips.

He released her breast from his mouth with a delicate kiss to her nipple, then tantalizingly scraped his teeth up over her throat. With a whimper of growing desire, she tilted back her head and curved the long column of her neck against his lips. He seized the invitation and placed long, open-mouthed kisses over her neck and along her bare shoulder.

Except for soft sighs of desire, she made no sound as he stroked his hands over her. He *had* to touch her, not just because he ached for the solace she offered, but to make certain that she was real, that he wasn't dreaming.

Then she took his hand and slowly guided it between her legs. She begged with a whimper for him to pleasure her as she cupped his face between her hands and brought her mouth to his, her golden hair falling around his head and shoulders as she sat perched over him. He gladly did as she bade, and beneath his teasing fingers, her quivering folds turned slick with evidence of her desire.

With every panting breath she inhaled, the ache in his loins grew more intense. Every nip and lick and kiss she placed to his lips and neck hardened him, every shudder of her thighs made him shake. And when a throaty moan rose from the back of her throat at the feminine need he stirred inside her, he couldn't stop his own answering groan.

She reached between them and unbuttoned his trousers, freeing him into the cool morning air. Then she took his hard length in her hand as she rose up onto her knees above him.

"What sacrifice?" she repeated his words against his lips and lowered herself. As she slowly sank over him, sliding him inside her tight warmth, she shivered at the intimate connection of their bodies and answered, "The duty of surviving, the responsibility of holding him in your memory for the rest of your days and keeping him alive in your heart as long as possible."

She shifted her hips and settled completely over him, taking him deep inside her. Her breath came fast and ragged, and every small pant pulsed through her into him, racing along the length of his cock like a lightning rod to his heart.

"That's the sacrifice you have to make." She wrapped her arms around his shoulders, her breasts pressed flat against his chest, and placed a kiss to his temple. "The sacrifice of living."

Then she began to move, rocking her hips against his in a smooth and loving rhythm. All thoughts of Fitch and the Home Office fled, until there was only Diana. Until all he knew was the exquisite feel of her tight warmth bearing down around him, the strength of his embrace encircling her.

He sat up and pressed his hands against her bare back to keep her close, and in response, she locked her ankles at the small of his back. With each roll of the boat beneath them, he rocked into her in a steady rhythm, one as natural as the open air and sea around them. The sky came alive as the sun peaked over the horizon and flooded its golden light over her shoulders.

He whispered her name and gave himself over to the sensation of their joined bodies, of him buried inside her and her clenched around him. They mixed until he couldn't tell where he ended and she began, until their heartbeats pounded fiercely in unison. They were shamelessly exposed to the dawn, yet neither cared about anything but moving together toward bliss.

This wasn't sex. This wasn't even making love. It was absolution, and in her arms, he was finally healed.

"You're not leaving me this time," she whispered into his ear, her legs tightening their hold around his waist. "I want you, Christopher. I want all of you, in every way."

He couldn't stop the hot shiver that sped through him, the tightening coil she twisted inside his gut until he wanted to explode. He took her hips in his hands and guided her movements against him, keeping himself buried deep inside her.

She came with a soft cry as he rocked her gently to release. Her body spasmed around his as she broke in his arms, and he followed a heartbeat later. He spilled himself inside her with a shudder, and her sex flexed around him as her body attempted to coax every drop from him. To claim every bit of him that she could.

Neither of them loosened their hold as they both struggled to regain their breaths and slow their heartbeats, their bodies still entangled around the other. Dawn had broken. A new day had washed over them, but Kit wanted nothing more than to keep holding her like this forever.

# CHAPTER 21

Diana stared shamelessly at Kit's muscles as he dug the oars into the water and rowed them toward the docks. Sweet mercy, he was heavenly. Her own god, like those in Lord Elgin's marbles...sculpted, hard, larger than life. Even his blond hair shined like spun gold in the morning sunlight. But underneath those rock-hard muscles lingered a vulnerability that she cherished.

A smile teased at her lips.

"You look like the cat that got into the cream," he commented, not pausing in his steady rhythm of rowing. When dawn had gotten too bright for them to continue to hide on the boat, he'd sailed it back toward shore and anchored it near a rowboat that had been tied to a buoy. Not wanting to take the chance that someone had seen them leave on the sailboat last night and would be looking for its return, he now rowed them back, with the docks growing closer with each stroke of the oars.

"I feel like Cleopatra on her Egyptian barge." She reclined back as far as possible on the bench and lazily waved a hand with all the imperialness she could muster. "Row on! Don't stop until we reach Cairo!"

He grinned at her. "Enjoying yourself, are you?"

*More than in my entire life.* She beamed and leaned up, leaving the steadiness of her seat only long enough to place a quick kiss to his lips before sitting back down as the boat rocked beneath her.

Oh, she *was* happy! Meri was safe and would be waiting at home for her when she arrived, her brother wasn't a traitor, the French had the diary and so had no reason to ever come after her family again—and she loved Christopher.

She nearly laughed at that. If anyone had told her a month ago that she would lose her heart to a Carlisle, and to the seemingly worst of the lot no less, she would have called them mad. *Mad!* But she'd gone and done exactly that.

"I would offer to help row, but..." She waved a hand weakly in the direction of the oars. "You know how we pharaohesses are."

He arched a brow. "Pharaohesses?"

She answered that with another imperial wave of her hand, then laughed at herself again. "Truly, thank you for finding the rowboat. I didn't fancy a swim."

"I serve at the pleasure of my pharaohess," he teased. Then his mocking amusement faded into one of affection, and he added tenderly, meeting her gaze, "And my angel."

Warmth swelled inside her, and she looked away before he could see the blush of happiness that pinked her cheeks. "It was fortunate that you were able to rent that sailboat last night on such short notice."

When he didn't reply, she glanced back at him, just in time to see a guilty expression cross his face.

"You didn't rent it, did you?" His guilty expression deepened, and her mouth fell open. "You stole it!"

"Borrowed," he corrected, not pausing in his rowing. When

that didn't appease the scolding glare she gave him, he added, "It was that boat or the hotel, and you'd just handed over military secrets to the French. Would you have rather spent the night in our room where everyone knew where to find us?"

Her shoulders sagged. "No."

Nor would she have given up a moment of being in his arms last night. But now that dawn had come, all that frightened her was once again revealed beneath the harsh light of day.

"You really think they would have come after us there?" she asked. "After they were given the diary?"

"It might not have been the French who would have paid us a call."

Her mouth fell open. "The *British?*"

"Possibly. I didn't want to take any chances."

"Then thank you for last night." She added in a husky voice, "Very much."

But the way he grinned at her told her that he knew she was thanking him for far more than appropriating the sailboat. So did the now familiar ache that stirred between her thighs.

"The French will leave your family alone now," he assured her as he glanced over his shoulder toward the docks. They were less than a hundred yards from the pier. "They think they have the real diary, so there's no more reason for them to come after Meri again, or you and the general."

Relief mixed with the happiness blossoming in her chest.

"When we reach shore, we'll go straight to the posting inn. You'll have to leave behind everything that's in the hotel. It's not safe to go back there."

He stopped rowing and reached into the sleeve of his jacket. His fingers fumbled for a moment beneath the fabric. Then he pulled out a small scabbard that had been buckled around his forearm. He slipped the knife out of its sheath to show it to her. The blade flashed in the sunlight.

He handed it to her. "To protect yourself."

She hesitated, then took it in her trembling hand and held it awkwardly. "What am I supposed to do with this?"

"Stab people with it." When her gaze darted up to his in shock, he gestured toward her legs. "Until then, keep it hidden up your skirt."

"Up my *skirt*?"

"It won't be seen there." He leaned toward her, his face deadly serious. "And if any man ventures beneath your skirt and finds it, then the bastard deserves to be stabbed."

A thrill coursed through her that he would be so possessive of her. "Except you?"

He answered with a wolfish grin that made her toes curl, and she longed to have him inside her again, once more making love to her.

Taking up the oars, he went back to rowing. They were only a dozen strokes now from drifting to the end of the pier.

He commented toward the docks with a preoccupied shake of his head, "I can't guarantee how everything will play out for your brother."

Her foolish heart skipped. The happiness that had warmed through her only moments before now seeped away like the water dripping from the oars every time he lifted them above the surface.

"I don't know when he'll return home," he continued. "Or if." He glanced over his shoulder, as if to gauge the remaining distance to the docks. "If the French discover that he double-crossed them, they'll kill him for it."

She blinked hard and turned her face away. *Please, God, don't let them find out what he's done.*

"There are too many players in the mix now to be certain about anything, too many agencies and operatives who all have a stake in this." He paused, a hesitation before the oars dipped back into the water. "Did he say anything to you about any of them?"

"No."

He pinned her with a glance. "Would you tell me if he did?"

She eased out a long sigh and let her hand skim the water along the side of the rowboat. "He said that Meri was safe and that he would see us at home again soon. That was all. He didn't say when or who he was working with."

"Thank you," he said quietly, acknowledging the trust she now placed in him.

"I have no more secrets from you." After last night, none at all. But she feared that he did. "You're still determined to arrest Garrett, then, aren't you?"

He looked away toward the mouth of the bay and the sea beyond. His face turned inscrutable. "No," he answered quietly. "I'm giving up the hunt for your brother. Whitehall and the French can sort him out between themselves."

Her breath hitched. If he was no longer pursuing Garrett, then… "Then why do I need this knife?" Her questions lingered on the salty air between them, implying so much more about the future than a simple coach ride home. "Won't you be there beside me to protect me?"

"No." His shoulders flexed as he dug the oars deep into the water, then he lay back nearly horizontal as he gave them a fierce pull. "I'm remaining in Bradwell."

She grabbed his knee and stopped him mid-row. "Why?"

"There are things that have to be settled here."

Wariness tingled down her spine. "What things?"

His answering silence struck icy dread inside her chest, and her fingers tightened on his leg. Desperate for answers, she searched his face, but he only returned her gaze with a stony expression.

"More secrets," she answered herself, releasing his knee and sitting back. Betrayal turned bitter on her tongue, and just when she'd begun to think they could fully trust each other.

He blew out a harsh breath and let go of the oars, his forearms resting across his knees as he leaned toward her. They were momentarily set adrift in the rowboat, to bob gently on the water.

"Whitehall is going to declare me a rogue agent."

"What does that mean?" The fear licking at her toes made her fear his answer.

"That I am beyond the Home Office's control. That I am using the Crown's assets for my own gains, damaging communication networks, and jeopardizing operations." He paused. "That I need to be stopped. At all costs."

*Stopped.* So did her heart for one brutal moment, because she knew exactly what he meant. "Why? You've done nothing wrong."

"More than you realize." His eyes softened on her, and he reached up to stroke his knuckles across her cheek. "In the past fortnight alone, I've interfered with Home Office operations and used communication links that I shouldn't have. And now I've crossed the Foreign Office by giving that diary to the French."

"But it's not the real one." She grabbed his hand and wrapped it in both of hers. "Garrett has that. And you did it to save Meri." Her voice choked. "And me."

"That doesn't matter. They'll see it as an act of disloyalty. I was already warned away once but ignored them. They won't give me a second warning. They'll come after me, and I want you as far away as possible when they do."

"No," she whispered, her fingers tightening desperately around his. "What you're saying— No! I won't leave you."

"Listen to me." He slipped his other hand behind her nape and drew her toward him, until he could place a kiss to her temple, then rested his forehead against hers. "It will take Whitehall a few days to learn that the French have the diary and that I played a part in handing it over. They'll track me to Bradwell. I don't want you here when that happens."

"No," she whispered. Dear God, she wanted to scream!

She wrapped her arms around his shoulders and pressed herself against his chest, until he had no choice but to pull her down onto his lap.

"Stop saying things like that," she ordered, rubbing her cheek against his shoulder. He was so strong and solid, warm...*alive*. He was with her, safe in her arms, where he was meant to be. "We'll explain that the French kidnapped Meri, that we had no choice but to hand over the diary, that all of it was my idea—they'll understand." Her hands clutched at his waistcoat, and the words choked in her throat as they tore from her. "For God's sake, the general will swear to it! They'll believe him—and your brother." Her voice rose as her hold on him tightened, each breath coming forced and hard. "They're both heroes. Whitehall will listen to them. We'll send messengers, and they'll come and—"

"Diana—"

"No!" If she didn't stop talking and planning, then he couldn't send her away. And if he couldn't send her away, then she would be right here with him, keeping him safe. The same way he had protected her and Meri.

She pulled back just far enough to stare up into his somber face, and what she saw there clenched like a fist around her heart. The fatalistic look of a prisoner marching to the scaffold. The same look she had seen from him once before, that night at Idlewild when he read the ransom note, when he agreed to bring the diary here to hand over to the French...

He'd known then. *Dear God.* He'd known days ago what

coming here would mean, how he would accept all the responsibility for it himself, how Whitehall would see what he was doing as disloyalty. He'd *known!* Yet he'd agreed to come here anyway. A trade…

A life for a life. His life for Meri's.

She grabbed at his lapels and shook him as hard as she could, all the fear and grief inside her for him striking out in anger. "You knew—for God's sake! You *knew!*"

She hit him in the shoulders with her fists. He'd known all along. Which was why he refused to think of any kind of a future with her, why he'd hesitated to make love to her—not because he feared getting her with child, but because he knew she would lose him, that she would grieve for him the same way she'd grieved for John.

He grabbed her to him, holding her so tightly that she could barely breathe as she choked back pained sobs. He rasped out, "It was the only way to save Meri."

"You had no right to make that decision!"

"I had every right. Because I would do anything to protect you, Diana. *Anything.*" He squeezed his eyes shut but couldn't stop the pain from gripping his face. "Which means that I would do anything to protect your daughter."

"Not this! Not your life." She clung to him as she shuddered violently. The anguish was unbearable. "I won't let this happen to you. You will *not* give up on me, do you understand? I won't let you."

"I'm not giving up." He placed a kiss to her temple, but she wasn't reassured. "I'm the best agent the Home Office has, remember? You said so yourself. I'll use that to my advantage."

The fury and fear boiled inside her belly, and her hands gripped him so hard that her fingers turned nearly as white as his neckcloth. "And this is how they treat their best agents—they slaughter them for saving innocent lives?"

He grinned somberly against her forehead. "That's my angel, always fearsome." He cuddled her in his arms, resting his cheek against hers so she couldn't see his face. "I knew that being an operative was dangerous, that it meant making difficult choices." His lips lingered against her ear as he murmured, "I'll never regret helping you and Meri. I need you to understand that."

"But—but we've come so far." Each word was little more than a pained breath on her numb lips. Her heart had broken like glass, and she couldn't find a way to ease the storm of roiling pain and fear that was consuming her. Hot tears stung at her eyes, and she swallowed them back, not wanting to break down in his arms. "How am I supposed to go on without you?"

"You will, and you'll be happy." His voice lowered to a hoarse whisper. "I want that for you, Diana, with every ounce of my being."

"I'll never be happy knowing that you…" The words strangled in her throat. A desperate solution shot into her head. "Don't stay here. Don't wait for them to come after you. Leave! Go to the continent, go to America—just *leave*."

"I won't do that." He took her chin and lifted her face to touch his lips to hers. In that kiss, she tasted his determination to see this through. "I'll stay and explain. I won't flee."

"Not even to save your own life?" A tear slid down her cheek. "Not even for me?"

"You would never suffer a coward, and I won't tuck tail and run." His eyes softened with sympathy as he brushed away the tear. "I couldn't live with myself."

"But you would be alive!"

"What kind of life would that be, never to be able to return to England, never again to see the ones I care about? Never to make love to you again?" He sucked in a long, ragged breath. "No. I have to make my stand here."

"Promise me—promise me that if they won't accept your explanation that you'll leave on the first ship out of the bay." Another tear followed the first, but she couldn't stop them. The grief was overwhelming. "At least give me that."

He paused, then somberly nodded.

She buried her face in his chest and held tightly to him for as long as she could. But in her heart, she knew that he had just lied to her.

# CHAPTER 22

*W*ith a punishing strain of his back muscles, Kit dug the oars deep into the water in a final stroke to propel the rowboat to the pier. He didn't dare look at Diana for fear that she would still be crying. For him.

He didn't want her tears, because he sure as hell didn't deserve them. Nor could he tell her what he now suspected about her brother. That he would be the one the Foreign Office would task with killing him. The same way he'd killed Fitch.

The little boat glided silently across the last few feet of smooth water, and he secured the oars in place as the hull bumped gently into the piling post, sending the pelican perched on top into a squawking and flapping fit at being disturbed from its early morning nap. He couldn't remember—were pelicans portends of bad luck for sailors, or albatrosses? Not that it mattered. He'd been living on borrowed time for the past six months. The end had finally arrived.

But damn the world that he had to hurt Diana!

She loved him. She hadn't said it, but he saw it in her eyes, felt it in her caresses. Only a woman who loved him would have come to him the way she did last night and healed him with her body and soul. Never had another woman offered herself to him the way she had, so vulnerable and completely trusting. *Never.* And he knew in his heart that no other woman ever would.

Grabbing the end of the rope in one hand and the iron rope tie with the other, he swung up onto the pier. He tied the boat off, still not able to look at her. Cowardly, he knew. But he wouldn't be able to do what had to be done over the next few days with the memory of her heartache at the forefront of his mind, that expression of inconsolable grief he knew would be marring her beautiful face even now.

No, he wanted to remember her as she was last night, with her golden hair falling softly around her bare shoulders, her body warm and inviting, and her heart...*his.*

The wharves were busy, given the early hour, and groups of people spilled down the long pier from shore. More than a dozen festival-goers were yet wide awake from last night's revelries and a good portion of them still swaying drunk. Sailors scampered over the pier and ships as they readied the boats that they'd brought to the docks specifically for yesterday's blessing, now hurrying to sail away before the sun rose much higher so they could continue on with their fishing or trade routes. Dozens of others completed the crowd—porters moving barrels and crates, merchants checking on their cargos, travelers checking on passage, and lightskirts yet hoping to find a man to pay for their pleasures before last night's festival became too much of a memory.

Thank God the place was busy. Because that meant that Kit didn't have to speak to Diana, at least not for a little while longer, when he could figure out how to make her understand that he was doing all this to protect her. That he didn't regret the decision he'd made. That he would give his life for her, without hesitation.

"Christopher."

Pausing as he knelt on the dock and tied off the boat, he steeled himself, then forced his gaze to meet hers as she still sat in the boat below, waiting to be helped onto the pier.

Her blue eyes glistened brightly with tears. "I really think we should—"

A scream tore through the early morning air from directly behind him.

Kit wheeled around, his hand going to his forearm before he remembered that the knife wasn't there.

A woman stood at the edge of the pier and screamed again at the top of her lungs, crying out hysterically for help and jabbing a finger at the water below her feet. Men rushed forward to help. But Kit reached her first.

"My baby!" she screamed. "There—in the water! Save him!"

Just below the surface, Kit saw white swaddling floating slowly downward toward the murky bottom of the bay. Without hesitating, he dove into the water and swam fiercely after the sinking baby.

He grabbed it, yanked it toward him, and kicked hard to swim upward as fast as he could. When he broke through the surface, he shoved the baby up into the air with one hand, while he grabbed with the other at a ladder of wooden boards that had been nailed haphazardly to the piling post. His smooth-soled boots slipped on the wet rungs, but he slowly and carefully made his way up to the pier, the baby securely in his grasp.

He reached the last step and held the baby toward its mother, who reached desperately over the edge of the boards on her hands and knees for her little son. When she snatched him into her arms, the abrupt movement startled the babe, who blew out a mouthful of water and began to wail.

"Thank God," she sobbed, cradling the screaming infant against her bosom.

Kit flopped his wet body over the edge of the pier and onto the boards with one last, large step. The seawater poured off him as he rolled onto his back and panted hard to catch his breath, ignoring the curious crowd that had gathered and pressed in around them.

The mother reached a shaking hand to Kit's arm and squeezed, barely able to force out past her grateful sobs. "Thank *you*. He would have drowned if you hadn't dove in like that."

"What happened?" he demanded as he sat up.

"A man grabbed him from my arms." She cried so hard with relief now, nearly matching the baby's ear-splitting screams, that Kit could barely hear as he shoved himself to his feet, dripping and cold to the bone. "He ripped him away from me and threw him into the water."

His blood turned to ice. "What man?"

She pointed behind him toward shore. But when Kit turned around, his heart stopped. The man was gone.

And so was Diana.

STEELY FINGERS YANKED AT THE TIES CINCHED SO TIGHTLY AROUND her wrists that the bindings cut into her skin. They ripped the straps off her hands, painfully scraping them over her thumbs and fingers. A fierce shove to the middle of her back—

Diana stumbled forward and fell, landing so hard on her hands and knees that skin scraped across the rough boards beneath her.

With her freed hands, she pulled at the burlap sack that had been flung over her head and shoulders to keep her from seeing where they were taking her. Or who. She'd been grabbed from the rowboat so quickly that she hadn't had the chance to scream before the cloth gag was forced between her teeth and the bag dropped over her head, all from behind.

But she had the chance now.

Tearing the gag from her mouth, she let out a scream so loud that it echoed off the wooden walls of the tiny room around her. No—not walls, not a room. Finely fitted boards forming the sides of a ship's cabin. She could barely see them as her eyes adjusted to the bright light pouring in through the row of tiny windows lining the top of the cabin wall.

"Shut up!"

Her gaze darted to a man in the doorway, and she sucked in a deeper breath to scream again.

"Let the bitch scream her bloody 'ead off," a second man reasoned as he came up behind the first and peered over his shoulder at her. "No one can 'ear her out 'ere on the water. No one'd bother checkin' out no screamin' woman i' th' first place, not on a ship wi' sailors."

As her eyes adjusted and she could finally make out their faces, the memory struck her like a blow. The two men who yanked her out of the rowboat and brought her here were the same two sailors who had chased her through the fairgrounds last night, the same men to whom she'd given her copy of the diary.

Her heart froze. Had they discovered that Garrett had switched out the real diary for a fake? Oh God—*Meri!*

The first man spat on the floor at her feet. "Demmed shame if the bitch found that gag shoved into 'er mouth again."

Flexing his hands into fists at his sides, a malicious gleam shined in his eyes as he stepped into the room. Her hand strayed toward her skirt and the knife strapped to her calf. If that man dared to come after her, she'd make him regret it.

The second man grabbed his arm and stopped him. "Redcoat said not t' touch 'er."

*Redcoat?*

"I ain't risking me skin fer 'er." The second man pulled the first back out of the cabin and into the gangway. "Ye'd not either, if ye had a speck o' brains 'bout ye."

Stifling a wince of pain, she climbed to her feet. Her hands had been scraped raw from the bindings and from the splinters on the floor. "I demand that you release me this instant."

Both men cackled loudly at that, but now she knew. Whoever Redcoat was, he'd hired them to come after her. And with a name like that, the man wasn't French. Had Kit been wrong? Had the Foreign Office arrived early in Bradwell and come after her for passing secrets to the enemy?

"Who are you?" She stood her ground, refusing to let the two men think they'd cowed her, even though they actually terrified her. "Who hired you to kidnap me?"

She took a step forward, just to see how they'd react. As she predicted, the two men stepped deeper into the gangway outside the cabin. They didn't like her, but they liked Redcoat even less.

So they had orders not to harm her. But given by whom?

"Was it the Foreign Office?" she pressed. "Or the people who took Meri?"

Her questions only gained her the same hostile stares as before. They had no idea what she was asking about.

"Redcoat'll be speakin' to you soon enough, I 'spect."

"Who is he?"

He answered the question silently with a grin that showed missing teeth.

"He hired you to bring me here." She fought to keep her voice calm and swallowed down her fear. "But I'll pay you more if you let me go—twice whatever he's paying you. My father's a wealthy general. You can take the money he'll give you and disappear."

"Just what we need, eh?" The second man slapped the first on the back. " 'Nother redcoat after us!"

"An' this one a general, no less. Guessin' we be climbin' the ranks, eh?"

They didn't know or care who she was. Yet they both feared this man named Redcoat who'd hired them, and especially violating his rules of not harming her.

For now, she would use that to her advantage. "I want to speak to Redcoat. Now."

"He'll tell ye what ye need to know when ye need to know it." He snatched up the gag cloth from the floor where she'd ripped it off. "Until then, shut th' hell up 'fore I'll make ye."

"If you lay one finger on me, I'll tell him what you did," she threatened. "I'll tell him that it was you who forced that gag between my teeth, who bruised my face and cut my mouth doing so. Apparently, I'm his prize, and I don't think he'd like to discover my face all black and blue and swollen because you two couldn't figure out how to handle a woman without abusing her, do you?" Her voice took on a fierce, burning intensity that pulled both men up straight. "Because I promise you that the only way you'll be able to put that thing into my mouth again is by force."

The man clenched his jaw and gripped the cloth in his fist, but he didn't take a single step toward her.

"Let me go," she tried again. "I'll make certain you both get paid well for your trouble, and I'll not have the chance to tell Redcoat how you mishandled me or to give him the chance to punish you for it." She reached desperately for whatever tendrils of hope were left to her, talking quickly but in a low, controlled tone, despite the pounding of her heart. As if they were in this together against Redcoat. "We can go back to shore. You'll be long gone before he realizes what happened, and he'll never find you."

The second man laughed. "Ye don't know th' man, if'n ye think that!"

"Rather have me life than blunt," the first man added. "So scream yer demmed head off fer all I care." He threw the gag onto the floor and spat again. This time the wad of saliva landed on her shoe. She kicked it off with a disgusted gasp, which only drew another laugh. "Redcoat'll make ye quiet soon 'nough, I wager."

He slammed the door shut.

She ran forward and threw herself against the door to force it open, but the solid boards didn't budge. The light clanking of metal against metal reverberated through the panels as the door was fastened from the other side.

A cry of frustration tore from her. She pounded her fists against the door, screaming and beating until her throat became raw and pain shot up from her hands into her forearms.

When she was too exhausted and upset to raise another hand to strike the panel, she turned around and sagged against the door, then slid slowly to the floor. She held her head in her bloodied hands and choked back the self-pitying sobs that would do her no good.

Lifting her head and blinking until her stinging vision cleared, she swept her gaze around the cabin.

Small and cramped, at less than eight feet long, six feet wide, and barely big enough to contain two built-in bunk beds and a small side table...clearly an officer's berth, but not grand enough to belong to the captain. It was the first mate's. Or one that was booked by wealthy passengers. She and her family had lived in one almost identical to this on the voyage back from India, located just below the aft deck of the ship and tucked away in the stern. Mostly likely, this one was the same, which meant that there was no way out through the tiny row of windows on the far wall. Even if she had been able to fit through one of them, a twenty-foot drop waited for her on the other side, straight into the cold water below. She'd drown within minutes.

The only way out was through this door.

*Patience.* She would have to bide her time before she could act. But she hadn't been blindfolded and tied for long, which meant the ship was still anchored at Bradwell, although the rise and fall of it on the waves told her that they were anchored far out in the bay and close to the choppier water of the Channel. Which meant that she was still near Christopher and Garrett, still near their help...if only she could find a way to shore. Because neither of them knew where she was.

The brutal truth was that no one was coming to save her. She had to find a way to save herself.

# CHAPTER 23

$\mathcal{K}$it raced down the hallway of the Mermaid toward the room they'd taken yesterday, praying to God that Diana would be there.

She *had* to be here! The moment he'd realized she was gone, he'd frantically searched the wharf for her, calling for her and shouting out at the crowd if anyone had seen a young blonde woman in a blue dress. For Christ's sake, he'd even crawled down beneath the pier itself, in case she'd fallen out of the rowboat attempting to climb out.

*Nothing.* She was gone.

He desperately wanted to believe that she'd simply become too upset by their earlier conversation, enough to flee from the docks the first moment she had the chance. That she'd come back here to collect her things, though he'd told her not to. That she was even now in a hired post-chaise and bouncing her way across the countryside toward home, cursing him with every passing mile.

His pounding heart didn't hold much hope. Yet he had to search first all the most probable places where he might find her. And then...

No. There was no *then*.

There was only finding her.

He flung open the door and charged into the room. "Diana!"

He stopped just over the threshold, and his chest sank. She hadn't returned. Her things were still here. Her dress still hung on the wall hook, her little bag still tucked beneath the chair where he'd put it. The room was exactly the same as when they'd left last night, for nothing more than a stroll through the festival grounds.

"Carlisle." A man stepped into the room behind him.

Kit lunged. In one smooth movement, he grabbed the man around the throat with one hand and by the right arm with the other. He threw the man back against the wall so hard that his back whacked loudly against the plaster and cracked it, so hard that the air whooshed audibly as it ripped from his lungs.

Kit forced his forearm beneath the man's chin and against his windpipe, pinning him to the wall. The man gurgled, his eyes wide.

"Where the hell is she?" Kit pressed his arm harder against the man's throat.

He reflexively gulped for air, his toes nearly lifted off the floor.

"What have you done with her?"

"Morgan," the man rasped out breathlessly, his fingers clawing at Kit's forearm to move him away. "Morgan…sent…for you."

Kit leaned into the man with his full weight, carefully keeping his lower body positioned at an angle to make it harder for the man to suddenly find a burst of strength and kick him in the bollocks. "Why?"

"He wants to meet with you." A second man's voice was punctuated by the metallic click of a cocked pistol.

Kit didn't move except to slice his gaze sideways to the man standing in the doorway, pistol drawn and pointed directly at him. "The hell I will."

Behind his forearm, the man continued to struggle weakly, receiving just enough air to stay on his feet and keep from falling unconscious. Kit ignored him. The intruder in the doorway was now the bigger threat.

"Morgan warned us that you might not cooperate," he drawled from behind the pistol. "He said we might have to be more persuasive. That we might have to divulge that the meeting regards his sister Diana."

Slowly, Kit stepped back and lowered his arm. The man fell limp against the wall, then slid to the floor. His hand went to his throat, and he wheezed as he struggled to gulp back his breath.

Kit toed the man in the leg with his boot and chastised, "You should have said so sooner."

With every muscle in his body alert and ready to spring, he faced the second man, then nodded toward the gun. "You should put that damned pistol down before it goes off and hurts someone."

The man's eyes glinted, yet he lowered the gun. Keeping the barrel safely pointed away, he eased down the hammer, then tucked it into the holster beneath his coat.

"Who the hell are you, and who are you working for?" Kit demanded.

One of the players in this game had taken Diana. Now it was just a matter of discovering who. And then killing the bastard when he caught him.

"Answers come later." Gesturing into the hall, he stepped back from the doorway. "Now, we have to leave."

"Not until you tell me about Diana."

"She's safe for now." He tugged at his leather gloves. "But not if you keep delaying. Morgan will explain everything."

Grudgingly, Kit followed him out of the room. Behind him, the other man moaned softly, still curled in a ball on the floor.

As he stepped past the man in the hall, Kit stopped and leveled his gaze on him. Hard. He leaned closer, making no mistake that he would kill him if necessary.

"Let me be clear," Kit said slowly. "If one hair on Diana's head is harmed, I will hunt down you and all of your associates." His voice lowered to an icy threat. "And I will slit you open from your throat to your balls."

The man gave a knowing nod. "We were warned about that, too."

He stepped away from Kit, leading him out of the hotel and through the village.

They walked side by side in silence, neither man glancing at the other, but both ready to strike at a moment's provocation. They walked not toward the docks as Kit had suspected, but up the winding street leading away from the waterfront, where stone and brick row houses lined the road.

"The last one." The man gestured toward an abandoned weaver's cottage, then glanced cautiously up and down the street to make certain no one was following them.

When they reached the house, the man rapped his knuckles against the blue-painted door. A knock answered from within. He silently lifted his gaze to Kit's, then knocked three times, paused, and knocked once more.

The door opened with a soft clanking of its old metal latch and a rusty groan of its hinges. Kit could see nothing inside the dark row house as he peered into it from the footpath, but he followed the man inside, despite the wariness that prickled at his nape. He had no other choice but to follow.

"This way." The man signaled to the guard at the door to lock it behind them, then led Kit up the narrow stairs to the attic room.

The space where a former occupant had surely once worked a loom now stood empty, except for a makeshift table near the windows that was constructed of a board laid across two tall barrels. A handful of men crowded around it and argued, pointing at a map spread across the board.

But the man in the center crossed his arms over his chest and listened intently, not saying a word. Until he glanced up at Kit.

Garrett Morgan didn't move a muscle or a give a single twitch of his facial expression, but Kit sensed a change in him. A hardening. The same way a lion would tense when it saw its prey.

Or the same way the prey would when it saw the lion.

"Carlisle."

"Morgan," Kit answered, his face held carefully inscrutable as he stopped in his steps, when what he wanted to do was leap over that table and grab the bastard by the throat.

The men who had been arguing fell silent and exchanged looks as they glanced between the two of them. One reached a hand slowly beneath his jacket for a weapon, but he was smart enough not to withdraw it.

"You've arrived." Morgan raked an assessing gaze over Kit, head to toe. "Good."

He drawled, "How could I have refused such a gracious invitation?"

Morgan's mouth twisted, but he never moved his gaze from Kit. Not even when he turned his head slightly to address the others. "Leave us."

The men complied, casting curious glances back at Kit as they shuffled down the stairs. They knew who he was. There was no mistaking the way he and Morgan had squared off across the room.

"So." Kit hit right at the crux. "You're a double agent."

"And you've gone rogue." He slid another gaze over Kit, this time more deliberate. "You'll be dead in three days."

"You'll be dead sooner if you've done anything to harm Diana or Meri."

The icy threat hung in the air between them for a long beat before Morgan answered, "I would never do anything to harm them." Determination underpinned his voice. "I'm here to save them."

Kit stepped forward, his eyes narrowed on Diana's brother. How could this man be Garrett Morgan? He knew Morgan from before Fitch's death. Had seen his weak attempts at gambling, drinking, and whoring in London, had heard his excuses for everything that had gone wrong in his life. Especially the blame he'd heaped upon the general for being an unforgiving father who expected too much from his only son.

This man wasn't the Garrett Morgan he knew.

He stood tall, straight, and solid, with his shoulders broad in his shirtsleeves as he crossed his arms over his chest in a casual pose that belied the tension crackling between them. Not a trace of weakness was visible anywhere in him, right down to the steely stare of his eyes. *This* wasn't a man who was a failure.

Apparently, nothing was as it seemed.

"Explain," Kit ordered, stopping in front of the makeshift table.

"This all began years ago." Morgan reached into his waistcoat and withdrew a small book. The general's diary. He tossed it onto the table in front of Kit. "You're just the most recent player to join the game."

He placed his palms on the board, ignoring the diary as he bracketed it between his hands and leaned toward Morgan. He repeated in a low growl, *"Explain."*

"I was twenty-two, out of the army and hating university. My family had just returned from India and set up household at Idlewild when I was approached by the Foreign Office. A story similar to yours, I understand." Kit's inscrutable expression never changed at that, but Morgan answered the unasked question, "Of course I researched you. The moment I heard that you were at the tavern the night of the failed exchange I knew you were more than simply an earl's wastrel brother."

Ignoring that, Kit demanded, "Why did they want you? The Foreign Office isn't in the habit of recruiting untried men. And failed soldiers."

"I *did* leave the army, but not for the reason you think. I wanted to make my own mark, but in the ranks, I was only General Thaddeus 'Never Surrender' Morgan's son. There was no way to prove myself there. But there was with Whitehall, even if I had to keep my work secret until the mission was completed."

"What mission?"

"Whitehall had heard that a British army officer was selling military information and War Department secrets. Because of my father's rank and influence, I had access to army officers at all levels, in all assignments. So I spent two years tracking down the leak." He grimaced. "Imagine my surprise to find the man right in my own household."

Kit knew... "Paxton."

"Yes."

He shoved himself away from the table and straightened to his full height. "But he's still in place, still working with the general. Why?"

"Once the Foreign Office knew what Paxton was doing, the decision was made to feed him false information that he could pass along to the French. More good could be done that way than by hanging him."

Suspicion tingled at the backs of Kit's knees. "You were doing more than simply reporting back on Paxton. You're actively involved with the French. They think you work for them."

Or did. Until a few weeks ago, when he vanished.

"Only recently," Morgan explained, "when it became clear that Paxton's access to information was drying up. Since the general's retirement, the major was becoming less and less valuable to the Foreign Office, and they needed another way to funnel false information to the Continent. So I agreed to work with the French. I let them believe that I was so angry at my father that I was willing to sell out my country for personal revenge. They believed it."

So did everyone else. All of society believed that Garrett Morgan had been at odds with the general for years. Including the general himself.

Morgan nodded at the diary. "And then that surfaced."

Without invitation, Kit picked up the little book and flipped through it. It was the original, right down to the scratch marks where the leather cover had caught on the wooden splinters when the general had twisted it out of the mangled cabinet. No one would have known to forge those.

"The French suspect that one of the men in King Louis's court is working with the British, but they have no evidence of whom. So they turned to their British operatives, hoping someone would be able to provide it. And Paxton did just that." He stepped back to lean against the wall, but even that casual pose signified a man who was never completely at ease. Another trait that Kit recognized in himself. "I went into deep hiding three weeks ago to travel to France, to find out what exactly the French wanted with the diary. I let everyone believe that I was visiting an old friend in the North."

"Because you couldn't pass along false information until you knew what the real secret was, the secret that you needed to keep hidden." Not a guess. A part of normal Whitehall operations.

He nodded. "Paxton was desperate and acted before we were ready. He knew what was in the diary and convinced the French that it contained the information they needed. But Paxton never had access to the diary itself and so had no idea where the general kept it, except that he kept it under lock and key in his study."

"But he thought Diana did," Kit murmured. "And convinced her that you were being held for ransom."

Which was why the Frenchman had refused to take the memoir pages at the tavern when she'd so adamantly offered them, and why the man had come after her a second time at the party. Paxton had no idea that she knew nothing about the diary.

"The major set up the meeting between Diana and the French, then undoubtedly helped them slip into the house." His eyes narrowed. "But you were there to stop them. Both times."

"Three times," he corrected grimly. "I was also there when Meri was taken." But that time, he'd been too late.

"I know where Meri is, and she's unharmed. Unfortunately, we can't yet bring her home for fear that Paxton will hear of it and know that we're watching him. For now she's safer where she is."

Morgan was right, damn him. "And the diary? What's in it, *exactly*, that makes the French want it so badly?"

He didn't answer.

"You brought me here," Kit reminded him, looking down at the map on the board that the men had been arguing over. A drawing of the bay and harbor, the village, the roads that spread out beyond the town toward London and Dover... What were Morgan and his men planning? "You need me, or you would have just ignored me. So answer my question."

"I brought you here because you're the only man right now whom Diana trusts."

That pounded through him like a hammer strike.

"She told you about me and our meeting last night."

That wasn't a question, yet Kit answered, "Yes."

"And she told you the truth about Meri and Captain Meredith."

Kit remained silent. He wouldn't betray Diana's trust by answering.

Morgan nodded slowly, visibly pleased to be proven right by Kit's silence. "And we'll need that trust if anything goes wrong when we rescue her."

In frustration, Kit tapped his finger against the diary's cover. "What do the French want with this? Tell me, or I'll leave and find a way to rescue Diana on my own."

Morgan's jaw tightened, but sitting back on the windowsill, he grudgingly explained, "The general was present at the windmill at Brye for a meeting between Wellington and the Prussians, two days before the battle at Waterloo. Also in attendance was a French general named Pierre LeFavre who didn't want Boney back in power and was there to hand over Napoleon's battle plans. LeFavre is now a highly regarded counselor in King Louis's government who still keeps the British informed of French maneuverings. If they discover that, they'll assassinate him, and England will lose our best informant in the French court." He pushed himself away from the window and stepped forward. "Without that diary, they know nothing for certain. When I found out that the French were attempting to use Diana to get it, I left France immediately and arrived in England just after Meri was taken."

"It isn't like the French to come after a child."

"Because it's not the French. It's Paxton himself."

Which was why Paxton had been the one to find the ransom note, how Meri had disappeared without struggle or shouts... because he had been the one to take her.

"That's why I came here, to place myself between the diary and Paxton," Morgan explained. "He had to believe that he was being given the true diary, or the French would never stop looking for information against LeFavre or leave my family alone."

Morgan's involvement was more self-serving than that. "They would also know that they had a double agent in their midst."

"That, too. So the exchange had to go on as planned. I'm very good at copying my father's handwriting, so I made a forgery of the diary and switched it out last night during the festival. I'd hoped that by the time Paxton realized he'd been had that Diana would be safely home and that he would be arrested. But his men were too quick."

"Now they have Diana," Kit murmured. "They'll want to ransom her for the real diary."

"And we'll hand it over, just as they want. I've already sent messages to the Foreign Office in London to inform them of what's happening."

"So you're not a traitor," Kit drawled, his eyes narrowing. "Just a murderer."

Morgan stiffened. "I had nothing to do with Fitch-Batten's death."

"You were *there*, God damn you," Kit muttered, his hands drawing up into fists at his sides.

"I was in that alley, but he was dead by the time I found him. Your partner was investigating routine communications, not knowing that Paxton had used those same channels himself to contact the French. Or that Fitch-Batten's contacts were pointing him directly at Paxton. When the major learned of it, he wanted to silence any chance of being discovered, which meant killing Fitch-Batten."

Or Kit, if he had been there as he should have been. With no warning that any of this had been going on, that the Foreign Office had been closing in upon Paxton and making him desperate enough to murder an operative, it so easily *could* have been him.

"I had no option but to walk away. Doing anything else would have revealed my position and destroyed all that we'd put into motion. More good men would have died, others forced from their posts—I made the decision to remain silent, and I don't regret it, knowing the alternative. It's the same thing you would have done. As *any* good agent would have." Morgan fixed a hard gaze on Kit. "Direct your anger at Paxton where it belongs. You'll have your justice when we arrest him."

"And Diana?" he demanded.

"Paxton's holding her on a ship anchored in the harbor." Morgan pointed a finger at the map. "We know exactly where she is, but we can't get to her. If we try to take her by force, they'll see us coming, raise anchor, and sail away."

"Or kill her," Kit added quietly.

"That, too. So we have to make Paxton bring her to us." Morgan murmured as his eyes scanned the map, "And we use the diary to do it."

"No." *Absolutely not.* "I won't make this into a trap for Paxton. I don't give a damn if the French get away with the diary. This will be an honest exchange for Diana, that's all. I will *not* put her at risk."

"Neither would I."

"Then we're clear on that point." He placed his palms back onto the table and leaned toward Morgan. "Let's be clear about something else, then, too. You don't like me, and I sure as hell don't like you."

Morgan's eyes narrowed for a beat, but the man wisely said nothing.

"But I will do whatever it takes to keep Diana safe, understand? Including handing you over to the French, if I have to."

"Good. Because I would do no less with you."

Clenching his jaw, Kit straightened. "Then call your men back. We have a rescue to plan."

# CHAPTER 24

*K*it stood alone on the end of the empty pier and stared out across the blue-green water of the bay through the small spyglass. Overhead, seagulls rose and fell on the afternoon air, calling to each other and frantic to capture the small fish and shellfish carried into the harbor on the rising tide, while boats bobbed at anchor across the bay. Despite the sunshine, the sea breeze carried a small chill. It stirred his blond hair as he stood there hatless so his face would be easily seen and brushed his black greatcoat around his legs. Nothing else about him moved.

His eyes never left the little dinghy as the boy slowly rowed it across the harbor toward a ship anchored near the mouth of the harbor. The ship where the French were holding Diana. The lad's red hair shined beneath his blue sailor's cap and made it easier to gauge his distance as the boy conveyed the message from Kit that he'd been paid well to deliver.

*I know that you have Diana Morgan.*

The boat bumped into the hull of the ship as the boy finally reached it after half an hour's rowing, with Kit standing there on the dock, unmoving, the entire time.

The lad called to the sailors on the deck and gestured for them to unfurl a rope ladder so he could climb up. Shouts were exchanged, but the boy didn't give up and pressed the sailors again. But of course he did, because Kit had told him that he wouldn't get paid unless he delivered the message to the men on the boat and brought back a response.

*I am offering a trade—the diary for Miss Morgan.*

Through the spyglass, Kit watched as the sailors onboard finally tossed a rope ladder over the side. The boy scurried up the swinging rope rungs like a creature born to the sea. When he reached the top, one of the sailors grabbed him by the back of the breeches and hauled him up and over the rail, to unceremoniously drop him onto the deck amid hoots and jeers.

The lad climbed to his feet and brushed himself off. Then he reached beneath his black peacoat to pull out the folded note. One of the sailors approached him quickly and snatched away the message. When he grabbed the boy by the collar to warn him about playing games, the boy jabbed a finger back toward land. Right at Kit, who didn't lower the spyglass or look away.

*I have the real diary. I have had it on me all along, not trusting you to keep to your word. I suspected a double-cross and so prepared a forgery, and that is what you did last night by approaching the woman without warning or notifying me. Now, I expect a proper exchange.*

On the ship, the sailor let go of the lad and reached for his own spyglass hanging from a leather belt loop at his side. He pulled it open and looked across the harbor, his gaze coming to rest on Kit.

Kit put down the spyglass and picked up the lit lantern burning its small flame at his feet. To make a show of exactly how real his threat was, he flicked open the small glass door, then reached inside his jacket and withdrew the diary. He held it up over his head, to be certain that the sailor recognized it. Then he placed it into the flame, letting the edges of the pages singe brown before pulling it away and beating out the flames against his thigh.

*If you do not agree, I will burn the diary, and then you will never have what you want. You will never discover who in the French court is sending information to England.*

Kit tucked the diary back out of sight, lowered the lamp, and picked up the spyglass once more. Once more keeping an unmoving watch. Onboard the ship, the sailor lowered his glass and hurried away toward the stern, down the stairs, and below deck.

A short time later, he returned. He held a message in his hand that he shoved at the boy, then pointed at the pier in Kit's general direction. The lad nodded, tucked the note beneath his cap on his head, and headed back down the rope ladder to his little boat, to begin the long stretch of rowing back across the harbor to the docks.

Kit lowered the spyglass, smacked it with his palm to retract it, and tucked it into his breast pocket, not bothering to look through it again as he waited patiently. His heart pounded off the seconds with dread, although he forced himself to not show one bit of emotion on his face.

*Bring Miss Morgan to the old boathouse at midnight for the exchange. I will not negotiate other terms. The diary for the woman. That is all.*

After an interminably long wait, the boy reached the pier, right where Kit was waiting, his stance wide-legged beneath his caped greatcoat, his left fist pressed into the small of his back. He didn't move, not even to reach a hand to help the boy onto the pier when he tied the boat to the iron ring between Kit's feet.

*You know who I am and what I am capable of doing. You also know that I am a dead man with nothing to lose. Do not cross me.*

The lad panted hard, exhausted and out of breath from the exertion of rowing, as he climbed up onto the pier. He yanked off his cap and handed the message to Kit. He didn't bother to pull back his hand, waiting for Kit to place the sovereign coin onto his palm.

The lad closed his fist around the coin, gave the brim of his cap a tug of appreciation for payment as he returned it to his head, then walked away, shrugging out his tight shoulders as he went.

Kit broke the wax seal on the note, unfolded it, and read the short message. They had agreed to his terms.

Crumpling the note in his fist, he threw it into the harbor. He turned on his boot heel and strode off, down the long pier toward the village. He didn't look back.

*If you harm her in any way, I will slaughter you. Every last one of you.*

# CHAPTER 25

*I*n the dim light of a candle lantern that swayed slowly in time to the ship's gentle rocking, Diana slipped the tip of the knife into the narrow gap between the door and the frame.

Undoubtedly, this wasn't at all the way that Kit had expected her to make use of his knife. Not to wiggle it into a latch but to slice it into a man's gut. And yet...

"A woman has to do what a woman has to do," she whispered and slid the knife along the side of the door, feeling for the cabin hook on the other side.

In this case, a woman working to free herself.

When one of the men who had shoved her into the cabin brought her dinner several hours later—a dinner she took one glance at and had no intention of eating—she listened carefully to the door when it closed. Not the clink-click of a padlock locking her inside, but the clank-clink of a falling hook. Which told her that a cabin hook secured the door, the kind she remembered on the doors of the ship from India. The kind of hook-and-eye latch that could be pried open if she could just lift the little arm out of its eye, if she could slip something between the door and the frame to hold it open.

So she'd been patient and bided her time, until the right moment came to free herself.

Just as she'd listened carefully to the sound of the door when it had closed, she'd also listened to the sounds of the ship around her. The sun had set nearly six hours earlier—she'd kept track of time by the tolling bell of the parish church, which could just barely be heard across the water—and in that time, the ship had grown quiet and still. Only the occasional groan of boards, flapping of sailcloth, and the slapping of waves against the hull broke the evening calmness. Even the sailors had all settled below deck for the night, retiring to their bunks and hammocks. No one stood in the gangway, guarding her. Why would they? Where could she possibly have gone?

But she'd had all day to make plans, to run through scenario after scenario. And now it was time to act.

This ship was similar to the one her family had traveled on from India, and during those long weeks when she'd had nothing to do but mourn John's death, feel sorry for herself, and pace the length of the ship while her belly grew beneath her dress, she'd come to know that ship well. She could still remember where the crew kept the rope ladders they used to climb on and off the ship and to the little dinghies tied to the side of the boat or trailing behind the stern. She also knew where the crew stood to keep watch across the water and how to sneak around those places without being seen, not wanting to draw any more attention to herself then as possible.

Once she was free from this cabin, she would let down one of those rope ladders and climb down, cut free with the knife the dinghy tied below, and simply drift away into the darkness. By the time they realized she was gone, she'd be back on dry land.

"With Christopher," she whispered. Because this wasn't only about saving herself any longer. It was also about saving the people she loved. Which now included him.

*Ding!* The blade hit the bottom of the latch.

Holding her breath, she placed both hands on the knife handle and raised it straight up, slowly feeling the little iron hook lift from its catch on the other side of the door. With one hand keeping the knife in place, holding the hook freely in the air, she slowly opened the door. Silently, one painfully slow movement at a time, she carefully pushed the door open as she withdrew the knife in equal measure to keep it from jamming in the doorframe.

When the blade slipped free, the hook fell against the door with a soft jangle.

She froze. She strained for any sound that anyone was there in the gangway. But she heard nothing except the rush of blood pounding in her ears with every frantic heartbeat.

Deciding that it was safe to continue, she paused to tuck the knife back into place beneath her skirt, closed the door behind her, and silently returned the cabin hook to its place so no one would know she was missing. Then she glanced up and down the dark gangway. Pitch-black, except for a beam of moonlight falling inside through the hatch above the short set of stairs leading up to the deck.

The only way out.

She took a deep breath and started forward, feeling along the wall with her outstretched hand and keeping her eyes on the patch of moonlight. Each footstep was agonizingly slow, but she had to go carefully and silently, praying that any misstep would be mistaken for a creak of the boat in the changing humidity and temperatures.

When she reached the stairs, she grabbed the hatchway with both hands to help keep her balance and stepped up onto the deck. She flattened herself against the side of the aft cabin and glanced over her shoulder as she moved slowly toward the stern railing—

She smacked into a man's solid body. She jumped back, startled. Before she could scream, the man's face became visible in the pale moonlight, and the sound strangled in her throat.

Her mouth fell open. "Major Paxton?" Relief poured through her, so fiercely that she began to shake. "Thank God..." She reached for him, throwing her arms around his neck in relief as she choked out, "Thank God you're here!"

She'd never been so happy to see him in her life. With a prayer of thanks to God, she immediately regretted every uncharitable thought she'd ever had about the man. Oh, she could kiss him!

"Are we safe here?" she whispered, still too wary to speak at full voice. Around them, the ship was just as dark and silent as when she'd left her cabin. "Have your men taken over the ship, then?"

"In a matter of speaking."

A ragged breath fell from her lips with a soft little laugh that lay somewhere between hysteria and relief. *Oh, thank heavens!* She was safe. "And Christopher? Where is he?"

"On shore." A cold smile pulled at his thin lips. "Waiting for you."

An icy suspicion crawled up her spine. Something wasn't right. The ship was too quiet, too still, for a rescue that would have required approaching over water, then overpowering sailors on watch.

The truth pounded through her as she fisted the lapels of his uniform coat in her hands. His *red* coat.

"It was you," she whispered barely louder than the waves lapping at the side of the ship, stunned. "All along, it was you."

She released him and stepped back, staring at him as the monster he truly was materialized in front of her eyes.

"You sent the note about Garrett being kidnapped, and you told that Frenchman where the general kept his diary." Fury replaced her fear, and she struck at him with her fists, striking his shoulders. "You took Meri! You *bastard!*"

He grabbed her by the wrists and yanked her against him, forcing her to stop.

"You made me do it." He clenched his jaw, and Diana gasped at the anger for her in his eyes. "I wouldn't have had to take her away if you had handed over the diary like I asked."

Hatred for him stung like acid on her tongue.

"I gave you opportunity after opportunity. *You* put your daughter in danger, Diana."

*Your daughter.* Her stomach pitched sickeningly. "You...know?"

His eyes gleamed at her naïveté. "There's nothing that happens at Idlewild that I don't know about. Especially if it concerns you." He brushed his knuckles over her cheek, and she flinched beneath his touch. "You'd do anything to protect your family, which is why I convinced you that Garrett had been kidnapped. You were supposed to have handed the diary to the French that night at the tavern. I'd have gotten my reward and left England then. But you brought the memoir pages instead, and the French thought I'd double-crossed them. They nearly killed me for it."

"What a shame," she drawled. She yanked her arm away and stepped back from him as rage burned in her chest.

"That's why they came after you the night of the party. They didn't want to wait for me to deliver it and decided to steal it themselves. When the Frenchman couldn't find it in the cabinet, he thought he could force you into handing it over."

She would have, too, and gladly, if she had known where it was, if she had known all that the general's notes would place in jeopardy since that night. "Why not take the diary and give it to them yourself?" Her hands clenched into fists. "Damn you! Why did you come after an innocent little girl?"

"Because I didn't know where your father kept it. He never brought it out in front of me. He didn't trust me enough for that. So I had to get to it another way."

He took a step toward her, but she stood her ground. She would *never* let him intimidate her.

"As for Meri, yes, I used her to bring you here. But if I hadn't taken her, the French would have. So I acted first, knowing you'd do anything to protect her. You should be thanking me."

"*Thanking* you?" A laugh strangled in her throat. He was mad!

"But you always were ungrateful when it came to me. Down-right insulting, in fact."

Her breath hitched at his menacing tone. When he took a step toward her, she reflexively stepped away, only to hit her back on the cabin wall. She gasped in fear.

"That's the only thing I regret, Diana. That you had to make my intention to marry you so difficult."

He took another step closer, and she flattened herself against the wall to keep from touching him.

"It would have been beneficial for both of us. Me, to marry Thaddeus Morgan's daughter, when your father would have pulled every string he could to get me promoted and assigned to a coveted post, if only to make life easier for his daughter. And you —you should have been grateful that a man wanted to marry you at all, given your past. Let alone a man of my rank."

When he leaned toward her, she slowly reached her hand down her skirt toward the knife.

"But you were so distant, so cold—behaving as if I wasn't good enough for you, when all along you'd already been ruined. I could have saved you from all hints of scandal and disgrace." He reached up to her hair, to rub a stray curl between his thumb and finger. His touch snaked revulsion through her. "Who's going to save you now, Diana?"

As her right hand poised to grab the knife, her left fisted her skirt. She took a deep breath and resolved to pull—

"Redcoat!" A shout broke the stillness of the ship. One of the sailors who had tossed her into the cabin that morning strode toward them through the shadows.

Paxton stepped back immediately.

A ragged breath of relief escaped Diana, and she sagged back against the wall, her skirt slipping through her fingers and falling back into place. At her sides, her hands flexed open and closed at the shock of what she'd been about to do. To kill a man—and not just any man, but one she'd known for almost a decade, who practically lived inside her home and one her father considered family…

But she would have done just that if he had laid one hand on her.

"It's time," the sailor called out. "The boat's ready." He leered at her and held out a leather strap and piece of cloth to Paxton. "Ye'll find that gag t' be a godsend wi' her."

"I should use the gag and strap on you, you damned idiot!" Paxton snatched them out of the man's hand and threw them away. He took Diana's arm, and although she fought to keep from yanking away, she couldn't stop a shudder of disgust. "Tell the captain to get the ship ready. I want him to raise anchor and set sail the moment I return, understand?"

He led her to the railing, where a rope ladder had been draped over the side of the ship.

"Climb down," he ordered, helping her over the rail and onto the first rung of the ladder. "I'll be right behind you."

She hesitated, dropping her gaze down the ladder to the rowboat waiting below, lit by a small lamp sitting on its seat.

As if reading the daring thoughts running through her mind, he reached beneath his coat and retrieved a pistol. He handed it to the sailor. "If you do anything to try to escape, he'll shoot you."

The man flashed a toothy grin of glee. "Aye, sir."

Diana trembled and held tightly to the rope as she tentatively stepped down to the next rung. Then the next, and the next...one at a time, descending into the darkness toward the little boat below.

When she'd moved far enough away that she couldn't overhear, Paxton ordered the sailor in a low mutter, "Get Kearns. Grab weapons and come behind us in the second dinghy. I want to make certain we get away with both the diary and Miss Morgan." He added before climbing down the ladder after Diana, "And that you kill Christopher Carlisle."

# CHAPTER 26

*K*it stood in the main room of the old boathouse. Every inch of him was alert.

Around him, the building which had once served as a customs house was dark except for the moonlight that shined through the row of windows and lit the scarred floorboards. And silent. Only the soft lapping of waves on the lower level broke the quiet, pulsing against the wide stone ledge where ship officers used to tie up the dinghies they'd rowed to shore to record manifests and settle fees before unloading their cargo.

He'd been here since nightfall, and long enough that his clothes had dried. Using the night's first darkness for cover, he'd silently swum into the boathouse from the harbor. The sound of the waves had covered any noise as he climbed onto the ledge, collected the two pistols and a knife that he'd paid the boy to leave there for him, and made his way up the wide steps to the main floor above. Then he'd settled in to wait, marking time by the tolling of the church bell.

And thinking about Diana.

He allowed himself that small luxury of distraction when he

still had several hours to wait. How could he not? He'd thought of little else but her since the night he found her at the tavern.

Oh, he'd always known how beautiful she was, how intelligent and inherently graceful, with a touch of an imperial air that had been crafted from a lifetime spent as a general's daughter. But he'd had no idea that her outer loveliness was no match for her inner beauty, or the kindness that reached all the way down to her soul. Or how resilient she was. How utterly strong and fierce.

What still sent his head spinning, though, was that she cared about him. *Him.* Not the scoundrel second son he pretended to be, not even the Home Office operative he actually was. But beneath all that, she saw him as nothing more than a flawed man, yet she loved him anyway. The absolution she'd brought to him was the greatest gift he'd ever been given.

No—not absolution. *Salvation.* In her arms, he'd been redeemed, and he'd go to his grave a better man because of her.

But before that happened, he had one last duty to complete. He would make certain that Diana and Meri would be safe.

The sound of the water changed, and a tingle raced down his spine. His muscles tensing, he reached beneath his jacket and withdrew his pistol. Keeping it lowered at his side and pointed at the floor, he fixed his eyes on the stairs.

His ears caught the soft thud of wood against wood as oars were secured, followed by the scuffling of footsteps across the stone and the creak of the old stairs. Two dark figures appeared from the shadows.

"Paxton," Kit called out, wanting the man to know that he was there in the darkness, expecting him. And wanting Diana to know, as well.

"Christopher!" she cried out and impulsively took a step toward him, only to be yanked back.

With one arm wrapped around her waist to hold her in front

of him as a shield, Paxton pulled a knife from the scabbard at his waist and held its sharp end pointed at Diana's chest. The blade shined in the moonlight. "One wrong move from you, Carlisle, and I *will* kill her."

And Kit would shoot the man dead where he stood. His eyes not leaving Paxton, he called out to her, "Diana, are you all right?"

"Yes." But her voice was barely above a whisper. She was terrified, and damn that bastard for making her afraid!

"Good. Just do as I say," he assured her, "and this will all be over soon."

She gave a jerking nod, only for Paxton to pull her back against him, drawing a gasp from her.

"You're not surprised to see me," Paxton mused. "You figured it out."

Kit clenched his jaw. "Just as I discovered that you were the one who murdered James Fitch-Batten."

"Had to. He'd learned that I'd been communicating with the French and had to be silenced, or everything I'd worked so hard to achieve would have been ruined."

Acid formed on Kit's tongue, and he choked down the anger rising inside him. "So you killed him before he could reveal to Whitehall that you were selling General Morgan's diary."

"Oh, I was working with the French long before that," he corrected with a dark laugh. "How do you think I knew which passage from the diary to offer them? I've been working with their operatives and contacts since shortly after Waterloo, along with other countries across the continent."

"You've been offering up secrets to the highest bidder, you mean."

"If there's one thing that the wars taught me, it's that exclusive alliances are worthless." He smiled tightly. "Including those with England, even as part of His Majesty's army."

"Why do it? You were a hero in the wars."

"I still am a hero. Just not one of ours." He tightened his hold around Diana, and the fleeting look he darted at her when she cried out softly in fear registered exactly how much the man despised her and her family. "I did it for the same reason that Benedict Arnold switched sides in the American war."

"Self-interest?" Kit bit out.

His jaw clenched. "Lack of recognition and no chance of being given the position I deserved. I was passed over for promotion after the Battle of Toulouse because I was a brewer's son. But even then I still foolishly thought that I'd be recognized for my valor eventually, that I'd be given the accolades that I deserved. Then came Waterloo, yet I was rewarded with nothing. Nothing!"

"That's not how promotions work, you know that," Diana interjected softly. "There are only so many men who can—"

He grabbed her by the hair and yanked back her head, placing the knife at her throat. He leered at her, his face close to hers. Kit saw her eyes squeeze shut as Paxton half-panted out in anger, "The wars are over. My only chance for promotion now is by buying one. But how does a man do that when he's surviving on an officer's salary and not a member of the aristocracy? He's damned from the start. *That* was when I decided that I had to take matters into my own hands."

"By selling information to the enemy?" she choked out.

The terror in her voice made Kit's hand tighten around his pistol. But in the darkness, with Diana positioned in front of Paxton like that, he couldn't shoot without risking Diana's life. And that he would *never* do.

"All kinds of wonderful information, right there at my finger-tips, garnered through the general and his connections to the War Department. That's why I went with General Morgan into the damnable countryside, into self-exile at Idlewild. Even retired, he had access to so much, which meant that I had access to it by extension. When he wrote about his experiences in the Waterloo campaign, I knew they were worth their weight in gold."

"And you'd used a little girl and a woman in the process," Kit interjected, wanting Paxton's attention away from Diana.

"Lots of innocent women and little girls died in the wars," he countered, his arm sliding around Diana's throat to hold her pressed against him. He lowered the knife to her belly. "What difference do two more make?"

"You *knew* us," Diana accused. "For God's sake! Meri loved and trusted you."

"You didn't."

His reply stirred a low warning in Kit's gut. He heard it in the man's voice—*revenge*. Suddenly, this exchange had become so much more dangerous.

"The diary," Kit called out, again bringing Paxton's attention back to him. He reached inside his jacket with his left hand and retrieved the diary from his breast pocket. He held it up. "Release her, and you can have it."

"Toss it here to the floor."

"Release her first."

Paxton laughed. "You think I'm that stupid? She's the only thing keeping you from killing me right now."

All amusement vanished from his face, and he jabbed the tip of the knife into her belly. Diana gave a small scream.

"Yes, she is." Kit calmly raised his pistol, ice water churning in his veins. "So tread *very* carefully."

"Toss the diary to me," Paxton ordered. "Once I have it, I'll back down the stairs to the landing, then release her and row away."

Paxton pulled her back flat against his front, so close that he rested his chin on her shoulder, his cheek against hers. She shuddered with revulsion. His eyes glinted as he stared at Kit through the shadows.

"Toss it over, Carlisle. I'm done playing."

And Kit was out of options. Clenching his jaw, he threw the diary. It landed on the floor and slid to a stop at their feet. Carefully keeping Diana in front of him, Paxton reached down to snatch it up.

"Thank you." Then Paxton ordered, "Kill him!"

Two men rushed up the stairs from below, pistols drawn and running straight for him.

Diana screamed, "Christopher, look out!"

But he'd seen them coming. With a flash of light, his pistol fired, and the loud explosion echoed off the stone walls. The ball caught one of the men in the thigh. He collapsed to the floor with a howl of pain.

The other sailor charged forward. Kit threw his spent pistol into the man's face, and when the attacker threw up his arms to protect himself, Kit dove to the side. He rolled and came up onto the balls of his feet, crouched low with a knife in his right hand and a second pistol in his left. The blade flashed as he slashed it into the sailor's leg, then dropped it clattering to the floor as he tried to wrench the pistol from the man's hand.

Paxton grabbed her arm and pulled her toward the stairs. "This way, damn you!"

Fear spilled through her. If he managed to pull her down the stairs, nothing would stop him from rowing away with her. Nothing would stop him from killing her. Or worse.

She dropped to the ground, throwing her full weight to the floor to force him to stop.

Barely pausing in his stride, he grabbed her arm and jerked her back up to her feet, but her skirt caught on the toe of her shoe. It ripped up past her knees. With one hand, he shoved her skirt out of the way and hauled her forward, half-dragging her across the floor.

"I'd rather die than go with you!" she bit out, reaching for her leg.

As she rose upward, she slipped the knife free of its scabbard and sliced it into his arm. The metal blade cut through his coat and shirtsleeve beneath, then sank deep into his flesh.

Bellowing in pain, he released her with a shuddering jerk, and his hand reached for the bloody wound on his arm. "You bitch!"

He kicked her. The toe of his boot landed hard in her stomach, and her breath ripped from her lungs. The knife fell from her hand and clattered to the floor, beyond her grasping fingers.

His face twisted into a maniacal expression in the moonlight as he reached for her again, his teeth clenched and bared. Still desperately gulping back her breath, she didn't have the strength to stop him this time from jerking her to her feet and pulling her toward the stairs. She stumbled helplessly beside him. Every gasping breath sent an incapacitating pain jarring straight through her, from her ribs to her spine.

"Paxton!" Kit shouted.

As he spun around to face Kit, the major pulled her in front of him, once more placing her between him and Kit's pistol. His forearm returned to her throat to hold her still, while his other hand dove beneath his coat to pull out a gun. Instead of pointing it at Kit, he placed the tip of the barrel against her temple, and she cried out breathlessly in fear.

The two men stared at each other across the room, frozen in place. The two sailors now lay unmoving on the floor.

"Move, and I'll kill her," Paxton warned.

She barely heard the threat beneath the blood pounding in her ears with every heartbeat. But she saw Kit stiffen as his muscles tightened, ready to spring.

"Then I'll kill you before you reach the stairs."

He swung the gun toward Kit. "Not if I kill you first."

A dark smile stretched across his face as he said quietly, "I'm already dead."

"No," Diana whispered, finding an untapped resolve deep inside her heart. She'd lost one man whom she'd loved. She would *not* lose another.

She lowered her mouth and sank her teeth into Paxton's wounded arm.

He howled, and his arm jerked from the fresh pain.

Diana shoved herself out of his grasp. She ran forward, desperate to reach Kit and the safety of his embrace. She looked back to see Paxton raise the pistol with an animalistic snarl, his face distorted with fury and hatred.

Arms went around her, spinning her in a fast circle—*Christopher*. He shielded her with his body, twisting at the waist to raise his gun and point it back at Paxton.

Two gunshots ran out in rapid succession.

Before Diana could scream, the boathouse erupted around them. The windows smashed in a shower of glass and splintered wood as half a dozen men crashed through them. The door flung open, hitting the stone wall behind it with such force that it twisted on its hinges. Lanterns blazed to light, and from all around them came the metallic click of cocking pistols.

Paxton stood frozen in place, his white face contrasting against the scarlet blood dripping onto the boards at his feet. He sank to his knees, then fell forward onto his face. Dead.

Behind him at the top of the stairs stood Garrett. Smoke curled from the end of his spent pistol.

"But there were two shots." In confusion, Diana turned toward Kit and placed her hand on his upper arm, the same arm from which he held his pistol, still loaded and unfired. "If you didn't shoot, who did?"

Then she felt it...a sticky, wet warmth spreading beneath her fingertips as she clutched his arm. She stared up at him, her lips parting in sudden panic.

His face was hard, but his color was paling. Beads of perspiration broke out across his forehead.

"Diana," he whispered, dropping the pistol to the floor with a clatter.

"Christopher!"

Her arms went around him as he began to sway, catching him as his knees buckled. Using all of her strength, she lowered him gently to the floor. The blood from his arm blossomed like a red flower through his jacket sleeve.

"He's been shot," she cried out to Garrett as he rushed forward. "Send for a surgeon—now!"

Garrett shouted orders to his men, two of whom nodded and raced from the boathouse into the dark night.

"I'm going to be all right," Kit assured her, reaching to cover her hand with his and unwittingly smearing blood across the backs of her fingers. "Might have ruined my jacket, though."

"That's not funny," she scolded, the worry inside her growing more intense with every passing second that no surgeon arrived to help. Of all the times to joke— *So much blood!* She grabbed her skirt and ripped off the hem, then wrapped the fabric around his arm to staunch the bleeding. "Christopher..." Hot tears formed on her lashes, yet she choked them back as she cradled him in her arms. "It's all my fault... I'm so sorry."

"Shh," he whispered, reaching up to touch her face. Even now, his thoughts were focused on reassuring her and not on his own pain. "You couldn't have stopped any of this." He sucked in a deep but ragged breath. "I'm so glad…"

*Glad?* How on God's earth could he be glad about this? She wanted to scream!

"That you found me. You saved me, Diana…more than you'll ever know."

Dear God! Why was he talking like this? "I'm not going anywhere," she insisted. "Neither are you."

His lips twisted into a grim smile. "You did it." His voice grew softer, more breathless. "You stopped Paxton…before he got away…with the diary."

"*We* stopped him," she corrected, agonizingly aware of how long it was taking the surgeon to arrive, of how Garrett lingered nearby but didn't come closer. As if giving them time alone to say goodbye.

*No.* This wasn't goodbye—it wasn't!

"You used the knife." His smile widened slightly with pride. "Good girl."

"You did say that if a man ever tried to reach beneath my skirt that I should use it." Despite the teasing, her eyes grew so full of unshed tears that his face blurred, and she couldn't blink them away fast enough.

"I did," he murmured, his smile fading as he struggled to remain conscious. "But that…wasn't what…I had in mind."

"Then next time you need to be clearer."

"I will…"

*Please, God—please let there be a next time!* "Christopher…"

"Tell her," he ordered softly, his words now slurring. "Tell Meri…who you really are…"

"Christopher!" Panic rose inside her as she felt him slipping into unconsciousness. She clutched him tightly to her, terrified of losing him. He couldn't leave her now. *He couldn't die!* Not when she'd finally found him and allowed him into her heart.

She kissed him, but the warmth and life she tasted on his lips only made her fear that it was slipping away. So much left to be said, not enough words in the world, and all of them coming too late. Except—

"I love you," she whispered, her trembling lips barely able to form the words as tears dripped down her cheeks.

He whispered back, his voice little more than a gravelly breath, "You'd better…"

Then his eyes closed, and he went limp in her arms.

# CHAPTER 27

*K*it's eyes fluttered open, then slammed shut as a sharp pain slammed through his forehead. Good God, the sunlight was bright! Who'd opened the damned curtains? His head pounded, but he didn't remember getting foxed last night.

The fog of sleep slowly cleared, and what he finally remembered... *Dear God.* He wished he'd been dreaming.

He eased open his eyes again, and this time, with much blinking, they slowly adjusted to the light. But as he looked around, he had no idea where he was or what the hour...until he recognized the room that he and Diana had taken at the hotel. He was back at the Mermaid and waking up in the morning sunlight, as if none of the past few days had happened.

But they *had* happened. The pain and aching soreness that gripped his entire body proved it.

His eyes landed on Garrett Morgan standing near the window. *Not* the person he wanted to set eyes on the morning after he'd nearly died. Or the other man standing with him, the two of them speaking quietly—

Nathaniel Grey.

Well. Perhaps he wasn't going to survive the day after all.

He shifted to sit up. A piercing pain shot up his arm and into his chest, and he sucked in a mouthful of air through clenched teeth, freezing in place to keep the pain at bay. When the hammer had stopped beating on the top of his head and the lightning ceased flashing in front of his eyes, he panted down the pain and rubbed his hand over his shoulder where a large white bandage wrapped around his bicep. Beneath the sharp pain lay a dull ache that would take weeks—if not months—to heal.

The two men turned toward him, but otherwise remained where they were on the other side of the room.

"By all means," Kit ground out as he eased back against the pillow, giving up on the idea of getting out of bed, "don't rush to help."

In response, Morgan leaned back against the wall, and Grey crossed his arms over his chest.

"So you didn't die after all," Morgan mused, the smile on his face revealing how much he was enjoying seeing Kit incapacitated like this.

Grey added, "Looks like I lost that bet at White's."

"Not for long." Kit's voice was rusty with sleep. And pain. What he wouldn't have given to be able to dive into a large glass of laudanum or to the bottom of a whisky bottle. Or both. "I'm sure your men will see to that."

"My men have nothing to do with Home Office agents who have turned rogue." He knowingly lifted a brow. "Or been saved by women."

Well, *that* stung his manly pride. But speaking of women… "Where's Diana? Is she all right?" His chest tightened with concern as his gaze darted to the door. "And what about Meri?"

The two men exchanged glances. Morgan answered, "They're both fine. Meri was taken home last evening."

"*Last evening?*" Last evening, he still had the diary, and Paxton still had Diana. "For Christ's sake—what time is it?"

"Ten in the morning."

"Two days later," Grey added solemnly. "You've been unconscious for the past two nights."

Morgan shook his head. "Damnable shame you didn't sleep longer."

Kit clenched his teeth. One of them alone was barely tolerable. The two of them together was sheer torture. "Shouldn't you two be off somewhere, rescuing kittens up trees or whatever it is that the Foreign Office does these days?"

He clucked his tongue with mock offense at the idea. "When we could be right here, showing you our support?"

"Well," Grey corrected with a sideways glance at Morgan, "let's not get carried away."

Gritting his teeth, he swung his legs over the side of the bed. He took a deep breath to hold down the pain and shoved himself to his feet. He grumbled, "I think I'd rather be dead than suffer your *support.*"

His mutter drew amused grins from the two men at his expense. Despite their teasing, though, Kit could see concern darken their gazes as they watched him sway on his feet. But they also knew not to offend him by rushing to his side, thus pointing out how weak he was. How close to death he'd actually come.

Neither man said it, but he could see *that* in their eyes, too.

"Meri's safe," Morgan assured him. The teasing amusement that had been in his voice earlier was completely gone. "While the surgeon was still digging that ball out of your arm, I sent a message to the men who were guarding her, to take the general to her and escort them both home. She should have been tucked safe and sound into her own bed last night."

*Thank God.* Relief rushed through him. That news was better at easing his pain than any spoonful of laudanum ever could have been. "And Diana?"

"Asleep in the room across the hall." Morgan looked tired and older than Kit had ever seen him. He wasn't certain how he felt about Morgan's role with the Foreign Office, but the man loved his sister and niece. "She was awake for the last two nights. Never left your side. I finally convinced her at dawn that she needed to get some rest."

"Thank you."

Morgan shrugged a shoulder. "After all, what good would she have been at planning your funeral if she were at the point of exhaustion?"

Kit grimaced. "Thank you."

"That's what friends are for."

"Well," Grey repeated his earlier words with another glance at Morgan, "let's not get carried away."

Kit rolled his eyes in aggravation. "And the diary?"

Morgan pulled it out of his waistcoat and tossed it onto the foot of the bed. "Safe and sound. And, unlike you, free of bullet holes."

But dark brown splotches stained the cover. Paxton's blood.

"What will you do with it now?" he asked Grey.

"You're no longer considered a rogue agent," he answered, dodging the question. "I sent word to Sir Robert Peel at the Home Office in London yesterday morning, explaining that you were working on an extended assignment that involved the War Department, by special request of the Secretary of State for War. I also sent one to the Foreign Secretary that I have no intention of declaring you a traitor."

"How kind of you," he muttered wryly and rubbed at his shoulder. "After I got shot in service to England."

Instead of smiling in amusement at that, as Kit expected, Grey's expression remained somber. "Peel returned the message. You're not considered a rogue agent, but you still broke the rules. So you've been expelled from the Home Office. He's discharged you and asked the War Secretary to strip you of your army commission as punishment."

The news hit like a punch to his gut, and he took a long moment to recover. When he did, the bitterness consumed him. "Because I'm worthless to them now, you mean. Because I'm too visible." After ten years of loyalty to them, of putting his life on hold and risking his very existence—for this. For *nothing*. Discarded without a second thought, when he could no longer be of service to them.

"Because you defied orders and burned too many bridges," Grey corrected. Then he admitted grudgingly, "And yes, because there's no such thing as loyalty inside the Home Office these days."

Being right didn't ease his resentment.

"You'll need a different future for yourself now." Grey stepped toward him. "So unless you truly do want to become a vicar, you should consider the offer I'm about to give you."

Kit leveled his eyes on Grey. The two men were of the same height and build, just as tall and broad shouldered, and now, just as world-weary and experienced about the ways Whitehall mercilessly double-crossed the men who dedicated their lives to it. They respected each other, even if no trust lived between them.

Grey pulled out a note from his breast pocket and held it up. "A message from the Foreign Secretary. I told George Canning what you did tracing Fitch-Batten's murder to Paxton, how you protected General Morgan and his family. He's offering you a position within the Foreign Office."

Kit's heart skipped. He didn't know whether to jump for joy or run away. Hadn't he just left a life of secrecy and lies? No—hadn't he just been kicked out of that life? The question now…did he want to go back to that same hollow existence, living at the pleasure of Whitehall over his own wants and needs?

"No," he bit out.

"You wouldn't be an operative. They'd never allow that. Everyone in both offices will be keeping a very close eye on you in the future." He held out the note. "But he's offering a position in London equal in rank." Grey pressed, "Consider it."

"*Hell* no."

But a knowing grin quirked up at the corners of Grey's mouth. He laid the unwanted note on the bed and picked up the diary.

"I'll be going then." He slid a parting look between the two men as he headed toward the door. "Send word when you've returned to London. I'm certain the Foreign Office will want to question both of you."

*Oh no.* Grey wasn't leaving here that easily. Kit had traveled halfway across England and risked his life, the life of the woman he loved, and that of her daughter because of that damnable diary. No way in hell was Grey simply waltzing out of here with it. Not without the final answers he needed to put the last of the puzzle pieces into place.

"And the diary?" Kit pressed.

"It will be taken care of, be assured of it."

"Forgive me if I doubt you," Kit drawled in challenge. "And while you're at it, tell me this—why you? Of all the men in Whitehall, why send someone of your rank after the decade-old notes of a retired general?"

That stopped Grey just as he reached the door. He turned to face Kit, but his face gave away no answers.

"Even if it contained the names of half the French counselors in Paris, someone at your level in the Foreign Office should never have been put into the field after it." He eyes narrowed. "Why send *you?*"

Grey held his gaze for a moment, as if considering how much he could divulge. "I sent myself. Out of personal interest, you might say."

Weighing the diary in his hand, he turned toward the fireplace and tossed it into the fire.

None of the three men moved. All of them stood still and watched the little book burn, watched the flames eat it up and flare brightly in gratitude for being fed.

Grey stared down at the fire and said quietly, "Paxton had been slipping secrets out of the War Department for years and selling them for his own gain. Sometimes to France or Spain." His brow drew down into a troubled frown as he added quietly, "Sometimes to other bidders within Britain."

When only blackened pages remained, he picked up the iron poker leaning against the mantelpiece and jabbed it into the diary, destroying the charred clump until nothing remained but glowing ashes. Until there was nothing for the French to ever ask for again.

"Do you remember what happened to the Earl Royston?" Grey asked. "You should. It involved the Carlisles."

"Yes." That was how his cousin Richard Carlisle had so unexpectedly become Duke of Trent. Because his neighbor, the Earl Royston, had been found guilty of espionage and hanged.

"Royston had obtained a list of secret War Department operatives, men whose names he was selling off to the enemy, one by one. The same list that Thomas Matteson uncovered during a house party at Blackwood Hall. A list that contained his own name."

Thomas Matteson...the Marquess of Chesney, and the man who had married Kit's cousin Josephine. Kit had heard stories that the man had once worked in secret for the War Office, but always, he'd dismissed them as apocryphal. The creation of bored society gossips. But now he knew them to be real.

"No one knew how Royston had gotten those names, and he went to the gallows protecting the man who sold them to him." He returned the poker to its place. "It took me five years, but I finally tracked that list back to Paxton. And two months ago, I set the trap."

"What trap?"

He grimly lifted his gaze from the fire and locked eyes with Kit. "There is no French official at the Court of King Louis sending information back to the British. That was all an orchestrated lie to bring Paxton out of hiding."

The room tilted around Kit as Grey's admission sank over him. *Good God.* "That's why you didn't want me hunting down Morgan."

Grey acknowledged that with a nod. "I couldn't let you interfere, but I also couldn't tell you why."

Kit's gaze darted to Diana's brother, who registered absolutely no surprise on his face. Morgan had known all along yet given nothing away. Downright lied to him about it, in fact. The man was a good agent, Kit had to give him that. Even if he wanted nothing more at that moment than to plough his fist into Morgan's face.

"But why make a copy of the diary, then?" Kit asked. "Why not just let Paxton hand over the original and arrest him for it?"

"While men like Pierre LeFavre aren't giving information to the British any longer," Grey answered for Morgan, "they once did. We owe it to them to protect them. We couldn't risk that the original would end up in French hands and reveal a past now best left to history."

After all these months, the last pieces of the puzzle finally snapped into place. The feeling of resolution that swept over him like a wave stung at his eyes and throat, and he sucked in a deep breath to steady himself.

"In the end, I went after Paxton for the same reason you pursued Fitch-Batten's murderer," Grey stated deliberately as he moved toward the door. "For justice. He sold Thomas Matteson's name to the enemy—my best friend and a man I consider a brother." His eyes gleamed with dark resolve as he glanced back. "*No one* threatens my family and gets away with it."

Grey walked out of the room and shut the door behind him.

"You knew," Kit drawled to Morgan, yet kept his gaze on the closed door. "All this time..."

"Yes," Morgan answered impassively.

"And you lied to me that day in the cottage."

"Partially." He paused. "But so did you."

Kit swung his gaze sideways and narrowed it murderously on the man. His life was in upheaval, his future uncertain, and his damned shoulder throbbed with pain. He was in no mood for this.

Morgan sat down casually on the window sill and crossed his legs at his ankles, and arched an accusing brow. "You didn't tell me that you'd been intimate with my sister."

*Christ.* He was in no mood for *that* either.

"That's none of your damned business," Kit growled and stalked over to the washstand. With his good arm, he poured water into the basin.

"She's in love with you, you know."

Kit glared over his shoulder at him, then splashed water onto his face with one hand.

"Which is good. Because you're certainly in love with her."

He missed, and the water spilled down his chest. With a curse, he snatched up the hand towel.

"Are you going to tell me that's none of my business, too?"

His gaze shot angrily to Morgan's in the mirror as he wiped his chest. "If I thought it would do any good."

"It won't," he answered with a shrug of his shoulder. But then his teasing faded, replaced by grim sobriety. "My sister went through hell when John Meredith died, and she deserves to have a husband who loves her and would do anything to make her happy. And for some reason I can't fathom, she's fallen for you."

Kit could barely fathom it himself. Yet he'd seen the emotion in her eyes that dawn when she made love to him on the deck of the sailboat, had heard her soft declaration right before the darkness swept over him.

But he also saw the worry and fear that had gripped her when she'd spoken about finding a stable and dependable man to be Meri's father. He knew she didn't mean him.

"You will marry her," Morgan ordered.

He laughed darkly, regretting it when stabs of pain shot down his arm. As if he hadn't thought of that already! A hundred times since he first kissed her, in fact, and every time, he ended up at the same realization— "Your sister doesn't want to marry a man like me."

"Oh yes, she does. She just doesn't want to marry a soldier." He gave a curt nod. "Congratulations on your court martial."

Kit's heart stuttered. His blood began to warm with a faint tingle that started in his bare toes and worked its way up his half-dressed body, until the hair on his head felt as if it were standing on end. It fell over him slowly, the realization that his world had just been irrevocably changed. That everything his life had been was now gone. An unnamable sensation seeped through him that he was floating weightless, tied to nothing that anchored him in place...nothing that held him down. For the first time since he entered the army over a decade ago, his life was his own, wide open to be anything he wanted it to be.

That was the unrecognizable feeling that crept through him...*freedom*. A freedom that only a few months ago—only a few days ago, in fact—seemed impossible.

The door opened. The soft metallic click of the latch snapped him back to the moment, so did the slam of pain through his shoulder when he turned too quickly toward it.

"Christopher," Diana whispered breathlessly, stopping in the doorway and holding onto the door for support. As if she couldn't believe what she was seeing. The relief that flooded her face shot through him with the force of cannon fire. So did the bright tears that glistened in her blue eyes, despite her rapid blinking to clear them away.

Letting his gaze wander deliberately over her, he drank her in. Never—*never* had he seen a more beautiful vision in his life than Diana at that moment. The sight of her pierced him. To his soul.

"Well," Morgan drawled, pushing himself away from the window. "I know when I'm not wanted."

Ignoring Kit, he stopped in front of Diana on his way out the door. He took her arms in his hands to make her face him, even as she attempted to crane her neck to see around him, to keep her eyes on Kit.

"Carlisle's going to ask you something very important," Morgan told her. Then he brought her attention back to him with a kiss to her forehead. "However badly he mangles it, say yes."

Kit rolled his eyes. *Good Lord.*

Morgan left, closing the door after himself.

Diana remained where she was, on the other side of the room. So close that he could almost feel her softness, yet still a world away. The only movement she made was to bite her bottom lip.

Kit didn't blame her for being wary. Everything had changed between them. And when he finished telling her what he planned on doing with his newfound freedom and with the offer from the Foreign Office, everything would change even more.

He glanced at his bandaged shoulder and said quietly, "I got shot."

"I know," she replied wryly, staying where she was. "I was there."

Her soft answer pricked him with guilt at the hell she must have gone through that night.

He took a slow step toward her. "I'm going to live." He paused. "I think."

Pulling in a shaking breath, she jerked a nod. She couldn't find her voice to give him the set-down that flippant comment deserved.

"I'm no longer considered a rogue agent."

She held her breath. "That means..."

"That Whitehall isn't coming after me to finish what Paxton started."

A shudder of relief swept through her with such intensity that she swayed on her feet, and a long breath poured from her. All of her fear and worry for him expelled with it.

"I also got dismissed from the army and kicked out of the Home Office."

Her face paled, but he had no idea if that was a good sign or not. She choked out, as if unwilling to believe that he was telling her the truth, "You did?"

"Yes."

For a long moment, neither of them moved, neither spoke. But he saw the way that news seeped through her, the understanding of what that meant registering with faint hope on her face.

"You were..." She swallowed nervously. "You were going to ask me...something?"

"Yes, I was."

He moved to stand in front of her, but didn't yet reach for her. This was too important, and if he took her into his arms right now, he wouldn't stop kissing her long enough to finish this conversation.

"The Foreign Office has offered me a position in London. Apparently, instead of wanting to kill me outright, they prefer to slowly torture me to death by making me do administrative for them."

All traces of hope vanished from her face. Definitely not a good sign. Visibly, she steeled herself. "And your question?"

"Should I take the position?"

He felt her breath hitch, so attuned was he to this woman. *Everything* about her made his skin prickle and his soul ache.

"I don't know." She hesitated, lowering her gaze away for the first time since she came into the room and saw him. "Is it a good position?"

"Of sorts." He fought to keep his face inscrutable. This decision had to be hers. He needed to know whether she truly wanted a future with him, once he was free to become the man she needed and deserved. "A desk position. No more field work. No more pretending to be a shiftless second son." He forced a grin. "I can claim that I grew tired of waiting around for a living as a vicar and decided to throw my lot in with the sinners in government."

Her mouth pulled down. She didn't find that amusing, apparently. "It sounds like a fine opportunity." But the tone of her voice —pained and full of grief—told him a completely different story. So did the way her shoulders sagged when she added, so softly that he had to take another step forward to hear her, "But it's still in service to the Crown. They could still send you anywhere they liked, couldn't they?"

"Yes."

"Could you ever refuse to go?"

"No." The truth of that was brutal, and he felt that single word rip all the hope from her.

She gave a faint, slow nod of acceptance and blinked rapidly, still refusing to look at him even though he now stood directly in front of her. So close that he could caress her cheek if he lifted his hand.

"Is it what you want?" Emotion scraped her voice raw. "To work for them?"

"I might be persuaded to decline it." He murmured, "What do you want?"

"I want you…to be happy," but the words tore from her in a desolate whisper.

He took her chin and turned her head gently until she looked up at him. He repeated quietly, "What do *you* want, Diana?"

The pleading in her eyes told him that she couldn't bring herself to put her answer into words. She'd lived for so long at the heartless mercy of fate that she didn't yet dare consider claiming her own happiness. Didn't dare raise her hopes, only to have them dashed if he did want a life in service after all. A life that would never have room for the stability and consistency she needed in hers.

She wanted a future together as much as he did, he was certain of it. But she also needed to protect her daughter.

And he loved her even more because of that.

Her face darkened with grief. "When you said you wanted to ask me a question, I thought…" Her voice trailed off.

"I haven't asked it yet."

Her gaze flew up to his, to search his face for answers.

He gathered all his strength to keep from yanking her into his arms and kissing away her doubts. "So this Meri girl—you like her, do you?"

She blinked, her watery eyes widening at that unexpected question. "Pardon?"

"I mean, you like her enough to keep her around?" He fought to maintain a somber expression on his face as he teased her. "Feed her, clothe her...water her once in a while so she'll grow?"

"Christopher," she chastised softly, her shoulders sagging with exasperation. "Be serious, will you?"

"I couldn't be more serious. I've been shot. Something like that shakes a man up and makes him want to seize what's important." He rubbed at his aching shoulder. What he wouldn't have given to be able to crawl into bed and fall back asleep until he healed, with Diana in his arms. "You want Meri to have a loving home, don't you? Maybe give her a brother or sister to play with?" He murmured, "Or six?"

"A brother or..." Her breath caught, her eyes widening with understanding of what he was truly asking her. "Yes," she finally managed to choke out. "I think she'd like that. A great deal." She trembled and whispered, blinking rapidly, "So would I."

Kit knew what he wanted, then and for the rest of his life.

He opened his arms.

She rushed into his embrace, burying her face in his chest and clasping him around the waist. He pressed her close despite the pain in his shoulder and the fatigue that even now had him light-headed and unsteady on his feet. Although that could have also been due to Diana and the anticipation of a life together.

"I love you, Diana." More than he'd ever dreamed possible. He drew a deep breath and finally asked the question that was burning inside him. "Will you marry me?"

"Yes," she said, pulling back just far enough to cup his face in her hands. "Yes, I will marry you."

A smile beamed through her tears as she rose onto her tiptoes to kiss him. Then, lowering herself away, she arched a brow that told him she'd brook no argument.

"But I am *not* having six children."

He laughed as happiness swelled inside him, and he pulled her back into his arms, to never let her go.

# EPILOGUE

*Kingscote Park, Hampshire*
*Two Months Later*

*D*iana reclined in the bottom of the little rowboat and turned her face up toward the warm afternoon sun, relishing in a few moments of peace from the noisy party they'd left behind at the manor house. "Where are we going?"

"I told you. It's a secret," Kit answered, not pausing in his rowing as he moved them across the lake on his brother's country estate. "You used to like secrets."

A laugh fell from her lips, and she corrected, "What I liked were secret agents." She smiled flirtatiously at him. "*One* secret agent, actually."

"You'd better like me." He softened the warning with a smile, his hands not leaving the oars as they skimmed the water's mirror-like surface and took them further away from their own wedding celebration. "It's too late now to change your mind."

She watched the sunlight sparkle against her wedding ring as she lazily dipped her hand into the water. "I won't be changing my mind." With a happy laugh, she flung a handful of water up at him. "So tell me where you're taking me."

"Even pharaohesses don't need to know everything."

"Then how about your wife?"

He flashed her a grin, and her belly fluttered. *Please, God, never let me grow used to this feeling of Christopher smiling at me.*

"My wife is allowed to know everything," he promised.

His wife. *That* sent her belly into somersaults.

The new appellation would take some time to get used to, especially since it was less than four hours old. Even now, the grounds of Kingscote Park were filled with hundreds of guests of all stations, ranks, and association to them, from the Duke of Wellington all the way down to Angus Higgins, the steward at Idlewild who had once come after Kit with a gun…although at the time, Diana had had no idea how common an event that actually was. And something she prayed would never happen again.

The rooms of the grand manor house were filled to bursting with people who had come to help them celebrate their wedding, a small ceremony held that morning in the village church with only family and close friends in attendance. Even then, though, the pews had been filled with all the Carlisles and their growing families, the Winslows, the Mattesons, the Westovers—the Duke and Duchess of Strathmore's beautiful little girls took up a row of pews all by themselves—a scattering of Whitbys, and even Nathaniel Grey, along with his wife Lady Emily and their son. With Kit's brother, Ross, standing beside him as his best man, Miranda Carlisle as her matron of honor, Meri as the flower girl, and the general walking her down the aisle, it was a true family affair.

Diana wouldn't have had it any other way.

As she watched Kit row in his shirtsleeves, his jacket removed and the muscles of his shoulders and back rippling, happiness bubbled inside her. The most wonderful man in the world loved her, a man who also loved Meri and insisted that her daughter be publicly raised as their child...who had already hired a solicitor to start the adoption process, in fact, so that he could also make her *his* daughter. In every way possible.

Diana didn't want to create any more upheaval in Meri's young life, preferring to ease her into all the changes to come. Kit agreed. So when they returned to Idlewild after the events at Bradwell, the family and household servants quietly enacted their subtle plan. Now, Diana was referred to as Meri's mama, with Diana's mother as her grandmama and Garret as her uncle. Meri transitioned well, experiencing only a bit of confusion when everyone began to refer to the general as her grandpapa. They gently yet persistently corrected her whenever she referred to them by their old roles, and always without directly confronting her about it. By the time of the wedding, Meri had come to accept the new roles without a second thought...including referring to Kit as Papa.

There was no explanation for Meri, except that Kit was going to marry them. The truth would come later, when she was older and could understand. Then, she would be told the story of John Meredith, of what a good and brave man he'd been, how he would be proud to know that she was his daughter.

But for now, they would form their own new family and simply enjoy being together.

The rowboat rocked suddenly beneath her, and she grabbed at the sides of the boat.

"If I'm going to have to swim for shore," she teased, taking a different tack to discover why he'd brought her out onto the lake, "I'd like to know in which direction to head."

He nodded toward the little island in the center of the lake. "There."

Her heart fell with disappointment. "There?"

"Wooded and private, with a hermitage. One that is conveniently lacking a hermit at the moment."

"Convenient," she drawled a bit suspiciously.

"Very. Even more so since I asked the servants to get it ready for us."

She sat up. "Ready?"

Knowing that he'd pricked her curiosity and now had her full attention, he lazily described, "Flowers, wood for warm fires, soft bedding…lots of soft bedding." A wolfish gleam lit his eyes, and that predacious stare pulsed all the way down between her legs, where a soft ache began to throb in time with his rowing. "And a picnic basket filled with enough food and wine to keep us fed for days."

"Days?" The word emerged as a throaty purr, only for the tingles of excitement to be dashed by reality. "But someone will notice we've left the party and come looking for us. They'll find us by nightfall."

"They can't."

The smug way he said that made her ask, "Why not?"

"Because this is the only boat on the lake that's still seaworthy." He winked at her. "I scuttled all the others last night."

"You didn't!"

"*Days*, Mrs. Carlisle." He rested his elbows on his knees as he paused in rowing to lean toward her to punctuate his point. "Days and days of nothing to do but ravish you, thoroughly and repeatedly." He glanced regretfully over his shoulder toward the little boathouse on the far shore. "But I suppose we could go back and—"

"Keep rowing." She gestured her hand imperially toward the island and once more reclined on the seat. "Your pharaohess demands it."

Amusement danced across his face as he took up the oars again. "Yes, my queen."

She couldn't help but smile at him. He made her so happy that it seemed she'd never stop beaming. Which was perfectly fine with her.

The only dark spot so far in their lives had involved his work.

Just as she'd hoped, he'd declined Canning's offer with the Foreign Office, yet fate had brought him back to the Home Office. This time, thankfully, not as an operative but as an administrator, overseeing the Home Secretary's latest initiative—a metropolitan police force. One that would be organized, well-funded, and—unlike Bow Street—uncorrupt. One that needed a man exactly like Kit to develop and implement it. A man who knew England's criminal underworld but who also had connections with enough influential members of Parliament to ensure passage of the act necessary to establish it. So Sir Robert Peel had come hat in hand to ask Christopher to lead it.

He and Diana had a long conversation about what he wanted from his work, about what she needed from him. He was a man who wanted action in his life. And she needed him to be happy. The new police force would give both of them that. Moreover, the initiative would take years to implement, with the position based exclusively in London.

He'd finally become the respectable, settled, and dependable man whom Diana wanted for a husband and who Meri needed for a father.

The change in him had certainly shocked society, though. So had the unexpected announcement of their engagement. Hearts were broken across England, widows were aghast, and the book at White's received a thorough going-over to see what old bets had come due, waged over Christopher being leg-shackled to a wife. But whenever anyone at the clubs asked him about his old plans to become a vicar, he grinned and answered, "Why give my life to God, when I can give it to a goddess?"

Diana found it easy to embrace a new life with him, especially now that she knew her family was safe. The French had been notified by the Foreign Office that they had retrieved the diary and destroyed it, thus ending any more attempts to come after it. Yet the loss of the diary didn't stop the general from finishing his memoirs and publishing them to great acclaim, including grudging praise from Wellington.

Tension still existed between the general and her brother, despite his true role in all this being revealed. But their relationship was improving, and the two men were finally taking the time to get to know each other, as they'd never done before. Garrett had accepted the position with the Foreign Office that Kit had declined. It wasn't the daring work of a field operative by any stretch of the imagination, but it was important—a government position that the general could finally brag about his son holding, and one at which Garrett could be a public success.

The rowboat bumped against the island.

"We've arrived." He jumped out and pulled it up the bank, then held out his hand to help her from the boat. "Welcome to your honeymoon, Mrs. Carlisle."

Warmth bubbled inside her as she slid her hand into his and felt his strong fingers close around hers, only to gasp with surprise when he grabbed her into his arms and lifted her from the boat in a laughing circle. She flung her arms around his neck and clasped herself to him as he carried her away from the lake and down a wooded path toward a little stone cottage nestled among the trees.

"Will this do, my queen?" He nodded toward the hermitage.

*Perfectly.* Not trusting herself to speak, she answered by running her fingers through the dark gold hair curling at his collar and reveled in the contradiction of him. Of soft hair between her fingers and steely arms around her.

Since they left Bradwell two months ago, they hadn't had the opportunity to make love, having to settle for a few stolen kisses and touches. Now her heart pounded wildly in anticipation of being beneath him again, of wrapping her body around his and giving herself in sweet surrender. The throbbing ache between her legs was impossible to ignore, as was the way her nipples had already drawn up taut beneath the bodice of her wedding gown. Unable to keep still against her growing need for him, she shifted in his arms to rub her breasts against his chest.

His arms tightened around her, and his stride increased.

She laughed wantonly and untied his cravat, pulling it off his neck and letting it dangle from her hand before dropping it to the path. Then she placed her lips against his bare neck and kissed him, open-mouthed and with every intention of how else she planned on kissing him once they were finally hidden away inside the cottage.

But she couldn't resist touching him now. She unbuttoned his waistcoat as far as she could reach, then wiggled her hand inside his shirt to caress his bare chest. As he carried her over the threshold and into the cottage, a masculine groan tore from the back of his throat. He shut the door shut behind them with an impatient kick.

"The bedroom," she ordered breathlessly, her fingertip toying with his flat male nipple. "I can't wait a moment longer."

His arms shook around her as he carried her up the stairs, and she knew it wasn't from the exertion of carrying her from the boat.

The small attic room had been transformed, with a lace canopy draped softly over a large four-poster bed made up with satin sheets and a down-filled, velvet duvet. Red and pink rose petals lay scattered across it.

That he had gone to this much trouble... Her eyes stung.

"Make love to me, Christopher."

Her soft demand was tempered by a sultry, lingering kiss to his lips, one that surely tasted of her love for him and her utter happiness that he belonged to her. All hers. Finally and forever.

"Yes, my queen." He placed her onto the bed and followed down on top of her. "My angel."

# HISTORICAL NOTE

Home Office and Foreign Office and War Office...oh my!

One of the biggest difficulties I had in writing this novel was researching all the various government entities that would have had a hand in stopping espionage plots in 1824 and where their jurisdictions ended or overlapped, especially as their organizational structures kept changing. Because this book involved an army officer giving secrets to the French on English soil...oh, the confusion! So here's a bitty primer to help you keep them all straight.

To begin, there is the War Office. Under the auspices of the Secretary at War, this office was responsible for carrying out all the administration for the army, home and abroad. But it did not oversee the colonies or military policy—that was the responsibility of the Secretary of State for War and the Colonies, a.k.a. the War Department (we'll get to this one in a moment). In other words, it was responsible for the day-to-day minutiae that kept the army functioning rather than for grand strategy.

To confuse matters, the Secretary at War and the War Office

were considered subordinate to another cabinet level position, the Secretary of State for War and the Colonies, who was known colloquially as the War Secretary and led what was referred to as the War Department. This department was responsible for the supply of equipment to the armed forces, the pursuance of all military activity, and the administration of the colonies. Confused yet? I am...but wait! It gets worse, because in 1855, the two secretary positions were combined under the Secretary of State for War, and the terms "War Department" and "War Office" were used pretty much interchangeably from then on.

In 1824, when Kit and Diana's story is set, the War Office was still under the auspices of the Secretary at War. So, oversight of officers like General Morgan and Major Paxton, in their military roles, would have fallen under the overarching War Department, and under that, the subordinate War Office. Do you remember Thomas Matteson, Marquess of Chesney, from the *Secret Life of Scoundrels* series? As a former army captain, it would have been a natural fit for him to slide from the army into the War Office, where he could have become an operative within the War Department, keeping track of military affairs and information for Lord Bathurst, Secretary of State for War and the Colonies, a.k.a. the War Secretary. The same with Nathaniel Grey.

And then there are the Home Office and the Foreign Office.

Prior to 1782, all foreign and domestic affairs were governed by the Northern Department and the Southern Department. As their names imply, the Northern Department was responsible for all government interactions with northern European powers, and the Southern Department for interactions with southern European powers. But that wasn't all—the Southern Department also oversaw domestic, Irish, and colonial policy. So in 1782, when a new organizational structure was needed and department responsibilities were realigned, it was only natural that the Northern Department became the new Foreign Office, responsible for foreign matters, and the Southern Department would become the new Home Office, taking over domestic, military, and colonial responsibilities. (Colonial and military affairs—with the exception of the militia, which remained under the Home Office —were transferred to new offices by 1801.)

So the Home Office became responsible for domestic policy. Specifically—and most importantly to our story—it became responsible for operating the secret service within the United Kingdom. Likewise, the Foreign Office was responsible for all foreign affairs, except for India. (Interestingly enough, part of its responsibilities today includes housing the Government Wine Cellar. Now THIS is a government agency I could love!)

What made doing research for this story so confusing was trying to figure out where one office's jurisdiction ended and another began. Were Russian diplomats watched by the Home Office or the Foreign Office? Was it the Home Office's responsibility to stop French operatives on British soil or the Foreign Office's? If a Home Office operative like Kit Carlisle got himself involved with French operatives in England, who is responsible for stopping him? And, historically, many of the secretaries, under-secretaries, and other administrators frequently moved between the departments in service to the Crown, which makes Grey's movement from the War Office in *Along Came a Rogue* to the Foreign Office in this novel quite common (and a helpful plot device). Also, the offices were often collectively referred to as Whitehall, from their office locations near the former Whitehall Palace; this colloquialism for the British government is still in use today. That's why you'll see the government offices referred to collectively as Whitehall throughout the novel.

I did my best to keep them all straight, both here in this note and in the novel itself. I hope you enjoyed all the intrigue.

Now...how do I find my way to that Foreign Office wine cellar?

# DEAR READER

Hello! And thank you for reading AFTER THE SPY SEDUCES, book #6 in my Capturing the Carlisles series. This book was five years in the making, since 2014 when I came up with the idea for my first series, the Secret Life of Scoundrels. That series ended on a mystery—who provided the list of agent names to the Earl Royston that he sold to the French? I knew even then that I wanted to write a second series about the Carlisles and tie both series together at the end by revealing who had given over the names and how. I hope you enjoyed traveling this journey with me (and in seeing Diana Morgan finally capture her Carlisle!). Although no more full-sized books have been envisioned for this series, I am hoping to write a novella for Hugh Whitby...and who knows? Perhaps other books will follow in the years to come as ideas come to me. The Carlisles *are* a very big family, after all.

Haven't met the Carlisles yet? Then are you in for a treat! The three overly protective brothers from ***HOW I MARRIED A MARQUESS*** (a RITA Award finalist) have gone from being the scourge of Mayfair to the heroes of the *ton*. When they meet three very special women, they've met their matches—in more ways than one. A sneak glimpse into Book 1 in the series, *IF THE DUKE DEMANDS*, follows below.

Coming in the spring of 2020, I'm launching a new series with SourceBooks that I hope you will enjoy—The Lords of the Armory. Based upon Marvel comic book characters, the books follow a group of former soldiers who have banded together to fight an evil organization called Scepter...and who find love in very surprising places along the way.

Thank you again for reading this book. If you want to stay in touch and keep up with my latest releases, contests, and more (including all those pictures of the roses from my garden—I cannot help myself!), be sure to sign up for my **newsletter.** You can also follow me on **Bookbub** where you'll receive news of all my releases and on all my **social media sites.**

♥ Happy reading!
*Anna*

# EXCERPT FROM IF THE DUKE DEMANDS

A special glimpse of *IF THE DUKE DEMANDS* by Anna Harrington, Book #1 in the Capturing the Carlisles series:

*Miranda Hodgkins has only ever wanted one thing: to marry Robert Carlisle. And she simply can't wait a moment longer. During a masquerade ball, Miranda boldly sneaks into his bedchamber with seduction on her mind. But when the masks come off, she's horrified to find herself face-to-face with Sebastian, Duke of Trent—Robert's formidable older brother. Sebastian offers her a deal to avoid scandal: he'll help her win his brother's heart if she'll find him the perfect wife. But their simple negotiation spirals out of control. For the longer Sebastian tries to make a match for Miranda, the more he wants to keep her all to himself.*

Sebastian nuzzled his mouth against her ear.

Miranda gasped. That, oh, *that* was clearly not an accidental brush of whispering lips! He'd meant to caress her, and the warm longing it sent spiraling through her nearly undid her. Drawing a deep breath as she threw all caution and sense to the wind, she tilted her head to give him access to her neck, unable to deny the temptation of having his mouth on her.

With a pleased smile against her ear, he murmured, "What is it about my brother that draws you so?"

The tip of his tongue traced the outer curl of her ear. She shuddered at the delicious sensation, and his hand pressed tighter against her belly to keep her still in his arms.

The confusion inside her gave way to a tingling warmth that ached low in her belly. With one little lick, Sebastian had set her blood humming, making her body shiver and her thighs clench the way he had that night in his bedroom when she thought he was Robert. She knew who was kissing her this time, yet knowing he was the wrong Carlisle brother made no difference to the heat rising through her traitorous body. She should step away—this was *Sebastian*, for heaven's sake, and the most wrong man in the world for her, save for the king himself—but she simply couldn't make herself leave the circle of his strong arms.

"Robert is masculine," she breathed, her words barely audible above the aria swirling around them.

"Most men are," he answered, dancing kisses down the side of her neck.

When he placed his mouth against that patch of bare skin where her neck curved into her shoulder, a hot throbbing sprang up between her thighs. She bit her lip to keep back a soft whimper.

"He's handsome," she forced out, hoping he couldn't hear the nervous trembling that crept into her voice.

"Hmm." His hand on her hip drifted upward along the side of her body, lightly tracing across her ribs. She trembled achingly when his fingers grazed the side swell of her breast. "We're brothers. We look alike."

Oh, that was *definitely* jealousy! But her kiss-fogged brain couldn't sort through the confusion to discern why he'd be jealous of Robert. Especially when his hand caressed once more along the side of her breast.

"Not so much alike," she countered, although she'd always thought Sebastian would be more handsome if he wasn't always so serious and brooding. If he did more spontaneous and unexpected things…like licking a woman on her nape at an opera. *Oh my.* She shivered at the audacity of his mouth and at the heat it sent slithering down her spine.

"Very nearly identical," he murmured as his hand roamed up to trace his fingers along the neckline of her gown. Completely unexpected yet wantonly thrilling, the caress sent her heart somersaulting just inches from his fingertips.

"He's exciting…a risk-taker…" Her voice was a breathless hum despite knowing that in his rivalry with his brother he didn't want to touch her as much as he wanted to touch her before Robert did. At that moment, though, with his fingertips lightly brushing over the top swells of her breasts, she simply didn't care. At least not enough to make him stop. "He's thrilling."

When his fingertips traced slow circles against the inner curves of her breasts, she was powerless against the soft whimper that fell from her lips.

"Lots of men are thrilling." He smiled wickedly against her neck at the reaction his seeking fingers elicited from her. "I'm thrilling."

"*You?*" She gave a throaty laugh of surprise. "Sebastian, you're the most reserved, restrained man I—"

In one fluid motion, he turned her in his arms and pushed her back against the set wall, his mouth swooping down to swallow her words as he kissed her into silence. Her hands clenched into the hard muscles of his shoulders, and she stiffened beneath the startling onslaught of his lips, of his hips pushing into hers, all of him demanding possession of the kiss. And of her.

# EXCERPT FROM AS THE DEVIL DARES

Enjoy this special except of *AS THE DEVIL DARES* by Anna Harrington, Book #3 in the Capturing the Carlisles series:

*Lord Robert Carlisle never backs down from a dare. But finding a husband for scandalous Mariah Winslow is one challenge he instantly regrets accepting. Robert will have to use every trick in the book to marry off the woman known as the Hellion, no matter how stunningly beautiful she is. Mariah Winslow has no intention of being a pawn in Lord Robert's game. She knows he only agreed to play matchmaker to secure a partnership in her father's shipping company, a partnership that's rightfully hers. Battle lines are drawn, and she won't surrender—no matter how tempting and irresistible she finds him.*

"Mariah." Robert smiled against her cheek, and a stab of defeat pierced her. So Carlisle thought he'd won, did he?

Well, she'd prove to him that it would take more than a kiss to convince her to surrender.

When he stepped back, Mariah advanced.

She wrapped her arms around his shoulders and delved her

fingertips through the golden curls at his nape, then pressed her body so tightly against his front that his heart slammed furiously against her chest. When she brushed her hips against his, a low groan tore from the back of his throat.

Emboldened, she brazenly kissed him, and when he hesitated, stunned,

she slipped her tongue between his lips the way he'd done to her.

*That* was enough to snap him out of his reverie.

He grabbed her shoulders and demanded in a raspy voice, "What the hell do you think you're doing?"

Despite the racing of her heart, she forced a shrug of her shoulders. As if it

were the most obvious thing in the world. "Kissing you."

Then she pressed against him again, her lips making fleeting contact with

his before he set her away. An angry scowl hardened his face.

"Don't you want me to?" she prompted as innocently as possible.

Something dark and heated flickered in his eyes, and she thrilled at gaining the upper hand. Hiding her own quaking she leaned toward him as far as his restraining hands would allow.

She purred huskily, "Surely the notorious Robert Carlisle knows what to do with a woman who wants to kiss him."

Despite gritting his teeth, his gaze fell longingly to her mouth, and for a moment, she thought he might just kiss her senseless again. And if he did, she wasn't certain that she could withstand it this time without falling completely apart in his arms.

"Don't tease me, Mariah," he warned in a murmur. "You're playing with fire."

"Am I?" Pretending that he hadn't affected her, even as that tingling heat still throbbed achingly, she sadly shook her head. "Well, I certainly hope the other gentlemen I'll meet this season are better at this than you."

She slipped away before he could reach for her again. Or she for him. "Or I'll be too bored to consider marrying any of them."

He stared at her coolly as he wiped his mouth with the back of his hand. "You *will* be married by season's end, I promise you."

He took her arm and pulled her toward the door. He flung it open and led her into the hall so quickly that she struggled to keep up with his determined strides. Anger radiated from him as he led her out to the carriage waiting in the street.

He placed her inside the carriage. But when she yanked her arm away, it wasn't relief she felt but an inexplicable sense of loss. For one maddening moment, she wanted to blurt out an apology, to beg him to crawl inside the compartment with her and keep kissing her just as he'd done before, all the way home to her doorstep.

But the devil inside her couldn't help one last parting jab, and she sniffed with mock disappointment, "If I'm going to be forced to give my first waltz to such a boorish man, I certainly hope you're far better at dancing."

He rose up onto the step and leaned inside, bringing himself close. "Don't

you worry, minx," he assured her in a husky voice that twined down her spine. "When it comes to having a woman in my arms, I do *everything* well."

Her breath strangled in her throat. Leaving her to gape at him in stunned mortification at her own heated reaction to the beast-liness in him, he closed the door, then ordered the coachman to drive off.

The carriage rolled forward, and she slumped against the

squabs. A curse left her lips at him, followed immediately by several more at herself.

They'd fought their second battle, yet for the life of her she couldn't have said which of them had emerged the victor.

ALSO BY ANNA HARRINGTON

*The Secret Life of Scoundrels Series*

Dukes Are Forever

Along Came a Rogue

How I Married a Marquess

Once a Scoundrel

*Capturing the Carlisles Series*

If the Duke Demands

When the Scoundrel Sins

As the Devil Dares

How the Earl Entices

*Standalone Titles*

Say Yes to the Scot

A Match Made in Heather

No Dukes Allowed

# ABOUT THE AUTHOR

I fell in love with historical romances and all things Regency—and especially all those dashing Regency heroes—while living in England, where I spent most of my time studying the Romantic poets, reading Jane Austen, and getting lost all over the English countryside. I love the period's rich history and find that all those rules of etiquette and propriety can be worked to the heroine's advantage...if she's daring enough to seize her dreams.

I am an avid traveler and have enjoyed visiting schools and volunteering with children's organizations in Peru, Ecuador, Thailand, and Mexico, and I have amassed thousands of photos I unleash on unsuspecting friends who dare to ask about my travels.

I love to be outdoors! I've been hiking in Alaska, the Andes, and the Alps, and I love whitewater rafting (when I don't fall in!). I earned my pilot's license at Chicago Midway (To all the controllers in Chicago Center—I greatly apologize for every problem I caused for you and Southwest Airlines), and it is my dream to one-day fly in a hot-air balloon over Africa.

I adore all things chocolate, ice cream of any flavor, and Kona coffee by the gallon. A *Doctor Who* fanatic (everyone says my house *is* bigger on the inside), I am a terrible cook who hopes to one day use my oven for something other than shoe storage. When I'm not writing, I like to spend my time trying not to kill the innocent rose bushes in my garden.

https://www.annaharringtonbooks.com/